D0065048

the STRANGER UPSTAIRS

the STRANGER UPSTAIRS

A NOVEL

LISA M. MATLIN

BANTAM
NEW YORK

Published in the United States by Bantam Books,
an imprint of Random House, a division of
Penguin Random House LLC, New York.

BANTAM & B colophon is a registered trademark
of Penguin Random House LLC.

LIBRARY OF CONGRESS CATALOGING-IN-PUBLICATION DATA
Names: Matlin, Lisa, author.
Title: The stranger upstairs: a novel / Lisa Matlin.
Description: First edition. | New York: Bantam Books, 2023
Identifiers: LCCN 2022057985 (print) | LCCN 2022057986 (ebook) |
ISBN 9780593599952 (hardcover; acid-free paper) | ISBN 9780593599969 (ebook)
Subjects: LCGFT: Gothic fiction. | Paranormal fiction. | Novels.
Classification: LCC PR9619.4.M37563 S77 2023 (print) |
LCC PR9619.4.M37563 (ebook) |
DDC 823/.92—dc23/eng/20230112
LC record available at https://lccn.loc.gov/2022057985
LC ebook record available at https://lccn.loc.gov/2022057986

Illustrations based on the original images by Adobe Stock/alisaaig (wallpaper)
and Adobe Stock/~ Bitter ~ (bird)

Printed in Canada

randomhousebooks.com

2 4 6 8 9 7 5 3 1

First Edition

Book design by Diane Hobbing

For my Mum,
We always used to say, "One Day."
Today, I say, "Day One."

To my brother and sister,
For always saving my ass.

Dan, who on my darkest days said, "Don't give up. You're going to make it big one day . . . and when you do, please buy me a superyacht."

Joels, who thinks books are for nerds. Thank you for the prayers, the laughs, the sissy time, and for not murdering me in my sleep when we shared a room as kids. Love from the biggest nerd of them all.

To my husband: I still choo choo choose you. I always will.

To H: Your friendship has saved me over and over again.

With no thanks to: Everyone who thought I should get a real job instead of writing my stories. HAHAHAHAHAHAHA suckers!

PART ONE

Want a great deal on a house?

BUY ONE WHERE SOMEONE WAS MURDERED!

Here's the killer truth: A brutal murder can slash the price by as much as 50%. But would YOU do it? Bestselling author Sarah Slade would!

By Whitney Roach [@KeepingItWeirdWithWhitney]

Welcome to Black Wood House! The stunning Victorian Gothic, built in 1889, lies right next door to a 400-acre bushland reserve. The two-story house comes with four generous bedrooms and a library and sits on two lush acres in a quiet wooded estate in Beacon, southeast of Melbourne.

And on the morning of February 4, 1980, Bill Campbell walked into the upstairs bedroom where his wife, Susan, lay sleeping and bashed her skull in with a hammer. After murdering her, Bill drifted down the hall into his seventeen-year-old daughter's bedroom. Janet Campbell was getting dressed for school when her father walked calmly into her room and beat her with the bloodied hammer. She fled out the front door. Neighbors heard her screaming all the way up the road, "Don't kill me! Don't kill me! Don't kill me!"

When she was gone, Bill locked himself in the bathroom and took a fatal dose of acid and tranquilizers.

For 40 years, Black Wood House stood empty and silent. But on a quiet night, some people say they still hear the cries of Janet Campbell ringing out through the neighborhood.

Don't kill me. Don't kill me. Don't kill me.

But new owner, Sarah Slade, doesn't believe it.

"Oh, we're not superstitious!" Sarah laughs, leaning against her husband of three years, bartender Joe Cosgrove. "I see it as a business opportunity. Black Wood House has great bones, and we're confident we can restore it and make a tidy profit."

And she might be right! A murder house can be good business—if you have the stomach for it. After all, *the infamous Boyle Murder House in New South Wales just sold for $2.2 million. Two hundred thousand dollars over the asking price!* Slade and her husband were able to nab Black Wood House at a probate auction last month for $525,000—half the price of nearby properties.

"I know it has a dark past, but I want to fix that," Sarah insists, squeezing her husband's hand. "You shouldn't judge anything or anyone on their past."

And Sarah should know—she's a therapist with a bestselling self-help book: *Clear, Calm, and in Control.*

I have to ask: What on earth does a therapist want with a murder house?

Sarah smiles. "I'm a fixer," she admits. "I don't like broken things."

Joe (who is notoriously more camera shy than his wife and freely admits to avoiding all social media) says that he wasn't as convinced as Sarah. "To be honest, the place gives me the creeps. I'm not thrilled about living there at all. But"—he grins at his tenacious wife, who he lovingly refers to as "Lamb"—"there's no stopping my Lamb when she gets an idea in her head."

Sarah pauses before playfully slapping her husband's arm. "What my husband *really* means to say"—she grins and rolls her eyes in mock frustration—"is that we are *thrilled* to be moving to Beacon! We can't wait to meet our new neighbors and start renovating Black Wood House. You can follow the renovations on my website: SarahSlays.com."

And, fans, take heart! She's hard at work on her next book, a follow-up to the wildly successful *Clear, Calm, and in Control.*

With plenty of gruesome inspiration at her fingertips, her next book is sure to be a killer!

Keeping It Weird with Whitney—voted Top 5 Melbourne Blogger. Covering everything creepy and weird in Melbourne! If you've got a cool story to share, I'd love to interview you! DM your pitch @KeepingItWeirdWith Whitney.

Chapter 1

April 26

Welcome to Black Wood House.

This is the front door Janet Campbell burst out of. This is the barren yard she ran across, fleeing for her life. Those are her cries echoing down the lonely street for forty years now.

Don't kill me. Don't kill me. Don't kill me.

Upstairs is a bedroom with bloodstained floorboards. This is where Susan Campbell bled to death, and this is where I'll sleep. Some people think that's messed up.

I am not some people.

I carry a stack of moving boxes up the long stretch of dirt driveway snaking through the yard like a scar. It's silent except for the musical warble of a lone magpie and the half-hearted squabble of the cockatoos in the blackwood tree.

My eyes drift past it to the house. Not for the first time I wonder, Why the hell did someone build a Victorian Gothic in a stuffy country town like Beacon?

Black Wood House is sharp and strange and utterly silent. Its flaking paint reminds me of peeling skin, and the steeply pitched spire looks like a towering black sword. There's only one window on the front of the house: a pointed arch overlooking the lounge room and matching the front door. Whoever built Black Wood clearly did not want anybody peeking in.

A private, sprawling estate. That's how the probate realtor described it. It sounds beautiful, and it would have been. Back then. I can imagine it—pea-green lawns large enough for a dozen families to picnic on.

But after forty years of neglect, all that's left are stark, flat grounds ravaged by kangaroo shit and echidna burrows and choked with knee-high weeds. The property has a barren feel to it, like the very ground is grieving. Like it's stuck in the memory of that day.

And yet the house itself seems detached from the misery. Like it doesn't give a shit what happened here all those years ago. Like it wouldn't care if it happened again.

I haul the boxes inside, up the stairs, to my new bedroom. The *murder* room.

I don't know what's more sinister about this room, the faded blood-stain by my bed or the concrete-gray wallpaper. Corpse skin—that's what it reminds me of. And worse.

Etched into the wallpaper is a massive forest. The black trunks are taller than me, and high above the canopy is a sky dotted with stars. Back in the day, I bet it was a peaceful scene. I imagine Susan propped up in her bed, sipping a hot cup of tea and staring at the forest after a long day of cooking, cleaning, and whatever the hell women did back in the seventies.

Maybe she even felt like she was *inside* it, breathing in the clean air, far away from the pressures of motherhood and her soon-to-be homicidal husband. It would have been dove gray then. Pretty.

I dump the boxes on the floor and reach up on tiptoe to trace my index finger over a diamond-shaped leaf. It instantly flakes off and death spirals to the floor.

Nestled in the crook of a low branch is a family of blackbirds, staring at me with dead eyes. The baby birds look underfed and frightened; their rib cages seem to poke through their papery skin. The mother bird hovers over her children, her eyes sad and desperate. But she can't help them, because both her wings are missing.

My husband heaves our marriage bed against the back wall, then straightens up and wipes his hands like he's touched something filthy. He stopped sleeping with me months ago, and our queen-sized velvet bed stares at him reproachfully. Instead, he sleeps quite happily on our couch, though I never once asked him to. He plays the Xbox until the early hours, while I lie awake at 3 A.M., reflecting anxiously on all the things I need to fix. Like my marriage.

I don't like sleeping alone, but God, it's better than the crushing loneliness of sleeping next to someone who doesn't want you night after night.

"Thank you," I tell him awkwardly. "For bringing it up here."

My husband's eyes drift to the pillow-sized bloodstain on the floor. It's impossible not to stare at it. I wonder if he's imagining it—the morning after the murder, the blood all glossy red like lipstick.

Maybe it's Maybelline.

Or maybe it's murder.

"We'll need to replace these floorboards." He steps back, grimacing. "For now, just buy a rug to cover it with."

I nearly snort my laughter. That's him. Let's throw a rug over the issue. If you can't see it, then maybe all that ugliness isn't even there.

Maybe it's why he can't stand looking at me.

I follow him toward the door, thinking of the moving truck waiting outside, jammed full of our five-year life together. We've spent nearly everything buying this house, and the renovations will have to be spread out over the next year. And even though we've lived in Melbourne for two years, we don't exactly have any close friends we can stay with while we renovate. . . . Well, maybe Joe does, but I certainly don't. The fact that he was willing to make this move with me meant a lot. He's still here. Still willing to invest in this house and, more importantly, *us*. I haven't lost him yet.

I pass by the only window in the room, about the size of my laptop screen. It's a fixed window, so there's no way to open it unless I smash my fist through it. And I'm sure I'll be tempted after breathing in this stale air every night.

I stop and squint through the grime, looking out to my backyard, and the first thing I see are the graves. They're draped in ivy, stained sickly green, and covered with little scabs of moss and mold. Susan. Bill. Twin headstones for the former owners of Black Wood House. I don't know who thought it would be a good idea to bury Susan Campbell next to her husband. Her killer. But there they are, out my bedroom window, side by side for eternity.

I asked the realtor about it, but he didn't know who buried them. No one knows what happened to poor Janet Campbell after she fled the town. She could be dead. All she is now is a piece of folklore. A ghost story before she even died. Poor girl.

"Are you sure you want *this* room?" Joe asks. "What about the others?" He nods in the direction of the hallway, where three other garage-sized bedrooms lie dormant.

I shake my head and move to brush past him. He stopped kissing me this year, but he still lets me hug him sometimes. I have to time those coveted hugs correctly, or he'll rear back like a pissed-off horse.

A year ago, I would've tackled him to the bed. Or maybe I would've just thrown my arms around his neck, looked him full in the face, and said, "I'm so proud of us, Joe. Look how far we've come."

Now I slink sadly past him, a goddamn ghost of a wife.

I pad down the staircase, a spiraling black masterpiece that made me gasp the first time I saw it, and made Joe wince and murmur, "Bloody hell, what a nightmare." It's wrought iron, cool to the touch, and every time I descend, I feel like a Disney villain.

I *adore* it.

Joe calls down, "Don't you want a bedroom a bit less . . . I dunno, murdery?"

I reach the second-to-last step, breathing through my mouth. The house has been shut up for decades, and it smells like a sweaty sheet. "I'm good, thanks." I don't know how to tell him the truth, because it's strange even to me.

I didn't choose that room. It chose me.

Just like the house.

I pull open the front door, grunting from the weight of it. It's heavy oak, and once we get some linseed oil into it, it'll look like a flame-red candle in the dark. My flat-faced cat, Reaper, bolts out before I can stop him. He screamed the whole forty-minute car ride here while Joe turned up the radio and yelled, "Do we have to bring him with us?"

I ignored them both. Joe's been trying to get rid of Reaper ever since I stubbornly brought him home five years ago. I wandered around an adoption center, staring at wire cages and reading cutesy taglines: MEET LYNNY, A QUIET AND SWEET CAT! JACK IS THE LOVELIEST BOY!

I stopped in front of the last cage, and the tagline simply read, FREE. Underneath that in apologetic text, it said, THIS CAT DOESN'T LIKE KIDS, DOGS, LOUD NOISES, BEING PICKED UP, AND HE'S BEEN KNOWN TO GET INTO FIGHTS WITH OTHER CATS. HE'S VERY POSSESSIVE OF HIS BLANKET AND HIS FOOD.

I smiled and peered through the cage bars. And there he was— a silver-haired Angora cat wrapped in a filthy blanket, staring at me with angry blue eyes. I loved him instantly.

I step onto the porch and watch as Reaper climbs the blackwood tree in our yard. He's six now and still hates everything with an inexhaustible passion, and I really admire him for that. My boy.

I wrap my arms around myself, cold in the morning sun. You can't even see the road from here, and it's quiet now except for a lone cockatoo chattering in the tree. Reaper glares at the cockatoo murderously but makes no attempt to climb higher up the deeply fissured bark. I reach into my pocket for my phone and snap a picture of Reaper and the bird nestled in the bony branches. I quickly tap in a caption:

Moving Day at Black Wood House! These gorgeous guys approve! Head to my website for all the renovation updates! #BlackWoodHouse #cockatoo #Melbourne #reaper #murderhouse

I hesitate, wondering if I should use that last hashtag. It's a bit much, I suppose. But it would definitely drive in some much-needed traffic and maybe a sponsor or two. There's already interest in my website again, now that I've promised to document the renovations.

I hit the post button and automatically scroll through my feed, full of painful-looking yoga poses, watermelon salads, and a tutorial on how to fake a lip job with one million likes. My thumb hovers over the screen, and I surprise myself by clicking off my phone and tucking it into my pocket. There's something incongruous about standing on this hundred-year-old porch and scrolling through the atrocities of social media. It doesn't feel right. It's like the house disapproves. Like it wants me back inside, cutting apple slices and smiling adoringly at my shiny-haired children. Or maybe it wants me asleep in my bed so my husband can murder me.

Finally I step off the porch, head to the truck, and busy myself with the moving boxes. We have a surprising amount of crap, and most of it's mine. I have a shopping problem. And a bit of an alcohol issue. And oh, everything else. Doesn't take a therapist to realize I'm filling up the voids in my life with a whole lot of shit.

For the next few hours, my husband and I work together, unloading and unpacking. Reaper sneaks inside the house as soon as we unload the couch and spends the rest of the afternoon propped on a cushion, watching us lug the rest of our furniture in.

When the truck's empty, I pull out a six-pack from under the driver's seat. I really shouldn't be drinking on anti-depressants, but there are a lot of things I shouldn't be doing. Last week, I went up to a double dose, but Joe doesn't know this. There's a lot of things he doesn't know. Doesn't even care to.

He thanks me, reaches for the beer, and we walk in ear-splitting silence to our front porch as I chug mine. My doctor's voice rings in my head. He was scribbling out my prescription, raising an eyebrow. "You know not to mix these with alcohol, right?"

"Of course!" I scoffed.

Tentatively, Joe taps his beer against mine with a reserved little clink. "Well . . ." he begins awkwardly, looking out to our gloomy front yard. "We did it."

"Yes," I say firmly. "We certainly did."

Silence. We're not used to communicating anymore. If we could still speak, what would we say? Perhaps I would finally admit the truth: Buying this house wasn't just about building my brand and making a huge profit. I thought that renovating this house might help repair us too. I saw us working side by side, painting walls in amiable silence or sharing a beer as we pored over color charts.

After a while, Joe strolls off the creaking porch and disappears inside. I watch him go, wondering if I'm allowed to follow.

I lean over the porch railing instead, all bone dry and bleached from the sun. A bloated magpie lands with a squawk to my right, peering at me with dull red eyes. He tilts his head, waiting for food. I narrow my eyes at him. Nobody's occupied this house for forty years. Who's been feeding him?

"Sorry, mate. I got nothing for ya," I tell him.

I step off the porch and head inside. The magpie watches, still and disapproving. I'm close enough to touch him, and he doesn't even flinch. The neighbors must feed him.

Reaper perches on the back of the couch, watching Joe fiddle with the cords of his Xbox. It's the first thing he insisted on before he agreed to move in: Get the electricity and Wi-Fi going for the bloody Xbox. It delayed our move-in day for two weeks, but hell, at least he's here.

He switches the TV on, and the gigantic piece of modern technology clashes violently with the *Brady Bunch* kitchen and linoleum floor. The last time anyone lived here was the early eighties. It's been frozen in time ever since. All our sleek, contemporary furniture is laughably out of place, and even Joe notices.

He smiles a bit guiltily. "I s'pose the house has never seen an Xbox before."

I take a sip, swallow it down. "Shit, did they even have TV then?"

Joe reaches for the remote, adjusts the volume, and frowns. "Yeah, but only a few channels, I think."

"Maybe that's why he killed her."

He snaps his eyes shut like he can't believe I just said that, but his shoulders shake with guilty laughter. My heart glows. I haven't made him laugh in a long time. I study him quietly, looking at him properly for the first time in ages. My husband's handsome in a bland way. Average height, slim build—*too* slim, I think. I always have to remind him to eat, and if I don't cook for him, he either makes two-minute noodles or simply goes hungry. He has phobias of flying, large crowds, talking on the phone, and any TV show with a laugh track. I suspect he has generalized anxiety disorder, but he'll never get diagnosed, because the idea of picking up the phone and making an appointment terrifies him. Which is why I make all the phone calls. Which is why he needs someone like me: I get shit done while he wrings his pale hands and panics.

His eyes are watery blue, and his hair is thick and shiny black. We dyed it in a truck-stop bathroom when we fled Queensland, and we re-dye it every six weeks to cover up the roots. He's fair-haired naturally, with pale lashes that blinked a lot and hair so blond it was almost silver. Black hair is too heavy for him. Everything is too heavy for him these days.

People wonder why we're together. Joe, the nervy bartender. And me, the Instagram whore. But the truth is that underneath all Joe's beauty, he's every bit as ugly as me. I *love* him for that. Trust me, my husband is not so perfect. He has more secrets to hide than I do.

I drain the last drops of my beer, and Joe surprises me by asking, "Do you think the house wants us here?"

"The house?"

"Yeah," he says, half-joking, half-serious, gripping the controller like it'll give him strength. "I don't think it likes us."

"This house is gonna make us a fortune," I tell him gently before adding, "One point three million, Joe. That's the median house price in Beacon. Up 35 percent annually."

I can never say that last part without hugging myself gleefully. *Up 35 percent annually.* I've done the figures an unhealthy number of times. Once these renovations are done, I'm looking at a profit of at least 600,000 dollars. We are, I mean. Joe and I.

"Someone had to have the guts to do it," I say resolutely, "and *we* did."

Wasn't that what Rodney Peake, the real estate agent, said when all the formalities were over and we were signing the deed? "It takes a certain kind of someone to buy a murder house," he said grimly, sliding it over like he was disappointed in us. Joe paused for a fraction before scribbling his name on the paper. "Not really my idea," he mumbled. It might not have been his idea, but he's certainly keen as hell on raking in the profits. Like I said, my husband's ugly, too—only nobody knows that but me.

The realtor eyed me disapprovingly, and I don't know why I smiled, but I did. I signed the deed with two jaunty S's and a big, looping L.

"I guess you won't be coming over for a cup of tea, then?" I asked, handing it back to him.

Quickly he signed his own name, and I noticed how he never quite touched the paper. The way he was acting, you'd think it was soaked in urine.

Or blood.

"No," he said curtly, "I don't think I could."

I say good night to my husband. He looks so lost sitting there on our couch that I can't help myself. I bend down, kiss him softly on the lips, and he actually lets me. God, I've missed this. But I don't push it further. Not yet.

I reluctantly pull back and head for my room. I hear Reaper jump from the couch to follow me, and Joe calls out softly, "Good night."

I smile up the creaky stairs, thinking about the kiss and the realtor's words. You're damn right it takes a certain kind of person to buy a murder house. You have to be familiar with the very ugly side of human nature. And who better than a therapist? Haven't I heard it all? Haven't I encouraged, even *prompted,* my clients to talk about the big, bad things?

Most people sweep monsters under the bed. I pull the covers back and let them crawl in.

Chapter 2

My last clients of the day are the Millers. Their ten-year marriage is falling apart, and thank fuck for that. Nice to know I'm not the only one failing. When their last tear-filled session was over, I drove home whistling.

I hesitate before opening the door and ushering them inside my office, which is light pink and gray and perfectly matches the carpet, the couch, and, most importantly, my book cover.

If I'm being honest, my last clients, the Vickers, really rattled me. Our session finished ten minutes ago, and I can't stop shaking.

The Vickers. Young couple. Newly married and marinating in that "we're having great sex" smell. We're two sessions in. There's nothing much wrong with them, and they were a bit too smug when I told them that. Last week, I wished them goodbye with a beaming smile, which curdled the second they left the office pawing at each other. Then I trudged home and watched TV in bed with the cat. Joe's been working late shifts at the bar for extra cash, and maybe that's a good thing for now.

I can fix this, I tell myself again.

I can fix us. I will. I will.

I hyperventilate at my office door, breathing in the faint antiseptic smell of Amy Miller, who is standing on the other side, knocking. I can do this. I just need a smoke. A drink. And the delightfully fucked-up

Millers with their infidelities, credit card debt, and mutual simmering rage to make me happy again.

I throw the door open, my smile huge, my yellow diamond wedding ring sparkling, my bestselling book shining on the windowsill as the afternoon sun washes it in soft golden light as warm as a bath.

It's so perfect. All of it.

When I stand at that door, it's like I'm presenting myself: You can *feel* the Pinterest boards dedicated to excerpts of my book. I have a handsome husband, beachy waves, and teeth so white you could read by them in the dark. My baby-pink cardigan brings out the warm caramel of my hair and the forty-three-dollar Nars blush on my cheeks. I'm the human equivalent of Instagram. Sarah Slade. At your fucking service.

"Hi, folks!" I beam, waving them inside. "Come in, come in."

Folks. I stole it from the celebrity therapist on *Teen Mom.* He calls all his patients "folks," and the dim-witted, slack-jawed yokels seem to like it. He's speaking *their* language; he's *trustworthy;* he's *stern but relatable.*

Richard shuffles past me, mute and solemn as a wounded bird. Amy smiles tightly, clutching her python-print handbag and smelling of total despair. I eat their sorrow, swallowing it down like it's hearty chicken soup, and by the time I close the door, I'm feeling *so* much better. My clients look at me like I have the answers. Like I can help. It's healing, to be honest, at least for a little while. I am a giant goddamn wound. My clients are soothing little Band-Aids. But then I go home to my emotionally distant husband, lie awake in my bed, and scratch at all my sores until I'm breathless and frantic in the dark. Then I post some trite bullshit on Instagram about health and healing, and I hold my breath and bleed until the likes come flooding in.

Instagram is my other Band-Aid. It's toxic, I know. But the more likes I get, the less I bleed.

Nobody is speaking, so we all do that awkward silent walk from the door to the chairs. I peek behind me, hoping they glance up at the dove-gray wall where my book cover hangs in the exact center, blown up to five times its size. Look up, dammit. Give me validation. Give me praise. I'm empty. Fill me up.

Amy's matching sterling silver bracelets chime pleasantly, and by the time she's sat down, I've decided I want a pair for myself. It's a shame she doesn't take them off. Shame she hasn't unclipped them from her perfumed wrists and slid them deep into that Balenciaga handbag she always carries. If I thought I could get away with it, I'd steal them both.

She wouldn't be the first client I've stolen from.

I slip into my chair, a Gatsby velvet I wanted the second I saw it on some bony influencer's feed. On a good day, I kick the last client out at 5 P.M., wheel it backward, swing my legs like a child, and gleefully chain-smoke out my window. On a bad day, I gulp peppery Shiraz in the darkness until I can stomach the thought of going home.

And on my *really* bad days, I get sloppy drunk and wait until the building's empty. Then I throw the window open and yell "Fuck you" until it burns.

I can't tell yet whether today is a good or bad day.

Amy shifts miserably on the couch, casts an accusing glare at Richard that I nearly miss because my eyes are so fixed on her handbag. Nestled on her knees is that sexy Balenciaga, black and blood red. Her bracelets drape over it, adding a sparkle of silver. God, I want it. I want the bag. I want the bracelets. I want it all with an almost physical hunger.

I tear my eyes from it, cross my legs at the ankles. Smile.

"How's your week been, folks?"

I nearly cringe at the word, but I can't stop using it. When my clients are sitting silent on my white leather couch, I am Sympathetic and Relatable Therapist Who Is Totally Not Judging You. Sarah has her shit together. Sarah has a strong marriage. Sarah says things like "folks" and "How did that make you feel?" and "That must have been hard for you." Sarah is a *bullshit artist* who charges $120 an hour.

"Not very good, I'm afraid," Amy begins, darting a glance at her morose husband. "We're not in a good place at the moment."

Good, because if you were, I'd be broke.

But I nod sympathetically and wait. Truthfully, I don't judge my clients no matter how scandalous their sins. Believe me, I've done much worse.

For the next hour, I listen. I encourage. I ask open-ended questions. Standard stuff from the online diploma I didn't finish. Funny how I have all the answers without it. Even funnier that people listen when I speak.

As a child, people really confused me. Everyday conversations were like streets with no signs. I was always saying the wrong thing or nothing at all. Soon enough I noticed that people who said all the right things were adored, even if they didn't mean what they said. My sister was like that. She was the one slinking over an armchair at sleepovers, butting in with brilliant one-liners. I was the one listening behind the lounge room door, mouthing her clever words as if they were my own. God, I was a weird child. If it weren't for her insistence, none of the neighborhood kids would have spoken to me at all.

I knew even then that I wasn't who people wanted me to be, because I felt their judgment and disapproval right down to my DNA. So, I began a slow self-eviction, contributing nothing to my classmates or schoolwork. But inside, I was *starving.*

Then I met Joe. Lovely Joe, who didn't care when I said very strange things. On our first date, I was so nervous that I over-explained my favorite episodes of *Forensic Files*. But he listened. When I was finished, he gently pushed his phone into my hand.

"Watch these. You might like them," he said shyly. "Though not many people do."

They were YouTube videos. At first I couldn't figure out what I was looking at. Then I realized: uncensored shark attack videos.

I was fascinated, to be honest. By the videos. And by the beautiful pale boy who showed them to me. He was like a *meal* made only for me.

Joe. God, I fucking *devoured* that boy. Our strangeness was like a secret we shared: We must keep our madness to ourselves. Me and Joe. Just two weirdos.

But now I get to watch as my darling husband begins his own self-eviction from *me*. I shake my head almost violently and clutch the arm-rests until my knuckles turn white. It's not over between Joe and me. I won't let go of him—us—that easily.

4:58 P.M. Perfect. Show's over, *folks*. Time for me to deliver a parting line of wisdom. And since my book is full of them, I reach into my frontal lobe and try to pull one out. And of course, I can't remember. I open my mouth, then close it. Shit. Hang on.

What was it again? That great line from the marriage chapter. The one so popular that someone actually made it into a viral Twitter post. Something about not giving up, yada yada.

I smile toothily at the Millers and whip out my phone, pretending to check the time. But I'm really typing Sarah Slade+book+giving up into Bing, Google's crackhead brother.

Ah, there it is.

"If you give up every time it's hard," I say softly, leaning back to really nail the next line, "you're going to have a very short marriage."

It doesn't land well, and we all feel it. I'm an actor who just flubbed their line. But I'm too emotionally strung out to smooth shit over. In the excruciating silence that follows, Richard does the strangest thing. He clears his throat and looks right in my eyes. Really looks. Examines my face like a doctor looking for disease. I feel caught out, exposed. And for just a moment, I think he sees right through me. He's seeing the Shiraz I'll down in half an hour. The shit I'll impulse buy tonight.

I bolt up and practically shove the Millers out the door.

"Take it easy, folks," I babble, waving them off. I'm losing it. I'm slithering out of my Sarah Slade skin. I'm done with the show. Amy gives me an odd look before disappearing around the corner with her husband. I watch them go and remain in the doorway, exhausted and staring at nothing.

"Sarah?"

Oh, shit. I straighten up and smile automatically at Emily. Her office is directly opposite mine. Now we stand feet apart as she locks her office door with a soft *click* and peers at me with worried eyes.

"Are you okay, lovie?"

I imagine she asks that a lot as the grief and loss therapist. But oddly enough, she sounds genuine.

"I'm okay!" I call out far too brightly. Emily smells of lavender, and she has a thing for ankle-length paisley skirts and slide-on sandals. Motherly, you'd call her. She has a square, thickset body and a long blond plait as thick as a horse tail. There's something calming about the way she moves and talks. She has a liquid voice and languid eyes. It's no wonder there's a waiting list to see her.

"You have a good night!" I tell her.

"You too." She smiles warmly. Her hand slides off the doorknob, and she surprises me by reaching for my shoulder and patting it softly. "If you ever need anything, just sing out, okay, lovie?"

My eyes fill with tears, and I turn my head so she won't see. I thank her and dart back inside my office. The second her Nissan leaves the parking lot, I race to the bottle shop. And I'm pretty sure that by midnight tonight I'll be wasted and screaming out the office window again.

Chapter 3

I bolt awake and think, *Someone's in my office.* My heart thumps so hard it makes me cough in the dark. My office door is wide open, the hallway rolling out behind it like the back of a crocodile's throat. I can't see shit. But I hear something.

I squint in the dark, hold my breath. And I hear it again: footsteps creeping up the hallway. I freeze in my chair, facing the open door like a bird fallen out of its nest and waiting for the hungry cat to arrive.

I bolt up, and my chair gives a traitorous *squeak.* Shit. The footsteps come to a dead stop. They've heard me. I know it. I stand frozen at the window, and the moonlight casts a vague milky glow around the room. How long have I been asleep? Two bottles of Shiraz wait silently at my feet like good little soldiers, and I snatch the half-empty one in my fist. I wait there so long my head starts to throb with the birth pangs of a massive hangover.

I eye the other bottle, the empty one, and it eyes me back, all critical and accusatory: *Are you sure you're not imagining this, Sarah? You drank the shit out of me tonight and passed out in your office. And you really shouldn't be drinking on your meds, remember?*

I count to ten in the dark. And then I hear it: a foot stepping over the threshold of my office. My fingers go numb with terror, and my heart gives one giant thump. There's someone *right there.*

I scramble to my desk and fumble for the lamp, when out of the darkness steps a man. I scream, staggering back into my bookshelf, thrusting the heavy end of the bottle out to defend myself. Red wine sloshes out from the loose cap and trickles down my chin and collar like blood spatter.

"Get *out*! Get outta here!"

The man steps in, flicking the office light on. "Mrs. Slade?"

He's surprisingly young. Mid-twenties, hard eyes, ridiculously tall, stooped a little at the shoulders. His hair's combed forward and falling over his left eye. It's brassy blond, unnatural, the black roots poking through. Looks like shit. I've never seen him before, but I recognize the shirt he's wearing. It's slate gray with a logo on the left pocket: Quality Office Cleaning. The long-sleeved shirt is far too small for him, the cuffs ending halfway up his forearms.

I drop the bottle and exhale shakily. The office cleaners get here at five every Saturday and Wednesday morning and finish before I get here at eight. Shit, is it five already? I know I set my alarm to go off before the cleaners got here. I always do. Black Wood House is only a ten-minute drive from my office.

He gives me a quizzical half smile, and I take a small step back. What if he stole that uniform to trick me? What if he's snooping on me? He wouldn't be the first person hired to track me down.

"Are you okay?"

"Of course," I say automatically. Actually, my fingers are trembling so bad I thrust them into my pockets.

"You're Sarah, yeah?" he asks patiently. "I just started here last week. Haven't met most of the shrinks yet."

There's an *entire chapter* in my book dedicated to mastering the easy art of small talk! And yet I don't know what the hell to say. It's too early for this shit.

"Me missus read your book." He grins. "She was pretty chuffed when I told her I'd be working here."

My face feels itchy, like I've stepped into a spiderweb, and my heart won't stop pounding. I manage a weak "Thank you" and wish to God he'd leave. I wonder how he got this job. He doesn't have the upper-middle-class Beacon feel about him. And he definitely doesn't have the vaguely expensive Australian accent so typical of these areas where Dad's a construction manager and Mum doesn't need to work since Dad pulls in a shitload. If you could call an Australian accent expensive, anyway. It's more like the discount version of our English cousins'.

But this guy, he's got the true-blue Aussie accent going—a vernacular that couldn't be lazier if it tried. Everything is *darl, love, mate, bloke, fair dinkum, g'day, 'ow ya goin'?*

My accent, if I'm being honest. Dad was a mechanic, Mum a house cleaner. But the old man could never keep a job and was always storming home in his cloud of righteous anger. He crapped out on everything in the end, including us. Took the car and all my self-worth with him. Left Mum bewildered and broke and holding her breath when the cashier tallied up our weekly grocery shop.

I didn't need another reason for Beacon residents to look down on me. So I stole Nicole Kidman's accent. I liked that vaguely upper-class cadence, so pleasant to the ear. I watched, then re-watched her interviews on YouTube, until it felt like I had two accents fighting in my mouth. But I'm a very good mimic. The best. And that working-class accent? I finally bled that shit out of me. It slips out only when I'm angry. Like now.

"Whaddya doin' here?" I ask, face hot with indignation.

"Sarah Slade." He rolls it around his tongue like he's at a wine tasting. I wonder if he can detect hints of my deceit. Wonder if he can taste smoky blackberries and terrible lies.

Obviously not, because he nods approvingly. "Nice name."

We wait in a silence that's rapidly turning awkward. And dangerous. For me.

"Couldn't stand to be a shrink meself." He sniffs. "Don't see why *anyone* would want to."

I must've zoned out, because he snaps his fingers to get my attention. He's crossed the line now, if he hadn't already. There's something nasty about the way he does it. Slimy. Like I'm a dim-witted student and he's the smart-ass principal.

I close my eyes, cool my blood. I've got to be nice to this asshole in case he tells someone about this. Do he and the other cleaners have a friendly smoke in the car park after work and bitch about us, like we do about them?

I caught Mrs. Slade asleep in her office, he would say, puffing on a cigarette. *Pretty sure she'd been drinkin' all night.*

His cleaning friends scurry closer like a pack of insects. *Husband problems, I betcha. Not to mention that murder house she just bought.*

I heard she's gotta come up with another book, another says, taking a gleeful drag. *Pressure must be getting to 'er.*

This is bad. This is really bad. Terrified, I slip my skin on, brush the droplets of wine from my chin, and stretch.

"Goodness me, I must have dozed off." I even go for a playful half smile that says, *This is all so silly, isn't it? You, busting in like this. Me, shit-faced in my chair and ready to club you to death.*

He looks pointedly at the empty bottle sitting at my feet, raises an eyebrow. My heart squeezes tight, and for one hot second I wish I *had* smashed him over the head.

I *need* this job. The royalties from my book are falling alarmingly. The next book is proving a bitch to write. And all that's paying my eye-watering mortgage is Joe's paltry bartender wage, a few Instagram sponsorships I'm desperately grateful for, and my work here at Mercy Community.

I've been working for them nine months now. I knew I'd gotten the job the second Adria, the manager, shook my hand a fraction too long before blurting, "I've read your book!"

According to their website, Mercy Community "maintains the highest professional standards," which is absolute bullshit. Because if they'd done their research, I'd never have gotten the job. And they would've realized the two references I gave were paid actors on Gumtree. Cost me fifty bucks each. They rang only one.

He shuffles his feet at my door. "It's getting on anyway," he says dismissively. "Your husband's probably worried . . ."

I doubt that.

I haven't thought about Joe in hours, and now here he is again, sinking into my frontal lobe because he's just another problem I have to solve. I ignore Joe and focus on the more pressing problem of Chatty Cleaning Guy and how I can get out of this without looking so guilty.

And then it hits me. I reach for my phone lying facedown on my desk like it's ashamed of itself.

JOE: R u coming home or not
JOE: ???
JOE: Whateva im goin to Andy's

Wincing, I close the texts. Right there on the home screen, along with a picture of Joe and I when he could stand me, is the time: 3:07 A.M.

I turn the phone off with a soft click. "It's three in the morning," I tell him. "The cleaners usually get here at five."

Am I seeing things, or did he flinch? I see a way out of my mess and try to take back control. "You're here a bit early today."

It's a statement, not an accusation. But it sure feels like one. Maybe that's why his eyes narrow, why his back stiffens. He shrugs, sticks his hands in his pockets. "Had a few things to take care of."

His words hang there like a little rain cloud, and I want to reach forward and wring the truth out. But he's already turning away, and that little creak at the threshold makes my skin itch.

Had a few things to take care of.

"Hey?" I call out, and he stops stiffly. "You never told me your name." When he turns around, I'm surprised how cold his eyes are. A chill settles over my scalp as I wait for him to answer.

He slides his hands into his jean pockets. "Watta's it matter what me name is?"

Okay, I'm nervous now. I take a half step back. "Did you open my door when you got here?" My voice is harsh, accusing.

"No," he says firmly. "Was already open."

But I locked it. I *remember.* I rushed to the bottle shop after Emily left, and I remember sneaking back into my office with the booze. I locked my door and plonked myself at the window.

He's been in here. I can feel it. He was snooping around in here *while I slept.*

Had a few things to take care of.

Like what, exactly? Like sneaking into my office and lying about it? Before he slinks away, his cold gaze lingers on the wine bottles. *Careful,* his eyes warn. *You've got secrets too.*

If I lost this job . . .

So I shut my mouth and let him disappear into the dark. I wait there in the moonlight, gripping my desk and knowing I will keep his secret.

And I pray he will keep mine.

Chapter 4

Welcome to Beacon, where everyone is settled and safe and smug as fuck about it. I drive through the moonlit streets, still surprised I can call it home. There are no traffic lights in Beacon, population 1,831. It's a one-road town where children bike to the general store on lazy Sunday afternoons while mums hang lemon-scented washing on the line and dads gather in good-natured groups at the town's only pub.

Kids don't have curfews, though none are needed. There's no danger lurking in the darkness and no trouble to get into that can't be sorted out with indulgent neighbors. Cinemas and shopping centers are a half-hour drive away, and a trip into the Big Smoke is gently discouraged. Kids grow up sequestered from outside influences and kept so distracted they barely notice. There are plenty of good trees to climb, cricket teams to join, pools to splash about in, and nothing but room to run and run and run.

There's a waiting list to buy into this town, the realtor told us. No wonder. The only people who can afford to live here are older couples, long retired, who spend their day gardening and chatting with their neighbors of thirty years while their children wait impatiently for them to die.

Kids grow up slowly here, and some barely grow up at all. My colleague Becky inherited her three-story Grecian house when her mother passed two years ago. Now she works three days a week, plays tennis the rest, and has heated conversations about how entitled this generation is.

She has one kid, Josh, and when she dies, he'll inherit that stunning two-million-dollar house and complete the Beacon cycle, until the town is just one long bloodline.

I grew up in a two-bedroom shithole in north Queensland that smelled of sweat and smoke. Summer was a miserable stretch of forty-degree-Celsius days where sticking your arm out the car window felt like you'd shoved it in the oven. Little kids would wail red-faced in their strollers in the supermarkets while their exhausted mums fanned them with rolled-up pieces of paper and counted the days until summer ended.

Like the rest of the poor families on our street, we had no air-conditioning, and not even a quick, cold shower helped. Five minutes later you'd be dripping sweat down your nose, knees, and underarms and flopping on hard, tiled floors until you woke up dizzy an hour later with a pounding heat headache.

But the rich kids had it easy. They'd hide away in air-conditioned houses or splash in their sparkling pools before emerging fresh and clean and cool, and God, I hated them for it.

When Becky bitches about how kids have everything handed to them these days, I really want to punch her in the face. Aren't you lucky, Becky, you out-of-touch cow, that your grandparents bought your family home a hundred years ago, back when a brand-new car cost three weeks' pay, and your three-story Grecian house with the football field for a backyard was paid off in ten years? How lucky that you and the other Beacon grandchildren have no mortgage, no debt, and no fucking clue how the rest of the world works.

Some of us fought hard to get here, Becky. Some of us fought dirty.

I exhale slowly, pulling into our moonlight-soaked street. Life in Beacon was sheltered and safe for years. People attended the bi-weekly town meetings, chatted over the fence, and watched their spoiled children play cricket on the eucalyptus-scented streets.

So the murder at Black Wood House must have come as one big, goddamn shock. Something about that makes me smile. Makes me glad I'm its new owner even for a little while.

Before we moved here, Joe and I lived in Mitchell, North Melbourne, for two years. What can I say about Mitchell, except it smelled like petrol and despair, the streets were bleached of color, and the whole town just seemed *pissed off*? Mitchell. God, I hated that town. Took me an hour to drive here to work every day. Sometimes I'd park in the main street of Beacon, breathe in the clean air, and just watch how the other half lived. I'd always wanted to worm my way into an upper-class town like this. I jumped at the chance to buy Black Wood when I saw it on PeakeProbate.com:

BLACK WOOD MURDER HOUSE FOR SALE

I'd watched every episode of *Murder House Flip*. I knew I could document all the renovations and make a shitload. It felt like the perfect way to grow my brand: *I'm Sarah Slade! I fix people—now watch me fix this godforsaken murder house!*

Plus, it was the only chance I had to get into the Beacon market. Yes, it was an impulse buy but a clever one. I was packing my bags before I even looked through the due diligence checklist. And now I'm here, infiltrating the peculiar blood bond of this town like a sickness. Becky visibly grimaced when I announced I'd bought it, and I bit back a gleeful smile.

"Oh . . ." she stammered. "Well . . . welcome to the neighborhood, I guess."

But her eyes said, *You're not one of us. And you never will be.*

I drive slowly down the dark street, breathing in the clean night air. Beacon has that aromatic damp-forest smell of the Australian bush. There's nothing like it. When you wind down the window and gulp it in, you're breathing in the bright, chiming calls of the bellbirds. The chuckle of the kookaburras on the fiery branches of the bottlebrush trees. The smooth white trunks of the *Eucalyptus viminalis,* shedding their bark in long ribbons under the summer sun.

I peer down the empty street as the white trunks of the ribbon gums glow in the moonlight. I haven't seen any neighborhood kids, dog walkers, or even a damn car pull out of a driveway since we moved in last week. Joe keeps saying we should introduce ourselves, but I think the neighbors stay away on purpose. The realtor suggested as much. He'd cleared his throat and said too casually, "Black Wood House is a bit of a sore point in Beacon." We'd already signed the deed by then. "It's a fussy old neighborhood, not much new blood." He winced at the word and blurted out, "You shouldn't have any real issues with the neighbors, but if you do . . ."

Joe stared in alarm at the realtor and gave me a pointed look. My husband lives in fear of two things: people finding out about our sordid history and not being liked. I was worried he'd back out now that we were clearly about to be the pariahs of the neighborhood. The realtor must have seen the look on Joe's face, because he flashed a slimy smile and said, "Well, if the neighbors have a problem, there's not much they can do about it now, is there?"

I drive past a three-story Spanish revival house where the Whitmans live. Red-clay roof, ice-pink tulips, bubbling angel fountains. This is the pretty house Janet Campbell fled to after the attempted murder at my house.

Don't kill me. Don't kill me. Don't kill me.

She collapsed at their terra-cotta door, and the horrified Whitmans rushed her to the hospital. Forty years later, and the Whitmans are still there. I drive past, tree shadows falling over the car, leaving me in ghostly darkness.

Black Wood House is at the very end of the street. It must have taken Janet two or three minutes, at least, to flee down this road to the safety of the Whitmans'. Longer maybe, since she was barefoot . . . and her head was smashed in.

Don't kill me.

I come to the end of the road and take my foot off the accelerator. In front of me, lit up by the headlights, is Black Wood Forest.

I was excited about the idea of living right next door to it. I'd spend Saturday mornings jogging there, I decided. Maybe even the occasional picnic with Joe if we were having a good day. But that was before I saw it for myself. Black Wood Forest is an impenetrable mess of swampy woodlands, charred black pine trees, and carnivorous plants. I parked there after work last week, locked the car, and climbed over the waist-high gate. Immediately the blackwood trees swallowed the remaining light, and the air was so cold, it left me shaking.

Determinedly, I kept walking down that black path, trying not to notice how the hairs on my forearms stood up in clear warning. Some-where overhead a cockatoo cried out, sounding like a wounded child. I felt like I was walking down the dark throat of some feral animal. I turned around, colliding hard with a mountain gray gum that I was certain wasn't there a moment ago. Its blackened branches clawed at my face while the bird screamed and screamed, and I had the strangest feeling the forest was trying to grab me and keep me from leaving.

I ran then. Ran all the way back to my car, stumbling over fallen branches and rocks bigger than my fist. By the time I stumbled to my car, it was totally dark, though I'm sure I'd been in there only a few minutes.

Now every time I drive past, it gives me an uneasy feeling.

I stare out the windshield at the forest, and the headlights catch a pair of yellow eyes high up in the trees. Possum, probably. Slowly, I press down on the accelerator and pull the steering wheel to the right where a rusty gate, swallowed by ivy, issues a weak warning: KEEP OUT. Ours is a damn long driveway. When I'm hungover and late for work, it takes twenty seconds to drive the length of it.

I drive slowly, high beams on, scanning for potholes. Rabbits scurry across the front yard, running from the light.

Black Wood House is as still as a painting.

I turn the engine off and stare at it through my grimy windshield.

We've been here four days, and each day has been harder than the last. Joe and I are struggling to hang on to the excitement of owning our first house now that the grim reality of the renovations has settled over us. Joe thinks the roof is rotting. We weren't anticipating a total repair, and our bank account sure as hell won't be happy about it.

I eye the stark land with growing anxiety, gripping the steering wheel tight enough to strangle it. The Whitmans' is worth $1.5 million, I remind myself. Once the renovations are complete, *someone* is going to buy this house. Plenty of murder houses have sold without a problem. We'll double our money. Triple it, even. We'll fix it all up, and I'll plant a rose garden out front for a bit of color. Little bursts of coral red and pale peach. Anything to combat the starkness of this dead and grieving land.

I step out into the dark morning, and God, it's cold. Quickly, I loop my bag over my shoulder, tuck my key under my elbow, and wrap my arms around my waist. I keep my eyes on the shadowy ground, careful not to fall into one of the echidna holes and break my neck. What a way to die.

I unlock the front door and step into the dark. It's just as cold in here, and I'm not surprised. There's an icy dampness to this place that not even a roaring fire seems to fix. I hesitate at the fireplace, wondering if I should light it. The fireplace is one of my favorite things about the house. It's an original Victorian, cast iron, horseshoe shaped, with an art nouveau pattern. I've gotten into the routine of lighting a fire when I get home from work. But I'm too cold to bother right now. I walk past, shivering, breathing in the stale air. We can't get any of the damn windows open, and for such a huge house, there's a surprising lack of them. There's only one in the lounge room, north facing and smelling of rot. After years of weathering, the wood's warped so badly it'll have to be replaced. For now, we're stuck in a house that smells like it hasn't been aired since the murder. There's a staleness to it like old water.

I shiver in my thin jacket, dump my keys on the coffee table, and stare blankly at the empty couch where my husband should be.

Whateva im goin to Andy's.

I'd almost forgotten his earlier text. My husband. My darling husband who hates me. God, why is Joe just another problem I have to fix? I climb the stairs, clutching the cold banister in my right hand. It's so quiet that the sounds of my feet are deafening.

Thud.

Thud.

I don't know where Reaper is, and I'm surprised how much that stings. I need my boy tonight.

My room, the Campbells' old bedroom, is large enough to fit four king-sized beds. The only thing I've had time to unpack is our bed, and the vast emptiness of the room just swallows it up. And it's dark, always dark, despite the paltry window.

I'm too tired to shower, and the hot water system still needs replacing. I creep over to the bed and pull my phone out of my jacket pocket. 3:43.

I sit heavily on my side of the bed. Joe's side's always been the left, closer to the door, and though we haven't shared it in months, it's hard to undo that habit. I tie my hair in a tight ponytail, climb under the covers, and pull them up to my chin.

And of course, I can't sleep. It hits me that this is the first time I've been alone in the house since we moved in last week. I don't know when Joe will drag his arse home, but I know he'll be hungover and unreachable when he does.

I roll over and consider pulling up the Kindle app on my phone. But no, I dismiss the idea straightaway. Lately, reading just reminds me of work. It reminds me of that damn blogger shoving her iPhone under my chin and prompting, "When's your next bestseller coming out?"

I wished I could've shoved her phone down her throat. But I smiled instead, because of course I did. That's what Sarah Slade would do.

I clench my teeth in the darkness, staring at the floor.

Creeeeeeeeak.

I bolt upright.

Creeeeeeeeak.

You'd swear someone was walking up the stairs. I hold my breath and listen.

It's just the house settling, for shit's sake. It seems louder tonight because Joe's not here, the bastard. I exhale slowly, ignore my rattling pulse and the fact that it's just me, two barren acres, and a murder scene.

You wanted this, I remind myself.

I'm about to roll over when I realize I'm staring right at the bloodstain. It hits me that Susan Campbell was lying *right here* when her husband crept silently over. It happened in the early hours of the morning. Did he make any noise when he stalked over, claw hammer in hand? Did she hear a creak of footsteps as she lay sleeping?

I don't know much about their marriage. Only how it ended. And now I can't get it out of my head. I squint at the bloodstain like I'm looking for clues. I imagine Susan and Bill clasping hands, all shiny eyed and full of that sweet belief reserved for newlyweds. I imagine Susan's head on Bill's shoulder as they slow dance in that *Brady Bunch* kitchen.

I stare at the bloodstain, grimacing. How did it go from vowing to love, honor, and cherish to *that*? To *fucking* that?

I roll over, turning my back on the bloodstain. An old image of Joe flashes through my mind. Him on our wedding day. He'd bought a ten-dollar shirt from Kmart and tucked the severed head of a yellow tulip into the pocket. It looked ridiculous, but it made me laugh. I was happy to marry him. My boy. Mine.

Tears sting my eyes, and I brush them away. Behind me, the bloodstain laughs. *That's the thing about marriages,* it taunts me. *We all know the endings. Endings are loud. But we don't know about the middle.*

I open my eyes, and for the first time I wonder about the Campbells. Not the ending. I want to know *their* middle. I want to know when their marriage crossed that devastating line. When did Susan first have a clue that she was no longer safe with the man she married? Did she see it unraveling slowly, thread by fucking thread? Or did she know only when she held up her bloodied hands to defend herself?

The middle of a marriage is quiet. The middle is dangerous.

Joe and I are in the middle.

Creak.

Out of the corner of my eye, something moves. I stop breathing. At the threshold of my bedroom, something pads silently forward. Burning orange eyes glare at me in the darkness. My lips go numb with terror as the thing rushes forward, leaps onto my bed, and pins itself against my chest.

"Reaper!"

The damn cat hisses in my face like he's laughing at me. I swear in the darkness and reach for him. His tiny claws grip both sides of my neck like he's trying to strangle me.

Lovely.

"Reaper, get off!" I prize his paws away, but he holds me tighter. When he drops with a thud onto my chest, I realize. Something is wrong with him. His entire body is trembling, and he grips me tight enough to draw blood. A low, anxious howl begins at the back of his throat. It's that hideous shriek-howl cats give right before they attack each other. It's creepy, unnerving, and I wish to hell he'd stop.

With shaking hands, I reach for the lamp beside my bed and flick it on. He howls again and tries to bolt off my bed. I lunge for him and grip him in the crook of my left arm. I can't see any signs of trauma. His eyes are clear and bright, and there's no blood. I force his mouth open and swipe inside with a fingertip to make sure he's not choking on something. Clear. I roll him over onto his back, and he hisses and spits while I examine his chest and stomach. Nothing there either. I run my fingers through his tangled fur. I don't know what I'm looking for. A tick, maybe? A snakebite, even?

But I find nothing.

I pull him gently upright again and hold him against my chest. "It's okay," I say softly, patting him from ear to tail. "It's okay."

This time he doesn't struggle, but little tremors ripple through his body. I stroke his back and scratch behind his ear where I know he likes it. After a little while, the trembling stops, and so does the howling. It's the stress of the move, I tell myself. There's nothing wrong with him.

I wonder if I should take him to the vet tomorrow to make sure, but it's always an embarrassing disaster when I drag him in. "He's a bit highly strung, isn't he?" the last vet murmured, cradling her bloodied thumb where Reaper bit it.

And Joe snorted. "No, he's just an asshole."

"You're all right, Reap." I tuck him into the crook of my arm, and he rests his flat little face on my elbow. Finally, we drift off to sleep, the creaking house and my anxious mind like a horrible metronome in the darkness.

Creak.

Whateva im goin to Andy's.

Thud.

When's your next bestseller coming out?

Groan.

Had a few things to take care of.

Bang.

Don't kill me. Don't kill me. Don't kill me.

Chapter 5

If we don't fix the bloody shower soon, I am going to murder someone. The showerhead's been leaking since we moved in. *Drip, drip, drip.* All day and all night.

I swear I can hear it all the way down the hall from my bloody bedroom. *Drip, drip.* I stand on tiptoes on my bed, my husband beside me, smelling pleasantly of sweat and beer. Together we hold the giant piece of cream-and-gold wallpaper with our fingertips, trying hard not to make any creases before we press it on. We inch closer. Directly in front of me are four blackbirds in the crook of a tree. Watching.

"They look so sad." I grunt, struggling to keep my balance.

Joe presses his corner down first with the flat of his hand, and I watch the blackbirds disappear.

For the next few minutes, Joe and I work together, side by side, and for a moment I allow myself to enjoy it. I always loved these little moments of being married. We smooth down the paper, and once it's stuck firm, there's a loud knock on the door downstairs.

Joe and I exchange relieved looks. The plumber's here.

"I'll let him in," Joe says, jumping nimbly from the bed and disappearing out the door.

I stare up at the wallpaper, shocked by how much difference it's already made to the room. The cream and gold gleam softly, just catching the last light of the day. It's beautiful, but I wonder what the blackbirds think now that they're smothered underneath it all. I jump down from the bed and land right on Susan's bloodstain. Poor Susan. Poor little blackbirds.

I feel uneasy, like I've made the wrong move. Like I'm guilty of something but I'm not sure what. I head to the bathroom and peer in.

"Cracked seal," the plumber says laconically, inspecting the leak. "Won't take too long to fix."

Joe shoves his hands in his pockets, anxiety staining his face. "How much is that gonna cost?"

The plumber scratches the back of his beefy neck. "Three fifty."

Bastard. He quoted me $280 on the phone. Joe pales, and I lean against the bathroom door, seething. I clear my throat, and Joe shoots me a warning look. The truth is, I rang four plumbers to come fix the leak, but as soon as I gave them the address, they either hung up or were suddenly too busy to come.

"Three fifty is fine," says my husband. The plumber grunts in reply, and I press my lips together before asking brightly, "Would anyone like a coffee?"

They don't, and neither do I, but I need an excuse to head downstairs and calm down a bit. Truthfully, I can't stop thinking about those black-birds. I lean against the faded green kitchen counter, staring at the spaces where the light switches used to be. The electrician worked on them yesterday, and now they're just holes in the walls, blue and red wires poking out like exposed intestines. It makes me queasy just looking at them.

Slowly, I head back upstairs, gripping the banister because my legs feel oddly hollow. I'm resting at the top, breathing hard, when Joe steps out of the bathroom and gives me a questioning look.

"You all right?" He actually sounds concerned.

"Yeah," I say automatically, straightening up. "Wanna finish the wallpaper?"

I head to the murder room, and when Joe follows, he places a soft hand on my shoulder. I want to reach for it like a woman drowning, but

I don't. I'm in control, I tell myself. But why does everything feel so wrong? All of it. I just can't shake the feeling.

I step into the bedroom and stare at the back wall in shock. I freeze at the door, and behind me my husband calls out, "What the heck?"

The lovely cream-and-gold wallpaper we just hung now lies face-down on the bed like a dead person. Silently, I step forward and inspect the paper. A chill creeps down my scalp and settles around my neck like a scarf. I look up. The blackbirds watch me, silent and angry. I step back.

Joe and I hover around the wallpaper uneasily. I stare down the hall-way, thinking of the plumber, but Joe shakes his head.

"He was with me the whole time," Joe says. "We didn't leave the bathroom."

I press my hand to my abdomen, and my eyes drift up to the black-birds.

"Did *you* do this?" Joe finally asks. "Did you take it down?"

The anger in his voice throws me.

"Of course not!" I say too harshly. "Why *would* I?"

He doesn't answer, but his body radiates anger. Damn it. It was fun wallpapering with him this afternoon. It felt like the start of something brand new.

And now he's angry at me again.

And those bloody blackbirds glare at me from the wall.

You tried to cover us up. Don't do that again.

I feel like everything in this room is mad at me. I step back, and some-one screams. At first, I think it's the blackbirds. Or maybe it's the house. The house is mad at me for trying to change it. But then Joe rushes past me, and I realize the screaming is coming from the bathroom. I stagger out the door, everything feeling unreal, just as the plumber comes burst-ing out the bathroom door.

"What's wrong?" Joe calls out. "What's wrong?"

I see it then. The plumber stops mid-scream and stands, dazed, at the top of the stairs, clutching the back of his head. Blood gushes down both temples, dripping under his chin. *Drip, drip, drip.* He wobbles on his feet, his face drained of color, his eyes too wide, pupils too large.

"I knew I shouldn'ta come to this house," he murmurs, his lips dry and white. "This house . . . This bloody house . . ."

Joe catches him as he collapses, and I stand frozen, watching the blood run down the plumber's forearm and drip from his fingertips. *Drip, drip. Drip, drip.* Distantly, I hear Joe call my name, but all I can think is that the plumber tried to fix the dripping shower but the house didn't want him to.

Now the plumber is the one who drips.

SarahSlays.com

HOME   ABOUT SARAH SLADE   BUY MY BOOK   CONTACT

WELCOME TO BLACK WOOD HOUSE!

MAY 10

Hi there, folks, and welcome to my website!

My husband and I finally moved into Black Wood House two weeks ago, so it's time for the very first update! I hope you're as excited to start this journey as we are!

Let's start with the not-so-good bits: We had a bit of a hard time moving our furniture in due to the many holes in the yard (thanks, echidnas!). And unfortunately, the kitchen needs more work than what we anticipated (the kettle works at least!). We're looking at a major kitchen overhaul, so we've been a bit naughty and living off Chinese takeaway since. (Gah, I hope my Pilates instructor isn't reading this!)

Joe's been dealing with the electrical and plumbing details (yawn!). So if you want updates about all the really boring stuff, you won't find them here. (Who cares about gutters and roofing when there are gorgeous Tiffany chandeliers to obsess over!)

Speaking of gorgeous things! I had the greatest time with the folks down at Retro Renovations. If you're looking at re-painting your own home, check these guys out. (This is not a paid promo!) They helped me make my own custom color: a beautiful pure green I'm calling Avocado Goodness! (Photos below.) I can already see this all over the lounge room walls. (And I may have ordered the new kitchen appliances in the same custom color! Yikes! I hope Joe isn't reading this, lol!)

We'll be working on the hot water system this week, so yay for that. There's way more work to be done, and it's been a little bit tougher than we anticipated. But the house has been shut up and neglected ever since . . . well, I'm sure you know.

Check out the pics of Avocado Goodness and the matching custom kitchen appliances below.

And here's a link to the stunning kitchenware: CreateYourOwn CustomKitchen.com

(No discount code, I'm afraid. But . . . maybe next time? @Create YourOwnCustomKitchen Would LOVE to work with you guys!)

Take Care, Sladies and Gentlemen!

P.S.—Yes, I'm still working on my next book! It's going soooooo well, and I cannot wait to share it!

I gulp my coffee and hate myself. This is Media Relations Sarah. She uses too many exclamation marks, is Enthusiastic about Everything!! and loves nothing more than whoring herself out for a discount code.

I hover the cursor over the post button, cringing as I proofread the update. I've had five hours' sleep in two days. My eyes are sticky, and another headache worms its way into my skull.

I hit the post button before I change my mind. Then I lean back in my Gatsby chair and wince as it goes live. There. Done. People can stop asking me for updates now. I swear, every time I sip coffee in the work kitchen, Tim, the sports psych, hits me on the arm with a newspaper. "How's those renovations going?"

"That's right!" Emily pipes up. "You bought the Black Wood place, didn't you?" Then she adds, "You don't actually live there, do you, lovie?"

Well. Now I can finally dismiss them with "The details are on my website! You should check it out!"

Yes, Tim and Emily, go read my cheery post and my bullshit lies. I'll let the abundance of exclamation marks hide the awful truth: The renovations have been a fucking nightmare. *Everything* needs fixing, replacing, unscrewing, remodeling, *gutting.* I've hired three contractors, and none of them showed up. We're on our fourth now, and the price just keeps adding up. Turns out, even moving a goddamn light switch will cost a grand.

I sip my sugarless coffee and check the time. 1:50 P.M. Ten minutes until my next client. I refresh the page, and to my surprise, someone's already commented on my post. I scan the words, and my throat tightens in fear.

You are an absolute insult to the memory of the poor Campbells. I think it's disgusting that you bought their house, and even more sickening that you clearly hope to profit on it.

I'm so stunned my mouth falls open. Joe warned me that I might get some crackpots, considering how infamous the house is. It's been on the news for forty years, and the interest hasn't subsided. And even Joe admitted we'd need as much publicity as possible to sell the damn thing.

But I honestly wasn't expecting the hate so quickly. So viciously.

Actually, I wasn't really expecting it at all.

I hit the delete button, and the message vanishes, but my uneasiness remains. God, I hope nobody saw it. If it's going to be like this, I might have to disable comments, and I hate doing that. I love the little likes, heart emojis, and congratulations. I feed off that puerile bullshit. Without it, I starve.

My head's in my hands when another comment fills the screen.

Slowly, I raise my head and read it. It's just one word, but it makes my blood freeze. No, no, no.

Lizzy.

I lunge for the keyboard and smash the delete button. When it's gone, I lean back in my chair, guts twisting. Did anyone see it? Lizzy. Lizzy. My sister's face rushes to my mind, and I try in vain to push it out.

There are people from my hometown who know the story. All of it. And even after all these years, the thought still makes my breath catch in my throat. For years and years I've run and run, but never without darting panicked glances over my shoulder. And it's so much worse now because I've never had more to lose. I've got a steady job, hundreds of thousands of Instagram followers, and all my money tied up in a murder house that I won't be able to sell if my reputation's smeared.

I've seen it before. Last year, an author with three bestsellers lost her contract, her sponsorships, and shortly thereafter her house all because an unfortunate video surfaced. Thirty-four seconds of her in a messy college dorm, dancing drunkenly and groping her boyfriend.

She issued two lengthy apologies, but nothing stopped the hate train. Nothing much does.

There are no drunken college videos of me. I never went to uni despite what my CV says. But there's something much worse out there. Someone knows, and if they tell anyone, I'll lose my job and my reputation, and I'll be stuck with a murder house I can't get rid of.

If people find out what happened to my sister, I will lose it all.

Chapter 6

A stranger stands next to the blackwood tree. He rests his head on the fissured trunk like it's an old friend comforting him. His back is to me, and he's not moving. Not even when I speed up my driveway without bothering to go slowly over the echidna holes.

My mouth is bone dry, and for a second I wonder if I should turn and drive away. Maybe head into town and ring Joe. *There's a stranger in our front yard,* I'll tell him. *And I don't know why, but I've got a bad feeling about him.*

But my husband is useless with confrontations, so I shake my head. Bugga it, I'll handle this myself. I come to an abrupt stop, shove the car into park, and leap out. I position my keys in my fist, jutting one of them between my middle and ring finger. If this man makes any trouble, I'll . . .

What, Sarah? Stab him in the eye with your house key?

I hover there at my car door and watch him. The man's barely moved. He's still gazing up at my house, hands thrust into his pockets like he's staring at a horrible painting. There's something so intense about it that I actually feel like I'm intruding on a private moment.

I clear my throat, and his back stiffens. "Can I help you?"

Finally, the man turns around and fixes his eyes on me. The first thing I notice is that they're red-rimmed and wet. Two fresh tears roll down his weathered face, and he makes no attempt to wipe them away. There's something intensely sad about him. But as he stands there looking me over, there's a spark of something in his watery blue eyes. Fear.

Mr. Whitman. I recognize his face from a magazine article, something like, "Neighbor Tells His Harrowing Tale on the Fortieth Anniversary of the Black Wood Murder."

"So, you're the new owner?" he asks quietly.

"Yes, I am," I tell him lightly. "You must be Mr. Whitman."

You're the one who gave the interview with *Home Beautiful* magazine. The one who said, "I hope nobody ever buys the Black Wood House. It'd be such an insult to Susan's memory. God, she didn't deserve to die like that."

I breathe in sharply. *Such an insult to Susan's memory* . . .

I'm taken back to that damn comment on my website this afternoon. *You are an absolute insult to the memory of the poor Campbells.*

It was him.

I grip my keys nervously, running my thumb over the pointed tip of the house key. I want to go inside, lock the door, and get away from this man.

I open my mouth to spin some bullshit. Something polite with a firm undercurrent like, "It was nice to meet you, but I have to get dinner started . . ."

"My wife and I were friends with Susan," he says in an aching voice.

I didn't know that. I nod sympathetically and peek longingly at my front door. Silence. A cockatoo lands softly in the blackwood tree and peers at us with unblinking eyes. A cool breeze sweeps over the tree, rattles the dead branches, and leaves me cold. I wrap my arms around myself, and the key pokes into my side.

"Did you know Bill Campbell?" *You know, the murderer?* It's out of my mouth before I even realize I've said it.

Mr. Whitman's eyes drop to the patchy ground.

"He kept to himself. Susan was the friendly one, and Janet, of course. The girls were like sunny afternoons." He frowns. "Bill was a cold morning."

He shuffles unsteadily, and I wonder if he's been drinking. I don't want to call the police on a harmless old man. It'd be terrible for publicity. But the thought surges unwelcome into my head: Unless he's not harmless . . .

"Susan said Bill started changing when he moved here." He speaks again in his rusty-old-can voice.

I raise my eyebrows. "How?"

"This house . . ." He shakes his head, and again something flashes in his old blue eyes. He glances warily at Black Wood House. "It made him crazy."

I remember Joe's words from the night we moved in. *Do you think the house wants us here?*

"It's just a house," I say gently. "Houses don't make people crazy. People make themselves crazy." To soften the mood and get the hell out of here, I force a jovial tone. "And I should know. I'm a therapist."

He eyes me warily like I've told an inappropriate joke. I clear my throat in the awkward silence, and he continues staring like I haven't even spoken, looking me right in the eye like I'm a silly woman in distress and he's trying to get through to me.

He takes a shaky step toward me, and I step back. He's making me really nervous, and my voice comes out harsher than intended, "Why are you here?"

"I need to tell you something," he says urgently. "And I need you to listen."

I narrow my eyes at him, waiting. He shuffles a bit on the spot, like his legs are struggling to keep him upright. If I run inside right now, I think, he won't be able to keep up. I glance desperately at the front door, and he steps forward, blocking my path.

"I'm here to warn you."

The hairs on the back of my neck stand up. "About what?"

His entire body is trembling. He's wobbly and unfocused, and his eyes are wide with fear. He glances at the house yet again, like he's afraid to speak in front of it.

"What is it?"

He bites his lip, eyes flicking back and forth between the house and me. He leans in. "There's something in the attic," he whispers.

"The attic?" I repeat stupidly.

"That's what Bill kept saying." He jerks his head at our sloping roof, the one that'll cost us ten grand to fix. Urgently he whispers, "He said he heard noises coming from the attic. Especially at night."

"What did he think it was?"

He shuffles in his spot, and I notice how pale he's gotten. "He wasn't sure . . . but he insisted something was up there, watching them. He was so paranoid that he started sleeping up there." He swallows hard. "But he never did find out what it was."

"What did Susan say about it?"

"She was worried, but not about the attic. It was Bill she was concerned about. She thought he was losing his marbles. Plus"—he frowns—"they were arguing all the time." He glances nervously at the house again, like he's sure it's listening. "They'd sunk a lot of money into the house, and they couldn't really afford it. And Bill . . . well, he hid it as best he could, but he had some problems."

I fidget with my car key, running my thumb across the cool metal. "What kind?"

"Drinking, mainly. And"—his voice drops—"I guess you'd call them mental issues these days. But back then we just said he was highly strung."

Marriage, financial, and mental health issues . . . Huh, same.

Mr. Whitman stares grimly at the front door. "The house made him crazy," he mutters. "I know it did. Plus, there was something that didn't add up about Bill. We always felt he was hiding something about his past."

Aren't we all?

He wheels so quickly that it catches me off guard. His red-rimmed eyes flick over me. "Where did you say you were from again?"

I tilt my chin up. Look him straight in the eye. *Trust me,* my eyes say. *I've got nothing to hide.* I open my mouth, and my lies come out so smoothly you'd think I'd spent hours and hours practicing them.

Which I have.

"Oh, I moved around a lot." I smile blandly. "My parents never liked to stay in the same place for long."

"Where are your parents now?"

I can answer that truthfully, at least. "Dead."

He flinches. "I'm sorry."

I'm not.

"Thank you." I shuffle from foot to foot and hope he'll get the message. Then I remember what Joe said about being nice to the neighbors. That's Joe. He needs to be liked, adored even, but not by me apparently.

I chew on my lip, thinking. If we intend to sell this place, it will help if the neighbors are on board. It might put off future buyers to know the neighborhood hates their guts. So, I add grudgingly, "We'll have to have you and Mrs. Whitman over for coffee sometime."

"No!"

Now it's my turn to flinch. He's staring up at the house again with that nervous look. He turns back to me, his mouth a grim line. "I'm sorry, but I don't think I could ever step foot in that house again."

He doesn't say it, but I can hear the accusation plainly: *And I don't see how you could either.*

I don't know how to answer him, so I click the lock button on my car key and start walking toward the house. I issue a firm goodbye, hoping he never comes here again. But he doesn't move out of my way.

"You'll be careful, won't you, Sarah?"

I blink in surprise. "Of what?"

He pointedly doesn't answer.

"Houses don't make people crazy," I repeat, firmer this time. Without meaning to, I put on my "soothing therapist who knows better than you" voice. I even tilt my head so my expensive caramel hair falls over my shoulder like a curtain, closing the conversation. "I know what happened here was a tragedy, but—"

"Sarah." He cuts me off, staring desperately into my eyes, like he just can't seem to make me understand. "You don't know the half of it."

Behind me a car creeps up the driveway. Joe's home, thank God. Mr. Whitman frowns at the interruption, then leans forward until his yellowing teeth are an inch from my face.

"If you see or hear anything strange," he says in a croaky rush, "you know where we are."

A car door slams behind me, and as soon as I turn to look, Mr. Whitman's hand shoots out. He squeezes my wrist, his fingers as smooth and cold as a snake's belly. I gasp, frozen still. "When it happens, we'll be right down the street," he says in an aching voice.

Joe calls out behind us, atoms of panic in his voice. But it's Mr. Whitman I can't stop staring at. I hate myself for asking, but I can't seem to help it. "When *what* happens?"

He doesn't answer. I snatch my wrist away, and he lets go, stuffing his hands into his pockets and looking up at the house once again.

"I'm sure we'll be fine," I say firmly, rubbing my wrist. "Look, I think you need to—"

"The others thought that too," he says quietly.

"What others?" I finally snap.

Joe's soft footsteps crunch up the driveway, and I want to yell at him to hurry up and help me. The sound distracts Mr. Whitman, who finally takes his eyes from the house and looks over my shoulder.

"Is something wrong?" Joe strides forward, eyes wide and scared, anxiety splashed all over his face.

Mr. Whitman stares almost sadly at my husband. "You shouldn't have bought the house, son. It doesn't want to be fixed, and it doesn't want you here."

Before he backs away, he says something under his breath so that Joe doesn't hear. But I do. His words ring warning bells in my stomach, and I swallow hard, ignoring Joe when he asks uncertainly if I'm okay.

No, I'm not okay.

Because all I can hear is the last thing Mr. Whitman said.

You shouldn't have bought the house, son. It doesn't want to be fixed, and it doesn't want you here.

And it's going to make you pay.

Chapter 7

I slump onto the couch and stare blankly out the one lone window. We haven't cleaned it yet, and it's just a blurred mess of moss and forty years of grime. Outside, the sky is graveyard gray, and everything looks dry and soulless. Dead.

A flock of galahs scuttle in the bushes, their fragile cries sounding eerily human. I cover my face with my hands and breathe through the cracks between my cold fingers.

It's going to make you pay.

The front door bursts open, letting in a terrific gust of icy air that sneaks under my jacket and makes me shiver. I don't even mind. The wind is clean and burning and *alive*. Maybe if we leave the door open long enough, it will finally soak through all this sadness. Maybe it will make it clean again.

I wrap my arms around myself, trembling. Joe slams the door shut and steps forward until he's hovering behind me. I hate when he does that.

"Mr. Whitman's gone," Joe finally says. "I . . . I told him not to come back for a while."

It must've been hard for Joe to do that, but I don't quite have it in me to thank him. "It couldn't have been easy for him, coming here," he adds quickly. "Maybe one day . . ."

He doesn't finish, but I know him too well. Maybe, Joe thinks, we can have the Whitmans over for a barbecue, and we can drink beer like old friends, and we can all ignore the fact that their friend was beaten to death upstairs.

I glance over my shoulder at my husband. His cheeks are red with cold, and he shuffles from foot to foot. Skirmishes with people always leave him jittery.

"I don't want him here again," I say flatly. "He's not welcome."

And before he can argue, I hold my palm up to stop him. "It's not your problem, Joe. I'll handle the Whitmans." I turn back to the window, staring moodily at a rain-heavy cloud. "I'll handle anyone that tries to mess with my plans."

"You always do."

It's the way he says it that makes me flinch. I'm shocked how much resentment he can cram into three words.

Well, now it's my turn.

"You're just as bad as me," I say quietly. "In fact . . . you might be worse."

I swear I can feel him bristling behind me. "The fuck does *that* mean?"

"You know," I say simply.

Silently, Reaper crosses the room, oblivious to the tension between Joe and me. Or maybe he *is* aware, but he's learned to ignore it. He leaps onto my lap and perches on my left knee. For a moment, none of us move, and it must be a strange picture. Me, trembling and silent. My cat on my knee like a disapproving statue. And my darling husband, hovering behind us like he can't make up his mind if he wants to kill us or not.

Joe finally moves. He stalks across the floorboards, and they groan loudly like they're mad at him. The front door bursts open again, and the wind shrieks in. A splatter of rain begins to fall, and Joe ducks his head as he half runs out to his car.

Reaper and I watch him flee. We watch his white car speed down the snaking driveway and listen to his tires screech around the corner. Gone.

Reaper gives me a look that says, *God, he's a dickhead.* He jumps off my knee, and I slowly get to my feet. I close the front door, then find myself wandering into the kitchen, standing in front of the pantry door. The longer I stare, the angrier I get. The wood is rotting, the paint all blistered like sunburned skin.

Stuff this.

I lunge for the hammer on the kitchen counter and smash it against the pantry door. I strike it over and over until I'm sweating and breathless and near tears. Joe. I don't even know where the hell he goes when he flees from me. Part of me envies him. I've never had a safe place to run to.

Smash. Smash. Smash. I bring the hammer down with all my strength, hitting the wall so hard I feel it in my elbow. Sweat and tears run down my face, and from somewhere far away I hear a faint voice.

Stop it. Stop!

I hesitate mid-strike, the hammer an inch from the door. I wait in the silence, my ears ringing, sweat staining my armpits. The voice doesn't speak again.

Because I imagined it. Obviously.

I slump forward and rest my forehead against the pantry door, clutching the sweaty hammer in my right hand. I hold my breath and wait. And I swear the house does too.

Idiot, I scold myself, the house isn't talking to you. It doesn't care what you do to it. But when I drop the hammer, I swear I feel the house begin to breathe again.

It's nearly 10 P.M., and Joe still isn't home. Every time I go to call him, I distract myself instead, but I keep my phone in my pajama pocket, just in case he rings me. Just in case he says, "I'm sorry. I'm coming home now."

I pull my work clothes out of the washing machine and dump them into a basket to hang on the back-porch clothes rack. When I lug the basket to the back door, I stare into the darkness. We have no outside light, and sometimes the roos like to come up from Black Wood Forest to stand around in the backyard. In the morning or arvo, it's actually kind of nice seeing those big, dopey bastards just hanging out. But at night, it's terrifying. You can't see them, but usually you'll hear them. Breathing. Grunting. Grinding their teeth. Sometimes you won't even hear them. You'll think you're alone out there, until something comes rushing toward you. *Thump, thump, thump.* When we were kids, my sister and I used to dare each other to run around the outside of our house at night while the roos watched from the darkness. She'd stroll out, taking her time, and appear back inside the house, unruffled. I'd run the whole way, shrieking.

I wait at the back door, gripping the basket. I'm reaching for the doorknob when I hear an ear-piercing *creak.*

The sound came from my left. The library. The bloody door is wide open again. I freeze, heart in my mouth. And then I hear it again. *Creak. Creak. Creak.* It sounds like someone is walking around in the darkness.

I drop the basket and dig into my pajama pocket for my phone. I hate the fact that I check first for any message from Joe. Idiot. I turn the torch on and shine it toward the doorway.

"Hello?" I call out, wondering what the hell I'll do if someone calls back.

But no one does. There's nothing there.

The library is creepy. I hate the abandoned books, the blackened floorboards, the musty darkness. Plus, the weird thing is . . . every time I walk past it, the damn door is *always* open. I confronted Joe and asked him to stop opening the library door. And he said, "What are you talking about?"

He narrowed his eyes at me like I was losing it and he wanted nothing to do with my unraveling. He held up his hands and said, "I've never opened the damn door. Why would I?"

"Well, someone's opening it," I snapped. "And it isn't me."

I locked the library door before I went to work this morning. And there it is again.

Wide open.

I stand on the threshold, shining my little light into the darkness. I pull my robe tighter and step inside. It stinks like stale air in here. This was Bill Campbell's personal library. Bill the murderer. Is this where he sat and plotted his wife's death? Did he come in here after work with a nice hot cup of tea and think, *Tonight's the night?*

I shiver in the doorway and turn to leave.

Then I see it.

The book is lying facedown in the middle of the floor. It's impossible not to see it. That's how I know it wasn't there this morning when I closed the door.

I step forward, shining the beam on the book. It's very old, hardback. I squint to read the title.

Dante's Inferno

Slowly, I bend down and pick it up. The pages are yellow and as brittle as butterfly wings. I leaf through them, not sure what I'm looking for.

Until I find it.

One sentence is underlined. I stand there in the middle of the cold library and read it over and over again.

I found myself within a forest dark,

For the straightforward pathway had been lost.

What the hell? I drop the book and half run out of the room, slamming the door shut.

I climb the stairs quickly, the passage roaring through my head. Did Bill Campbell underline that passage? Was he crazy by then? Am I? Because the funniest part is, I understand.

I understand exactly how he felt. I reach my room, shut the door, and sit heavily on my bed.

For the straightforward pathway had been lost.

Is Bill Campbell trying to tell me something? Is his ghost wandering around this bloody house?

No, of course not. But someone placed that book on the floor for me to find.

Who?

Chapter 8

May 14

SarahSlays.com

HOME   ABOUT SARAH SLADE   BUY MY BOOK   CONTACT

There are two graves in my backyard. Yes, in my bloody backyard. One grave belongs to a murder victim. The other, to her murderer.

Susan. Bill.

Sometimes I creep out onto my porch and stare at them. The headstones are moon silver and half-buried in moss and ivy.

Susan Campbell, beloved wife and mother.

Beloved . . .

Beloved until her husband took that hammer to her skull, anyway.

So, dear reader, do you . . .

A) think Susan had no idea what was coming for her that morning?

or

B) think she lay in bed, waiting for the sound of footsteps up the stairs, knowing they signaled her end?

I choose A.

If there's one thing I've learned, it's that we have no clue what horror is coming for us. Especially from those we love . . .

I hit the delete button and hold it down, but the final line lingers unwelcome in the murder room.

We have no clue what horror is coming for us.

God, when did I get so morbid, so paranoid? I blame Mr. Whitman's rabid warnings, and that fucking plumber, too! That rat bastard spent a few days in the hospital, rambling to anyone who'd listen that there's *something wrong* with Black Wood House. That was he "attacked from behind" in the bathroom. For God's sake, he's alive and well, isn't he? Just a minor concussion. Fucker probably slipped on the tiles. He's making me paranoid, the bastard. And there are still months of renos to go before we can put the house up for sale. I grit my teeth and keep my finger on the delete button, wishing I could erase my mood.

When my website is blank and shiny and waiting for my next (overdue) update, I shove the laptop away and sit heavily on the edge of my bed.

I breathe in the forty-year-old air and wish I could open the damn window in my room. It's the sort of night that calls for fluffy socks, two jumpers, and mugs of steaming coffee. How lovely it would be to curl up on my bed with Reaper in the crook of my legs and a breezy window open. I wouldn't care how cold it got. I long to let the cold night air in. To flush out the staleness of this dead air.

I lie flat on my bed, hold my breath until it feels like I'm the one who's dead. I imagine Bill Campbell standing over me, thrusting out his hammer, readying it to strike against my skull. Only, when I close my eyes, it's not Bill's face I'm seeing.

It's my own husband's.

I bolt up, heart pounding. I press my palms against my head, cradling it. I've had so many stress headaches lately that I've demolished boxes of ibuprofen. I stand up so quickly my vision goes murky red and black. Shit. My left knee buckles and hits the bloodstain next to the bed.

Poor Susan. Poor dead, *murdered* Susan.

Pain shoots through my kneecap, and my head spins in dizzying circles. I shut my eyes tight. My heart speeds up frantically, then slows down, down, down. I kneel there, eyes closed, counting woozily to ten. The back of my throat aches, and I desperately crave a sugary drink.

My fault. I finished work three hours ago, and I haven't eaten all day. I haven't eaten much all week, actually. But I've sure made up for it with the drinking. I've had a shitload of red wine, so at least I've been getting my grapes.

I reach up to my desk, slowly opening my eyes. Carefully, I swallow three more ibuprofen, then crouch back down, right on the bloodstain.

We're starting the kitchen renovations tomorrow morning. A kitchen remodel can increase the resale value up to 40 percent . . . if you sell it, that is.

Shakily, I pull my laptop down and balance it on my right knee. God, I wish I'd never agreed to all these damn updates on Black Wood House. I've done only one since we bought the bloody thing, and I still haven't gotten any paid sponsorships.

There's an edge to people's questions now when they ask how it's all going. An accusation hidden in their chirpy words. My co-worker Tim cornered me after work today. "Are you *okay*, Sarah? You look a bit . . ."

Shit. I look shit. That's what happens when you aren't sleeping or eating and you have a twenty-four-hour headache that *won't stop pounding*.

"How's the renovation going? I haven't seen any updates on your website lately . . ."

Oh, piss off, Tim. I muttered something, jangled my car key like I had to go, and he squeezed my shoulder not unkindly. "Maybe get some rest, yeah?"

I glare at the blinking cursor and begin to type.

SarahSlays.com

HOME   ABOUT SARAH SLADE   BUY MY BOOK   CONTACT

Hi again, folks!

I have awesome news! Are you ready for this? (Drumroll, please.) We're officially beginning the renovations of Black Wood House! Joe and I are demolishing the kitchen tomorrow, and our builders have been uh-may-zing. Shout-out to the guys at Handyman Dan's!

Over the next month we'll be removing all the flooring (goodbye, hideous Formica!) and installing a gorgeous new onyx marble splash back.

Now comes the fun bit! We'll be installing all new cabinets, counter-tops, and lighting, which I've already splurged on (links below—no discount code yet, I'm afraid!).

Can't wait to share the before and after pics of the kitchen. You're going to be amazed!

Sarah x

Thank fuck that's done. I disable comments and hit post. Then I snap the laptop shut and crawl into bed, and minutes later, I'm asleep.

I dream of an office full of clients sleeping in overstuffed armchairs. I step inside. It's warm in here, *cozy.* I shrug off my coat and realize that everyone has fallen silent. Their eyes are blank and soulless. I wait at the door, stomach churning.

And that's when I realize. The clients in the armchairs aren't asleep at all.

They're dead.

I stagger back in the dream, throat seizing up with panic. My back presses into the closed door, but I still don't run. I cover my mouth with my hand, holding back a scream, and a young woman comes charging forward.

Her face is hard. Her eyes glisten with angry tears. She is all teeth and tears.

She is my sister.

She points at me, poking me hard in the shoulder. *How could you? How could you?*

I wake up, gasping.

Lizzy. Lizzy.

It's been months since I dreamed of my younger sister. I swipe at my eyes with the back of my hand. God, I miss her. I wish I could call her, wish she'd listen. I haven't heard her voice in years.

I stare at the ceiling, my pulse beating hard in the base of my throat, Mr. Whitman's warning ringing in my head. *The house made him crazy.*

"Houses can't make people crazy," I say breathlessly. I roll over and plump my pillow. "And I'm not crazy either."

My words hang there like a lie. So I say it again, firmer this time. "I am *not* crazy."

Creak.

I lift my head off the pillow and listen. There's something outside my door.

Creak, creak, creak.

I stop breathing. It's dark now, my room lit only by the blue light of my phone charger. It casts an eerie glow around the room, washing the forest scene in a murky blue.

Meowwww.

Reaper. I fling the cover off my bed and pad quickly to the hallway, not even remembering to bring my phone with me. The unwelcome memory of Reaper springing onto my bed, frantic and shaking, spills through my mind. God, what if he's sick again?

Meowwwwwwwww.

"Reaper?" I call out, wrapping my arms around myself. It's freezing, and my hands are stinging with cold. The hallway is dark as shit. There's no light switch here yet, only a narrow strip of darkness.

"Reap?"

Meow.

I sense he's close. I step forward into the gaping dark, keeping my hand on the wall, trailing my fingers across it. I keep my eyes down, afraid I'll step on him. I must be halfway down the dark hallway when I finally spot him. I freeze. My hands are numb with cold and fear.

I lick my lips and call out uncertainly, "Reap?"

My cat is sitting in the middle of the hallway, white tail flicking back and forth like a windshield wiper. His eyes are wide, unblinking. "What's wrong?"

I let go of the wall, crouch in front of him, anxious to get him in my arms and make sure he's okay. Make sure we don't have a repeat of that episode a couple weeks ago. But the moment my fingers sweep his fur, he turns his back on me, tail shooting up like a warning.

Meoooooooowwwwwwwwww.

He howls so loudly, I feel it in my teeth. I'm freaking out now. I grab for him, but he slinks farther down the hallway, a tiny puff of white in the darkness. I chase him, swearing under my breath, hoping he doesn't think this is a game. But he pauses, turns around, meows again. *Follow me,* he seems to say. My chest tightens, but I follow Reaper. Funny how we trust our pets more than human beings.

Reaper and I pad silently down the hallway. Finally, he raises his head, sniffs the air.

And stops. He whirls around, looks me dead in the eye.

Meowww.

Here, he says. *It's right here.*

God, I hope it's not a dead parrot. I step forward, scanning the area where he sits, my jaw tight.

Empty. There's nothing there at all but Reaper, sitting still and silent on the floorboards, tail whooshing back and forth, faster now than before.

I exhale impatiently, scanning again. I crouch, grab him, and sweep my hand over his body for any sign of discomfort. The only thing out of place is his heartbeat. It's way too fast.

I let him go and rock back on my heels, shivering. I have that horrible, sweaty feeling you get right before someone jumps out and screams, "Boo!"

And then he does something I've never seen him do. He tilts his head back and stares pointedly at the ceiling. Shit. I bolt up, terrified. It's too dark to see the ceiling, but my brain helpfully fills it in. I imagine horrific things: someone stuck to the ceiling like a spider about to pounce and hammer me to death. Bill Campbell about to come down from the attic and hammer me to death.

Wait.

The attic.

Reaper is standing right under the attic.

I gasp, and he gives me a look that says, *About time you figured it out, dipshit.*

A small staircase is tucked under a panel in the ceiling, directly above him. How the hell does Reaper know about the attic? He's never been up there. He couldn't have. The only way to get in is by pulling the cord anchored in the ceiling.

I tilt my head up, and there it is. The little cord to open the attic. Slowly, I reach up and close my fist around it.

He heard noises coming from the attic. Especially at night.

I drop my hand, swallowing hard. I'm so scared I'm panting. Bill Campbell heard noises in the attic . . .

I scoop Reaper up and press his soft fur to my face like a shield. His heartbeat is wild under my fingertips. "Did you hear something up there?" I whisper into his neck.

I'm glad he can't answer. I wait below the attic, debating whether to pull the cord or not.

Meoww?

I make up my mind. I turn around and carry Reaper back up the dark hallway, my face still pressed into his neck. I'm not going up there. Not tonight anyway.

Creeeeeeeeak.

My heart stops. I freeze. Reaper's heartbeat slams against his ribs. I'm inches from my door, but I can't move. I heard it. I know I did. Up in the attic, something moved. *Someone* moved.

I force myself to move as quietly and calmly as possible back to my room.

And I don't want to admit this.

But, I swear to God, I feel like someone's upstairs in the attic, watching me leave.

MURDER HOUSE STRIKES AGAIN:

BODY DISCOVERED IN BLACK WOOD HOUSE

June 30, 12:35 p.m.

ABC News, Melbourne

A body has been found under suspicious circumstances at the infamous Black Wood House. The Victorian Gothic was the site of one of the most publicized murders in 1980, when its original owner, Bill Campbell, murdered his wife and attempted to murder his young daughter.

But the neighborhood has been rocked by news of a second tragedy today.

Officers arrived in Beacon, 45 minutes southeast of Melbourne, at 11:40 this morning. A body was found at Black Wood House shortly after. Police are treating the death as suspicious and have declared it a crime scene.

A source said, "I can't believe this is happening again. There's something really wrong with that house."

Fans of true crime will know that bestselling self-help author Sarah Slade bought the house two months ago. Police have refused to confirm the identity of the body.

But friends admit Slade and her husband had been having difficulties lately.

"Ever since they bought that damn house, Sarah's been acting . . . strange," one friend said.

Another friend commented, "She was becoming paranoid. She thought she was being followed. And there was that scary business with her cat."

Alarmingly, Slade told friends that she believed her cat was being poisoned.

"He was getting sicker and sicker, and I think she accused one of the neighbors of poisoning him," said a source. "The neighbors were angry that she and Joe bought the house. It's pretty well known that nobody wanted them there."

None of the neighbors have responded for comment.

BREAKING NEWS IN BLACK WOOD CASE:
CHILLING VOICEMAIL DISCOVERED

By Whitney Roach [@KeepingItWeirdwithWhitney]

Keeping It Weird with Whitney—voted Top 5 Melbourne Blogger.

Wednesday, June 30, 1:25 P.M.

Oh. My. God.

You might remember that I interviewed Sarah Slade just before she moved into Black Wood House. If you've been watching the news, you'll know that a body was discovered there today. I just reached out to Tim Holmes, colleague of Sarah Slade at Mercy Community. . . . And, ladies and gentlemen, have I got news for you: Shit just got WEIRDER!

Sarah left Tim a chilling voicemail at 2:34 Saturday morning, four days before the body was found at Black Wood House.

"I didn't listen to her message," Tim said. "We're not that close, so I figured it was a butt-dial or something. She never really calls me."

But Sarah did. Three times in a row.

"I only played her voicemail this morning, and I called the police straightaway," he said. "If the body they found was hers, I'll never forgive myself."

He dials his voicemail.

At first there's nothing but heavy silence. Then static for ten seconds. Tim holds the phone up to his ear. "Can you hear that?" he asks before holding his breath again. "In the background . . . it sounds like someone's sobbing."

Then out of nowhere the static clears.

And a voice cries out,

Don't kill me.

Don't kill me.

Don't kill me.

Chapter 9

May 16

I step onto the wraparound porch, and it squeaks a progression of minor-key notes. It's like standing on an out-of-tune piano. I rest my forearms on the porch railing, and it wobbles alarmingly. It's quiet this afternoon except for the warble of a magpie. *Quardle oodle ardle wardle.* The air smells of eucalyptus as I lean forward and gulp it in, hoping it will heal me. A dull headache throbs at my temples, and I'm still finding it hard to keep food down.

Joe's car creeps up the driveway, and my heart lifts. He hasn't been home since our argument. I texted him an hour ago, asking him to come home. Told him I was sorry. God, I don't even know what I'm apologizing about anymore. I just want him here.

I raise my hand and wave hello as he parks near the porch. I hold my breath, hoping he'll wave back. He doesn't.

He gets out of the car, shuts the door, and I'm so anxious that I call out stupidly, "Hi!"

"Hey," he says softly, climbing the porch steps. He won't meet my eyes yet.

It's amazing how much you want to say during these tense, silent marriage moments.

Where have you been?

Do you hate me?

Are we okay?

Instead, we stand awkwardly on our porch, avoiding all eye contact. I chew the inside of my cheek, bursting with all the things I want to tell him—the strange events at Black Wood since he left. Like the book on the library floor. How Reaper led me to the attic. The feeling that someone was watching me from up there.

Joe turns his attention to the porch banister. He picks at a bit of flaking paint and peels it off in one long strip. "How've you been?" he asks grudgingly.

I chew my cheek hard enough to bite a hole through it. "Yeah, I'm all right. You?"

He doesn't answer. Just keeps peeling the damn paint. I lean against the railing again and notice my hands are trembling.

"Actually"—I hesitate, staring at the front door—"it's been a bit weird here."

I wait for him to ask why. I'm so tense I want to grab the banister in both hands and scream my head off. Instead, I reach out timidly to my husband and place my hand on his.

"A few nights after you . . . left," I begin, "Reaper woke me up. He made me follow him down the hallway."

Joe smiles a little. "He *made* you follow him? How, exactly?" He gently pulls his hand away, places it in his jean pocket. God, that hurts.

"I think he heard something in the attic."

Joe gives me a withering look. "Like what?" Why does it feel like there's an edge to his voice? Like he's angry at me? What have I done but try to let him in?

My throat aches with unshed tears, and I just want something—fucking *anything*—to hold on to. I have spent our entire marriage reaching for my husband. He's never once reached back.

He sighs loudly. "Are you pissed at me now?"

I straighten up. "Forget it."

Joe shrugs, but his jaw is set, and I know he's angry. I don't know why.

I never know why. He strides to the front door and pushes it open when a loud bang rattles the whole porch, making me jump.

"What the hell?" Joe calls out angrily.

He's an inch from the front door, staring at it in shock. His right hand hangs loosely from the doorknob.

"What happened?"

Joe doesn't even look at me. "The door," he says finally. "I just opened the front door, and it slammed shut on me."

I shrug. "Maybe it's the wind."

He frowns and takes a small step back. "There *is* no wind," he says quietly. I look over my shoulder to the blackwood tree. The top branches are still and silent. Joe's right. There's not a breath of wind.

"I pushed the door open and went to step inside"—Joe replays it in a high, nervy voice—"and the door slammed shut like someone kicked it."

My eyes sweep the barren fields. The flaking porch. The front door Janet Campbell burst out of, fleeing for her life.

"Maybe the house doesn't want you back," I murmur, eyes on the blackwood tree.

Maybe I don't either.

I shake my head and open my mouth to apologize, but Joe whirls around, eyes flashing. "Thanks for that," he says shortly.

I've stuffed this up so badly I could cry.

"I'm sorry," I say automatically. "I didn't mean it."

I don't think I did, anyway.

We wait in tense silence. Joe swipes a hand through his too-black hair, muttering something under his breath. I can't stand it anymore.

Slowly, I walk past him, push the door open. "You coming in?" I ask timidly.

I've left the door open wide for him, and he stares longingly at his car. Then he straightens up. "Oh, wait. I forgot," he mumbles.

He steps off the porch. "I've got something for you," he calls over his shoulder.

A present for me? I can't remember the last time he bought me anything. I sit on the couch and wait nervously. Reaper appears from nowhere and jumps into my lap. He looks up without interest when Joe comes back inside.

"Here." Joe stalks across the floorboards and dumps a package over my shoulder. It's a medium-sized envelope the color of sand. I don't know what to say. I stare at the present uneasily while Joe hovers behind me. This doesn't feel right.

"Open it," Joe insists.

Slowly, I unwrap it. The house feels too quiet, like it's watching, waiting, listening. I fumble with the wrapper, hands cold and trembling until I see what the present is.

I drop it so fast Reaper lifts his head in surprise.

It's a DVD. *Good Will Hunting.*

An image of my sister flashes in my head so clearly, it's like she's sitting right next to me. She's curled up on the couch, a soft pink blanket pooled around her knees. *One day I'm going to be a therapist.*

Shakily, I stand up. Reaper bolts out of my lap and perches atop the DVD. But it's my husband I fix my eyes on.

"What the hell is this?" My voice comes out all wrong. It's like someone's grabbed my throat and I'm squeezing out strangled words. Joe raises his eyebrows, and I want to hit him. I actually want to hit my husband. My heart burns so hot it *hurts.*

"What do you mean?" He's giving me that feral-cat look that says, *Is this about to turn into a fight?* In the past he'd have backed down at this point. Now he straightens his spine, stares me down.

"The post office emailed me today. I had some time after work, so I thought I'd pick it up for you." Under his breath he mutters, "And I stupidly thought you'd be grateful."

He thrusts his hands deep into his pockets.

"Why would the post office email *you?* Is this your idea of a sick joke?"

I stare my husband down, and the thought hits me. Maybe they contacted him because he's the one who bought the fucking thing.

Joe's mouth tightens. My husband is not a confrontational man. He's one of those passive-aggressive guys who holds it all in and pouts about it for weeks after. We've never crossed the line with each other, but God, we're both getting close to it.

Rain begins to thunder down, and when Joe fixes his eyes on me, you'd swear he was blaming me for it. For everything. The house. The state of our marriage. The rift with his shitty mother, who's hated my guts since the day she met me. But mostly, he hates me for that one unspeakable August night five years ago that ended in police sirens and screaming.

I hold my hands up, backing away from the couch. From him. Reaper watches us from the coffee table, tail flicking back and forth.

"I didn't buy this," I say hotly.

He raises an eyebrow, snorts. "You sure? You buy a lot when you're . . ."

Drunk.

I shake my head, and my heart pumps so hot and fast it's making me dizzy. I want to *get out of here.* I want to sprint out the front door, right into the soaking rain. "I wouldn't buy this," I say quietly. "Not this."

"Why? What is it?"

Quickly, I bend down and launch the DVD at him. It lands with a thud in the center of his thin chest. He catches it clumsily.

I wrap my arms around myself, but I can't stop shaking. Silently, Joe inspects the DVD. In his pale hands is the mustard-yellow cover with Matt Damon and Robin Williams. Joe turns it over and over again, grim-faced and silent. I know he's thinking about my little sister. He knows it was her favorite movie. I know he, too, can see her perched on our old couch, telling anyone who'd listen, *One day I'm going to be a therapist.*

Every marriage has silent rules. Ours is, *Don't speak about the past. Don't speak about Lizzy.*

Joe and I met five years ago. We've been married three of them. And in all these years, he's never brought up my sister.

I fold my hands behind my head and wait, eyes on the rain.

"Did you buy this?" I ask quietly.

I made the dangerous move, and we both know it. I've picked up my queen and nudged it forward.

His jaw tightens, and when he looks up, I'm chilled by the look in his eyes. Murderous, you'd call it. In our hometown, Joe was famous for his easy smile, and now he carries the heavy energy of a bad storm. . . . God, where did that boy go? What have we done to each other? I glance desperately at the door, wondering if it's too late to undo this. Undo everything. He drops the DVD, and it lands on the ground with a sick thud.

"Why would I send you this?" he asks softly, but there's an edge to his voice. "Huh? Why would you think that I would send you this?"

To fuck with me? To punish me?

I can think of many reasons, and what a shame that is. My fingers are numb with fear and cold, and the rain roars down like it's angry at us.

"For God's sake," Joe says hotly, "you're the one who . . ."

He doesn't finish. I swallow hard, not even sure what I'll say. I stride forward so quickly that even Reaper flinches. I'm scared and angry, and I'm all up in my husband's face, hot breath on his cheek.

"My sister . . ." I breathe. "You know this was my sister's favorite movie."

It was my sister who wanted to be a therapist . . .

"Don't," Joe says shortly, eyes flashing.

Is it just me, or is the house listening to our fight? It's the strangest thing, but something flashes through my vision again. A pulsing black heat, coming from the heart of the house. It feeds off our dangerous anger, *relishing* it.

Joe steps closer, the tip of his boot prodding mine. Cold rage radiates through his thin body. I *feel* it. I hold my fists steady at my sides . . . in case they're needed.

The lightbulbs flicker, dimming, brightening, dimming, and the warning from Mr. Whitman bolts through my head. *The house made him crazy.* But that's not true. Not true. Not true. It's the storm that's making the lights flicker. The storm.

In a soft, dangerous voice Joe says, "Just. Fucking. *Don't.*"

It's not the house making Joe and me crazy. We don't need any help with that. We're perfectly capable of fucking things up on our own.

Chapter 10

If anyone knew the truth about my bestselling book, I'd be a fucking laughingstock. I never wanted to be a writer. But Gina did.

Gina Hampton was my co-worker at Kmart back in Queensland. It was my first job, the pay was terrible, but it got me away from my mum for a few blessed hours after school. Gina was fifty-one, with a permanently red face and a giant laugh. One of those jolly women who makes you feel less alone. For two months we folded T-shirts side by side in our ink-blue uniforms, and she'd tell me about the self-help book she was writing.

"Who knows?" She'd nudge my ribs. "Maybe it'll get picked up by one of them big publishing mobs in the city!" She'd stop then, holding a folded T-shirt against her large chest, dreaming her big, bright dreams. I envied that. Badly. Wanted that feeling for myself. If I could describe myself as anything, it'd be an emperor penguin. I swoop in, steal eggs, and raise them as my own. Only, I don't give a shit about eggs. I steal futures.

I became a bestselling author because I answered this ad: *Provocative and quirky pop-culture magazine on the hunt for a superstar writer!* It was the first job I landed after Joe and I fled Queensland and landed in New South Wales. I was desperate and broke with nothing at all to lose since I'd lost it already. The magazine was called *Sabrina*. A start-up. One of those *We're different and edgy 'cause we expose the truth and say "fuck" a lot.*

The boss, Sabrina Pond, was nineteen and an Instagram influencer. She earned a shitload through paid sponsorships. She was always selling something: nail polish, perfumes, candles, sunless tanner. Within three years, *Sabrina* magazine had half a million subscribers, and my Instagram following skyrocketed. I wrote edgy opinion pieces about hardcore porn, birth control, and Justin Bieber.

It was all right, I suppose. It was a job anyway, and the pay kept increasing. Maybe it would've stayed that way were it not for a feature I wrote titled "Clear, Calm, and in Control: How I Went from Panic to Power." It was a hastily written thousand-word fluff piece. Mostly lies, of course. I wrote about my decade-long anxiety struggle and how I overcame it through healthy eating, wellness, and a BA in psychology.

It fucking smashed. People shared snippets of my post on Twitter and Pinterest, and people around the world commented, "So true!" "Love this!" "This was *so* brave of her!" and my favorite, "#SarahSlayed Anxiety."

Nobody had to know that I barely graduated high school, had never practiced healthy eating in my life, and had no fucking clue what *wellness* even meant. The anxiety thing was real, though. But it wasn't the only thing I'd been diagnosed with as a teen. Nobody needed to know about the other one. And while the hashtags were still warm, I spent three weeks turning the thousand-word fluff piece into a fifty-thousand-word self-help book. I published it myself, linked it to my Insta, and *Clear, Calm, and in Control* became an instant bestseller. Still is.

Sarah Slade, the author bio said, *qualified therapist, with a BA in psychology.*

On my guilty days, I tell myself it was a victimless crime. Truth is, you probably *can* ease anxiety with healthy eating, wellness, and therapy. I just choose to heal mine with Lexapro and Instagram likes. And yeah, I'm not a qualified therapist, but I did most of an online counseling course. I know enough to cover my arse.

Eventually, I left *Sabrina* magazine, drove four hours south to Victoria, and applied for therapist jobs with my brand-new fraudulent degree in psychology to match my fraudulent driver's license. I was hired within a week. I've been practicing ever since and selling my shit all over social media, of course. Not that there's much to share now, since the Black Wood renovations are going terribly.

I sip cold coffee on the couch and watch the dying flames in the fireplace as the builders chat in the kitchen. They got here an hour ago, and I trudged downstairs in my bathrobe and let them in, not even caring how greasy my hair was. I'm pretty sure Dan, the beefy foreman, winced when he saw my cat slippers.

Since then, I've lit a fire, and watched it burn down to nothing, while the builders have stood around, hands on their hips, as Dan marked measurements with a fat red pencil. I need to get out of here for the day, but I have nowhere to go. I distract myself instead with a list of errands I keep putting off. I've got to pick up my anti-depressants and cat food. But first, I'm going for a run.

Silently, I take my laptop back to my room and plug it in. I pull on leggings, a T-shirt, and a hoodie and lock the bedroom door behind me.

On my way out the front door, I call to Dan, "Be back in a few hours."

The builders wheel around to stare at me like they've forgotten I live here, and I hesitate at the front door, feeling foolish. Dan gives me a distracted wave. He doesn't care if I'm home or not. Neither does my husband, I guess. He didn't come home again, and I'm both relieved and upset about it. He's probably at work now. We'll see if he comes home tonight.

Cheeks burning, I step outside into the cold morning sun. I zip up my hoodie and start to brush past my car. Then I see it. A yellow sticky note is stuck to the windshield, tucked under a wiper. I stare at it for a moment, wondering if one of the builders put it there. I reach forward, pluck it out, and read.

Did you enjoy the movie?

My stomach drops to my feet. What the hell? I reread the note, my heart pounding harder with each word.

Did you enjoy the movie?

Who else knows about the DVD? Who else fucking knows it was my sister's favorite movie? I analyze the writing. It's hastily scrawled, messy. I don't recognize it. I stare desperately at the front yard, and a cockatoo gives me a curious look from the blackwood tree.

Did you enjoy the movie?

Chapter 11

Sweat drips down my jaw, and the only sound is my shoes pounding the wide, empty road. I picked up running in my early twenties, and my ex-therapist approved. But she wouldn't have if she'd known the truth. For most people, running is a way to unwind. To lose themselves in the rhythm of the music and the language of their body.

Not me. I don't listen to music when I run. I think. I seethe. I *plot*. And this morning as I sprint, there's only one thing on my mind.

Who. Knows. About. Lizzy.

My feet slap hard on the pavement like I want to punish it. It's an icy morning, and the sky is thick with clouds hanging so low, I feel I could reach up and tear off chunks of them.

But it's the note that I can't stop thinking about. The note that I'm running from.

Who.

Knows.

About.

Lizzy.

Angrily, I swipe at the sweat over my eyebrow. It's Saturday morning, but the road's empty like always. No old ladies walking their yappy dogs. No kids pedaling their bikes to town. No cars pulling in and out of driveways. Nothing at all but me and my early-morning rage. And the shiver of the gum trees as they watch me run.

You'd swear this street was home to nothing but ghosts.

I sprint faster until the backs of my ankles burn and the neighbors' gardens rush past in smears of primary colors. Despite its reputation, it's still a pretty street. I'd be happy to be here, if it weren't for this Lizzy shit.

Black Wood was meant to be a fresh start. Another one. But if someone knows about Lizzy and what happened . . .

I brush away the sweat dripping down my jaw. The tree shadows look like angry hands trying to snatch me up. I run faster, the back of my calves uncomfortably hot. It hits me that Janet Campbell was running down this same street. But unlike me, Janet was fleeing for her life while her father swallowed tranquilizers in the upstairs bathroom.

God, that poor girl.

A sharp pain wrenches my chest. I slow down, but it's not my frantic pace that hurts.

I think it's disgusting that you bought their house, and even more sickening that you clearly hope to profit on it.

The comment from my website flashes through my mind, and for the first time ever, I feel a twinge of guilt.

Janet inherited Black Wood after the murders, but she never returned. No one has a clue where she went or what became of her. Even the estate's executor couldn't locate her. For all we know, she could still be in Beacon.

What would she say if she saw me knocking out walls and dreaming of six-figure profits from her childhood home? Of using the tragedy of her family history to make a name for myself? She'd be angry . . . maybe angry enough to send me threatening notes.

I walk for a bit, thinking, as a magpie warbles his morning song. I remember the magpie on the porch at Black Wood from moving day. Someone's been feeding it.

"Janet," I find myself whispering. "Where are you, Janet?"

It's strange to think of Black Wood House without the murder. Strange to think that to Janet it was simply *home*. A home where she ate cornflakes at the kitchen table while Bill read the paper beside her and Susan busied herself in the kitchen, packing a sandwich into her lunch box. I've seen pictures of Janet smirking at the camera as her parents stood stiffly behind her. She looked cheeky, spirited. The sort of girl who stuck her tongue out when the teacher's back was turned, maybe. She'd be in her late fifties now. If she's still alive.

She was a redhead, Janet. I imagine her as a young child riding her bicycle down that gigantic driveway, bag slung over her shoulder as Susan stood on the front porch, waving goodbye. I can also imagine Janet pointing an accusing finger at me, flame-red hair falling over her shoulders, mouth twisted in rage.

How could you? How could you? How could you?

But a moment later her face blurs like I'm seeing it underwater, and when it clears, it's not Janet I'm seeing.

It's my sister.

How could you? How could you?

A gleaming Lexus drives slowly toward me. I wave hello to the driver, an elderly man in his seventies with a silver goatee. He stares back, impassive and unsmiling. I drop my hand, embarrassed, and he zooms past.

I dart glances at him over my shoulder as he pulls into the driveway of a pretty colonial with a gable roof and double-hung windows. It looks like a giant dollhouse. He stops at the mailbox, climbs out of the car, leaves the door open. He reaches for his mail and pauses.

Then he glares down the street at me. We lock eyes, and I'm the first to turn away. So this is how it's going to be, is it?

I pick up my pace again, sprinting down the street like someone's chasing me. I've never been the type to let consequences stop me. Until now, I saw that as a strength. And for the first time, I have an uneasy feeling that maybe it isn't.

Maybe it never was.

I run with my head down, farther and farther from Black Wood. It almost feels like I'm running for my life. Like I'm Janet all over again.

I glance over my shoulder, feeling stupid, and eye the tangled mess of forest. The trees are still and silent, but I feel them watching me. I wonder if they remember a flame-haired girl on February 4, 1980, running for her life down this same street. Are they thinking of her as they watch me?

I haven't stepped foot in the forest since that first night. Some woods are inviting. Some woods are just sad. But Black Wood is full of secrets. I can't shake the feeling that it knows something and it's dying to tell me.

Joe and I drove past after our first inspection of the house. We stopped at the gate, staring uneasily at the massive gums blocking out the sun, and made half-hearted plans to picnic here. Joe idled the engine, peered at the droopy sign, and listed off the plant species. "*Drosera rotundifo-lia . . .*" He sounded out the word carefully. "A carnivorous plant."

The first thing I'd thought was, God, even the flowers are hungry there. My second thought was of my sister. We grew up in walking distance of a bushland reserve, home to a muddy creek, bellbirds, and carnivorous sundews. I'd crouch over a flytrap, force its mouth open, and stare in fascination at a half-digested black ant, its legs still moving. My sister would inch back, clutch her stomach, and urge me to stop.

We spent every weekend at that reserve, ordered outside while my dad roamed the house, looking for something to blame, and my mum lay on the spare bed, staring at nothing.

My parents gave me nightmares. I dreamed constantly that my dad was trying to set the house on fire. He'd stomp around, lighting matches, hate in his eyes, and I'd flee to the spare room and scream for Mum to make him stop. She never heard me. Never even blinked. She'd lie on that damn bed as the house started to burn, and I'd bolt awake, sweating.

The older I got, the worse I felt. Sometimes I'd sit alone for hours on end while my sister kissed the neighborhood boys and made excuses for my strangeness. Sometimes I'd hold my breath and pretend I was dead. Sometimes I'd climb to the top of a tree, ease out onto the highest branch, and feel it wobble under my feet. Then I'd tell myself to jump.

If I hurt myself, maybe I'd finally have an excuse to feel the way I was feeling.

My mother was distracted by her own misery, but one time, she noticed and dragged me to a doctor who clicked his tongue and announced, "It's unnatural for a child to be so still." She'd let me stay home from school that day and made me a cup of hot milky tea. Then she snatched the cup away before I could take a sip and scolded me for embarrassing her in front of the doctor. I was always embarrassing her in front of someone without meaning to. My sister, however, was the daughter she shoved forward on the rare occasion my mum brought a friend over. Everyone was charmed by my sister. Especially me.

I'm nearly past a three-story Greek Revival house, when a voice calls out, "Amanda?"

It's the way she says it that makes my head snap in her direction. Makes me stumble to a confused halt that jolts my spine. My lungs and ankles burn with the cold, but I forget it all.

The woman is at her mailbox, loosely clutching a stack of envelopes in her right hand. She has a salt-and-pepper bowl cut and lilac sneakers, and she's so still, I wonder if she's even breathing. Her left forearm is slung across her face as she shields her eyes from the morning sun. I breathe noisily, resting my hands on my sweaty hips, and for a long moment neither of us speaks.

"Amanda?" Her breath catches in her throat, and she makes a choking noise. The woman takes a small step toward me. Slowly, she lowers her forearm, her eyes wide and alarmed. I take a step back and wonder if it's too late to run away.

"My God," she breathes, placing a hand over her heart. "You look so much like her."

I stand there stupidly, not sure what to say. I wipe my forehead with the back of my wrist and tighten my sweaty ponytail with a useless tug. I'm a bit too conscious of the sweat stains under my arms.

"My name's not Amanda," I tell her.

She steps forward tentatively. I have the strangest feeling she's about to reach out and brush my cheek like I'm a frightened horse or some-thing. I step back again.

"My name's Sarah," I tell her. "Sarah Slade." I motion behind me, but she never takes her eyes from my face. "We bought the Black Wood House."

I wait for her to react. Wait for her to narrow her eyes in disgust, fold her tiny arms across her chest, and silently judge me. She doesn't. Her eyes are watery and sad. You'd think I just told her about my terminal liver cancer.

"Nice to—" Swiftly, she turns and scurries up her sloping driveway. "Meet you," I mutter.

A cool wind tunnels down the back of my T-shirt, making me shiver. I wrap my arms around myself and watch her leave.

Amanda? You look so much like her . . .

"I'm not Amanda," I say again.

I'm not Sarah. I'm not anyone.

I shiver in the empty street, wrapping my arms tighter around my body, afraid I'll disappear. I stand there until she vanishes inside her house and the tree shadows swallow me up.

By the time I return from my errands, the sun is setting in a brilliant smear of orange, and the wind stings my face when I hop out of the car. The builders' trucks are gone. Joe's still not at Black Wood. I sling the grocery bag over my shoulder and unlock the house.

It's empty and ear-splittingly silent. And the kitchen! I drop the bag at the door. My knees nearly give out. Nausea roars up my throat until it burns. The builders have started laying the black and white ceramic tiles. The wooden floor is gone, and I feel the loss physically, violently. I rush to the kitchen sink, grip it, and vomit until I see stars. Over and over in my head, the words pour out: The house doesn't want to be fixed. The house doesn't want to be fixed.

I finally finish and swipe my mouth with the back of my hand. My hands are hot and my legs numb. Get a grip. Please. You're just over-whelmed right now. You're not getting any sleep, and the fucking house doesn't have *feelings*.

I walk slowly, my stomach still churning. Shakily, I put the milk in the fridge and empty the fancy cat food into a red plastic bowl for Reaper. I make myself a strong coffee and carry it upstairs, taking small sips. I pause at the top stair.

My bedroom door is open. I freeze there, shocked. I locked the door this morning. I know I did. Maybe the builders went upstairs? But then, why the hell did they go into my room?

Slowly, I move forward and peer inside. Nothing seems out of place. My bathrobe is still piled in a pink ball on the floor, and my bed is un-made, just like I left it.

But then I see it. I cry out, dropping the mug to the floor. Hot coffee splashes up my leggings and burns into my ankle. But I barely notice. Attached to my laptop screen is another yellow sticky note. And I *did not* put it there. I scurry forward, heart in my mouth. I squint at the note, careful not to touch it.

Don't forget your anti-depressants and cat food!

I freeze. I read the note again. What the hell? I never told anyone I needed cat food or my meds refilled. I told the builders I was heading out. Did I tell them what I was doing? I chew my lip, trying to remem-ber. No, I didn't. I'm sure of it. I haven't even spoken to Joe today.

I stare at the note, reading it over and over, my stomach cramping in fear.

I'm certain of two things only.

I never told anyone what I was doing today.

And I did *not* write this note.

CLEAR, CALM, AND CONNIVING:

FAMED AUTHOR'S WEB OF LIES BEGINS TO UNRAVEL

July 1

ABC News, Melbourne

It's been less than 24 hours since a body was discovered at Black Wood House. Police are still tight-lipped about the victim's identity and the cause of death. But one thing's becoming clear: The current owner, famed author Sarah Slade, is not who we thought she was.

A source has come forward insisting on a closer look at the author's certifications. Slade has been employed at Mercy Community as a self-development therapist for eleven months. Before that, according to her book bio, she "graduated with honors with a degree in psychology."

But in a strange twist of events, it seems that her certifications are fraudulent. Slade has never listed her alma mater. The source claims Slade once said that she studied at the University of Sydney in 2015. Another source claims Slade said that she graduated from Macquarie University in 2016. But there is no record of a Sarah Slade graduating from Macquarie University, nor is there evidence of her studying at the University of Sydney in 2015. We've reached out to Mercy Community, but so far, there has been no comment from Slade's employers.

More strangely, there's little record of Sarah Slade before she published her bestselling book, *Clear, Calm, and in Control.* Slade worked at *Sabrina* magazine in New South Wales from 2015 to 2018. She developed her fan following there and moved to Victoria two years ago. Her history before *Sabrina* is unknown.

A source said, "She's always been sketchy about her past. She never really gave any answers about where she grew up, or her family, or any of that."

Another source said, "She doesn't have a degree in psychology, so what qualifications did she have to write her self-help book, then? She's a liar, and she should be exposed."

Slade's bestselling book has been in and out of the top 10 nonfiction list for over two years. It was an instant hit when it was published in July 2018, and fans have eagerly awaited another Slade book. But it looks like fans may not be seeing another.

Chapter 12

SarahSlays.com

HOME   ABOUT SARAH SLADE   BUY MY BOOK   CONTACT

Guess what I found in my mailbox today?

A rat.

A dead fucking rat.

Around its bloated neck was a rubber band, and tucked inside it was a charming note:

Welcome to the neighborhood, you rat bitch.

I lean back in my office chair, rubbing my temples with icy fingers. I swear I can still smell the rat on my fingertips, even after I scrubbed my hands over and over with lemon soap. I found it this morning when I left for work. Its tail was dangling out of the mail slot like a piece of yarn. It must have been left there overnight. I hurled the damn rat out of the mailbox, along with the note, and decided against telling Joe. Or the police. I don't need the shitty publicity. What I need more than anything is to hurry up and get the renovations done. We'll smash through them, put the house on the market, and move the hell away before the next buyer realizes their mistake.

I reach for the water bottle next to my laptop and notice my hands are shaking. I drink long and deep, closing my eyes and resting my head against the plush white leather.

A dog. That's what we need. We need a big, hulking bastard of a dog on our property. That'll stop anyone from trespassing. I rock slowly in the chair, wondering how I can casually mention the idea to Joe. Not that he's even speaking to me. He slinks in and out of the house like Reaper. Speaking of that bloody cat, I haven't seen him for two days now, and I'm starting to worry. He hasn't touched the food I left him, and it was the fancy $4.99 tin stuff he likes.

Unwillingly, I glance at the screen. It's 5:15 P.M. My last clients left ten minutes ago.

Firmly, I hit the delete button until the post is blank and waiting. I need to update my website for real, but it's getting harder and harder to fake it. I find myself opening it and just unloading the truth, and out it all comes like gushing blood. I've never kept a diary before, but I can see why people do it. It's lonely keeping secrets, but a blank page is secure and safe, and I've never had a safe place before.

My head pulses in pain just as someone knocks softly at my door.

Emily. She pokes her blond head inside and gives me an apologetic smile. "Got a minute to talk, lovie?"

Despite my headache, I find myself nodding gratefully. In swift, graceful movements, she steps inside, and her long skirt swishes like lapping water. She sits on my couch, smooths her skirt with her palms, and the little wooden beads of her bracelet click softly like ice cubes. I feel like I could watch her for hours. Even her name is pleasant. Em-i-ly. Em-i-ly.

"Just wanted to check and see how you're going," she says in her gentle way.

"I'm great!" I tell her as my eyes fill with tears. Oh my God. I quickly fake a sneeze and swipe the tears away. All this shit with the rat this morning is pushing me closer to the edge. And also, I can't even remember the last time someone asked if I was okay.

"Oh, lovie," she says, and it's amazing how much empathy she crams into two words. God, it nearly has me bawling. Wordlessly she reaches into her skirt pocket and slides me a tissue.

I wonder why she's so nice to me. My other co-workers skirt uneasily around me, backing out of the office kitchen when I walk in. It's been like that all my life. My sister used to save me from these situations, speaking for me or just stubbornly taking me along when I was excluded from birthday parties or whatever. Lizzy. Lizzy.

I smooth the lavender-scented tissue onto my lap, fighting hard not to cry. I don't even try with people anymore. I don't follow my co-workers to the pub after work. I go home to my murder house and my secrets, and I call it a life.

Don't lose it, I tell myself. Don't you dare, you piece of shit.

I slip into my skin and shift the focus from me. "How long have you lived in Beacon, Emily?"

"All my life," she says with a hint of pride. "It's a close-knit community. Everyone helps each other around here."

Only if you were born here, apparently. Otherwise they leave dead rats in your mailbox.

"I went to primary school with your neighbor, actually."

"Who?"

"Jeff Johnson. He lives up the street from you." She hesitates. "He tried to sell his house last year, but no one wanted it."

My heart drops to my feet. I didn't know that my neighbor tried to sell his house last year. And worse: that no one wanted it. Shit. What chance do we have of selling Black Wood if nobody will even buy the neighbor's house? *There's a waiting list to buy into this town,* the realtor told me. That lying bastard.

I sink into my seat, deflated. "What's Jeff like?"

"He's a bad sort."

My head starts to pound again. "What do you mean?"

"I grew up with him." She smooths her skirt again. By the look on her face, the memories aren't pleasant. "His uncle is Beacon's police sergeant, and his mum let him get away with absolute murder. He wasn't nice, even back then. But he's worse now."

My stomach tightens. "How?"

"They're just rumors," Emily says urgently, probably noticing my concern. "I wouldn't worry about it too much, lovie."

But I am. I am worried about it. "What else do you know about him? About Beacon?"

Gently, she rolls a wooden bead on her bracelet with her fingertip. "He left Beacon at eighteen like they all do," Emily says slowly, quietly. "Went to the Big Smoke and bided his time until his poor mum finally passed last year. He inherited the estate of course, all four thousand square meters of it." She shakes her head. "Moved in two days after her funeral."

I shake my head, too, but I'm not surprised.

"Rumor has it he's got some debts." Emily pauses, and I raise an eyebrow. "Gambling," she says meaningfully. "He's been trying to sell the house for a year now. He hates Beacon, though he's got no reason to . . . but he hates Black Wood House more," she reluctantly adds. "He can't sell his mum's house to pay his debts, and he blames your place for it. He tries to get Black Wood bulldozed every town meeting."

I tap a few meaningless words into the keyboard and notice a red wine stain near my foot. The uneasy scene with the cleaner plays through my head, and I forget the keyboard.

"Hey." I look up. "You haven't had any problems with the cleaners, have you?"

"Other than the fact that they don't do their job properly, you mean?" She grins. "We go through cleaners like you wouldn't believe."

I cover the stain with my foot, thinking of the bloodstain upstairs in Black Wood House. "Have you ever been to my house?"

She presses her lips together and smooths her skirt again. "No," she says almost apologetically. "I don't know how you could live there, to be honest." She gives me an admiring look. "You must be very brave!"

No, just stupid. Truthfully, I wanted Black Wood House the second I saw it. When I want something, it *consumes* me. My wants have always straddled the unhealthy-obsession line. When that bony look was in during high school, I starved myself with watery soup until my rib cage and limbs were picked clean of flesh.

When the quiet blond boy with the easy smile started dating my rival, I silently borrowed his mannerisms, hobbies, quick smile, and even his hair color for a while until he looked at me and saw himself. Two months later he was mine.

That was Joe.

It bewildered him when *I* started slowly emerging. But it was too late then because the Incident happened. The one we don't speak about. So, we left our hometown of Scarbour, north Queensland. Actually, we fled. A fresh start, I stubbornly called it. My life has been made up of very sudden fresh starts.

"Do you know much about the Campbells?" I ask.

She shakes her head, and her long blond plait swishes softly. "The . . . incident with the Campbells was a bit before my time." She hesitates, rolling a bead between her fingers. There's something she wants to tell me.

"Emily." I lean forward quickly, and my chair squeaks a protest. "What is it?"

She bites her lip. "Did anyone tell you about the previous owner?"

"The Campbells, you mean?"

She gives me a curious look. "Not them," she says. "I meant the last owner. The one before you."

I lean back. "What?"

"I had a feeling Rodney didn't tell you. Not that he had to, of course. But it would have been nice for you to know."

Know what?

"You bought the house through PeakeProbates.com, didn't you?"

Yes, we did. I found the house online and rang the agency without once discussing it with Joe. We inspected it forty-eight hours later.

I see Rodney Peake now, hastily signing the deed, careful not to touch the paper. *It takes a certain kind of someone to buy a murder house,* he said grimly.

I guess you won't be coming over for a cup of tea, then? I asked.

And he gave me a sour look. *No, I don't think I could . . .*

"Someone bought the house before us?" I fight to keep my voice steady, but even I can hear the wobble in it. The uncertainty.

"Black Wood was on the market for years, as you probably know," she says in a lower voice now.

I bounce my knee impatiently. "Forty, I was told."

"I mean, yes, that's technically true." She avoids my eyes.

"Technically?"

"Last year, someone else bought it," she says. "She lived there for a few weeks."

My knee stops bouncing. "I should have been told this," I blurt out a bit too aggressively.

She bites her lip apologetically. "It's like I said. Beacon's a tight-knit community. Suspicious of outsiders."

Like me.

My head throbs. "What happened to the woman?"

"That's the thing," she says quietly. "Nobody really knows."

"She can't have just *disappeared.*"

My door bursts open. Tim. The sports psych.

"There you are, Em!" He claps his hands together, and it's as loud as a gunshot. My nerves are so shot, I choke back a yelp. "Get your ass to the pub, girl." He grins at her and finally notices me. "Oh yes," he says too brightly, "you're welcome to join, of course."

Behind him, someone calls his name. Tim reaches out to high-five the stranger and steps out of my door, leaving it open.

Emily slowly rises to her feet. "Would you like to come with us, lovie? We'd be happy to have you."

I shake my head because I'm not thinking about the bloody pub.

"Emily!" I lean forward, my voice tinged with hysteria. "What was the name of the woman who lived at Black Wood before me?"

My mind drifts to the woman at the mailbox. The one who looked at me like I was a ghost. The one who called me Amanda.

You look so much like her . . .

Down the hallway, office doors are snapping open. Clients are escorted in and out. Emily clicks her tongue, thinking. "Let's see now . . ."

The back of my neck feels unbearably warm, like someone's pressing a hot scone against it.

"Amanda," she finally says. "Her name was Amanda."

Chapter 13

Let me introduce you to Friendly Neighbor Sarah! Friendly Neighbor Sarah is disarming, chatty, even a little clumsy! Harmless.

I knew a woman like her when Joe and I were living in Mitchell. Mrs. Short, her name was, though her husband had been dead for decades. She lived next door and was always popping over with a beaming smile, bouncing curls, and probing questions. Sometimes she brought scones, which were always slightly burnt. "Care for a scone, deary?" she used to ask, holding the paper plate up like she was offering me her heart. She was a dithery old dear who made a big fuss of Reaper—"Who's a handsome boy there!"—and tottered off with her cane after hugging me goodbye.

I was lonely and grateful for the company. And so was she, I thought.

One day, we were chatting in the sun at my kitchen table, glasses drained of cheap moscato, when I said something about growing up in Queensland with my sister.

And I swear to God her eyes narrowed like a bird of prey's. "I thought you were an only child?"

Amazing. She had easily gained my trust without me even noticing. Our kitchen conversations were interrogations disguised as friendly chat. Honestly, I was more impressed than angry with her.

Mrs. Short. This is who I will be today when I go to Kay Potts's house. Mrs. Short can be trusted with your secrets. So go ahead, fucker, and let them spill.

When I wave goodbye in a cloud of Gucci Bloom and disarming femininity, you'll think to yourself, *Isn't she a dear?*

And maybe you won't even realize you've told me everything and I've told you nothing at all. You won't even realize I've accessed all your valuable data like a hacker. Or a virus. I wrap an inch-long strand of caramel highlights around the curling wand and hold it there, pressing down until it burns. The mirror in my bathroom is cracked down the middle and stained with flecks of toothpaste. This is the bathroom where Bill Campbell killed himself.

I hold the curl longer, feeling the warmth of the iron against my chin. I release the curl, and it falls hot into my palm. I let it cool there, and while I wait, I glance slowly to my right. Bill was found slumped against the bathtub. The same one I'm currently staring at. The faucets are red-brown with rust, and the bottom of the tub looks like someone washed a pack of filthy dogs in there. I itch to clean it, but every time I try, something stops me. Last week I hauled a bucket of hot, soapy water over to the tub, and just when I was about to pour it in, I stopped. I felt like someone was tugging my arm urgently, pulling me away. I froze, the bucket hovering in the air, ready to spill, and I felt the wrongness of it right down to my bones.

The house doesn't want to be clean. It doesn't want to be fixed.

I turned around, trekked downstairs, the bucket sloshing in my arms. I carefully stepped out the back door and threw the hot, clean water out onto the blackberry bushes.

I didn't tell Joe about this incident. He thinks I'm crazy enough already.

I lightly brush the curls out and spray them until they're sticky and glistening. Critically, I inspect my Friendly Neighbor clothes. Blush-pink cardigan, cream slacks, and a gold pendant cross nestled between my collarbones. I feel like a sixties housewife. Mrs. Short would approve.

The neighbor at the end of the street, the one who called me Amanda, is a Ms. Kay Potts. A brief Google search informed me that she bought her house seventeen years ago. Husband worked at a bank and is now deceased. No kids. She's just the type of neighbor who might have struck up a friendship with the young woman who moved in down the street.

And then disappeared.

I apply a dusty pink lipstick and one spray of Gucci Bloom to each wrist, then nod slowly at myself in the cracked mirror. This time when I come face-to-face with Kay Potts, I will not be caught out in sweaty leggings. I'll bring a smile and a hundred innocent questions about the previous owner, who nobody knows about.

I spent hours after work googling Amanda, but I had little to go on. I don't know her last name, where she worked, where she came from. Still, you'd think there'd be some trace of her buying Black Wood House. Some documentation. *Something.*

And Mr. Whitman, who lives next door. He never told me there was a previous owner.

Why?

Uneasily, I slide my hands into my pockets and stare at my cracked face in the mirror. Why the hell is everyone so secretive about everything in this town?

I head slowly down the stairs, wincing at the sound of the builders talking too loudly in the kitchen. Joe's huddled among them, clapping backs and laughing. You'd think he was back in his football locker room. I hesitate at the final stair, watching my shiny-black-haired husband with his Tom Ford glasses and chinos among the barrel-chested builders and paint-stained work boots.

I feel a bit sorry for Joe. He's desperate to be "just one of the guys" again.

Quietly, I slip past them and disappear out the front door into the breezy morning. I stuff my hands into my pockets as the wind funnels down my thin cardigan. A rosella chirps in the blackwood tree as I walk down our driveway. I look out for Reaper, but I don't see him anywhere.

I reach the end of our driveway, and there's Black Wood Forest to my right. A great dark mess of creaking branches, rustling leaves, chattering birds, and awfulness. I shiver, turning my back on it, and stroll up the road to Kay's house. It's a terrible morning for a walk, all gray clouds and weak sunlight. I rub my arms to warm them as raindrops drip from the sky, splattering my shoulders and perfect hair.

I didn't notice Kay's house last time we met. She must have rattled me, because it's absolutely stunning. An impressive Greek revival with four creamy columns and a close-cropped lawn you could play golf on. But as I walk past the sprawling garden, I notice the roses are wilting and the orange tree in the front yard is heavy with rotting fruit.

I knock at the door, and instantly a dog starts barking. I wait there long enough to think she's not home. Or she is but she's not going to answer the door. I knock again, louder this time, and from behind the door I hear the frantic click of the dog's nails on floorboards.

Finally, the door opens a crack. "Yes?"

I peer through it, smiling. I can't see her face, only her bony hand on the doorframe. "Ms. Potts?" The damn dog gives two throaty barks, and she nudges it with her foot to stop it escaping outside.

"Hi there! It's me again, Sarah, your new neighbor!"

The dog keeps barking, and I keep smiling, fighting hard not to flinch. She remains hidden behind the door, so I raise my voice over the dog and half yell, "We met last week."

You know, when you thought I was the missing girl and nearly had a heart attack.

She bends down, and even through the small crack, I can tell it's painful for her. She moves too slowly, her head disappearing for a fraction too long as she scoops the dog up. A sigh of pain escapes her lips as she straightens up, and I feel guilty about disturbing her.

But I have to know.

The dog nudges the door open with its graying muzzle, and there's Kay in a messy bun and house slippers, eyeing me uncertainly.

I bend forward, clasping my hands between my knees. "Who's a handsome boy there!"

I don't want to touch it. But it's the only way to get her to open the door wider. The dog thrusts its bulky head at me. I make a fuss of it and try not to grimace when it sticks its tongue between the cracks of my fingers.

"What's your name, deary?" I coo.

"Tobias." Her voice is clipped, guarded.

"Lovely boy!" I remain there on her welcome mat, scratching the dog under its chin as if I have all the time in the world to chat.

She says nothing. Doesn't even nod. I peer behind her at a winding amber staircase and wilting bouquet of yellow tulips. The inside of her house smells like burnt toast.

I clear my throat, not sure what to say, and out pop the words, "Care for a scone, de—"

Shit.

"Last week when I met you," I say, recovering quickly, "you called me Amanda?"

Silence. I wait, watching the dog try to wriggle out of her arms. She holds him tighter as if he's her only shield against the world. Against me.

I catch her eye, finally, and my smile freezes. She stands limply at her door, looking at me with such genuine sadness it makes me jittery. She reminds me of a woman who's seen too much, heard too much. Lost too much.

Nervously, her eyes flick to the door as if she's debating whether to shut it or not. Quickly, I step forward and add, "I live at Black Wood House. Just bought it last month."

"I know," she says sadly.

"Amanda bought the house before me, didn't she?" I ask softly.

Silence again. Then finally, a tiny nod.

"Do you remember her last name?" I wish I could wrench the door open and force her to talk to me.

She shakes her head and takes a step back. "I never asked."

I reach for her dog again and scratch it under the chin so she can't close the door on me. "What can you tell me about Amanda?"

She must realize I'm not going anywhere, because she leans against the doorframe, sighing. "She was lovely."

My hand drops to my side. "Was?"

"Is, I mean," she says quickly. "I haven't heard from her for months, though. She just kind of disappeared."

"And nobody else in the neighborhood has heard from her?"

"She kept to herself. I don't think she talked to the other neighbors much." She chews her cheek as if there's more she wants to say but can't.

"Because they didn't want her here, did they?" I ask gently.

Her eyes are wet with tears. "No. Nobody wanted her to buy Black Wood," she says sadly. "The neighbors want it bulldozed. They bring it up every town meeting."

It's getting colder and colder outside. I wrap my arms around my middle, shivering. I'm surprised she hasn't let me in. "Do *you* want it gone?"

Her eyes drift over my shoulder, and she stares vacantly at the road. "Yes, I do," she breathes. "It makes me weep to see it."

She murmurs something under her breath. "Susan," I think she says. "Poor Susan."

The sky's growing darker and darker, and a distant rumble of thunder makes me pause. I stuff my hands in my pockets as a thought strikes me. I don't want to ask it, but I have to.

"Did Amanda encounter any resistance? After she bought Black Wood, I mean?"

She narrows her eyes in confusion.

"Did anybody threaten her?" I say unwillingly. "The neighbors, maybe?"

She straightens up, looks away. "I don't know anything about that."

I think you do.

I'm worried she's about to close the door, so I step forward. "Maybe she changed her mind about owning Black Wood House?" I suggest. "It's not for everybody."

She shuts her mouth tightly.

The thunder's closer now, and droplets of rain fall from the brooding sky. My Friendly Neighbor act is long forgotten. The hairs on my arms stand up, and my knees and ankles are freezing under my ridiculous cream slacks. I have this urge to mess my perfect curls up. To smear mud all over my blouse and quit with the bullshit.

"Kay . . ." I plunge my hands deeper into my pockets, feeling like a small child. "You think something bad happened to her, don't you?"

She won't meet my eyes. She's not going to say any more. I sigh and tell myself I'll try again another day. I'll keep coming back until she finally tells me everything she knows. I nod a reluctant goodbye and begin to walk away.

"She was hearing noises in the house."

I freeze before slowly turning around. God, Mr. Whitman said the same thing about Bill Campbell, the original owner, the murderer. Kay taps her foot, and her dog licks her face as if it can feel her anxiety. I wait for her to speak, pulse throbbing in my wrists. Lightning sears the sky in a quick, hot flash.

He heard noises coming from the attic. Especially at night.

I swallow. "When did she hear these noises?"

"At night," she says grimly, and I stop breathing.

Me too.

"What part of the house was she hearing them?"

Don't say the attic. Don't say the attic.

Kay chews her lip. "Upstairs, I think she said."

"The attic?" I blurt out.

"I'm not sure," she admits, sighing. "I told her not to stay there alone." She speaks more to herself than to me. "Told her she could stay with me if she was scared."

Kay chews the inside of her cheek, gives me a look that says, *I don't know if I should tell you this next bit.* I wait, holding my breath.

"And someone was leaving her notes."

Oh my God. My stomach flips as I remember the sticky notes on my car and laptop. I don't know what I was expecting Kay to tell me about Amanda, but it sure as hell wasn't this. "Where was she finding these notes?"

"In the kitchen, the lounge room, the dining room," Kay rattles them off, her face pale. She pauses for a moment, eyes wet with sympathy. "And in her bedroom."

Another bolt of lightning. Tobias yelps in terror. We both ignore him. "What did the notes say?" I half yell over the thunder.

She steps back as if she doesn't want to be a part of this any longer. "Strange things," she says shortly. "Things no one should've known about."

My heart squeezes.

Things no one should've known about.

Like me needing to refill my anti-depressants. Like Lizzy. Like the DVD. My forehead starts to sweat. Kay watches me silently, and for a long moment neither of us speaks. A car drives past slowly, and a silver-haired man stares at us from a tinted window. I ignore him. Kay glances fearfully at the driver, as if she's worried to be seen talking to me. But I can't leave yet.

"Which bedroom was hers?" I ask desperately. "Did you ever see it?"

"No," she says softly. "I never went inside the house. I couldn't."

I think that's all she's going to say. Then she shuffles from foot to foot. "Amanda used to come over here for coffee. Once a week, usually . . . Sometimes she'd bring Winter," she adds, her eyes watering.

I give her a quizzical look.

"Her black Lab," she explains, voice heavy with grief. "Beautiful boy. Young too."

She pats Tobias's head reflexively, and a lump forms in my throat. "Where's Winter now?"

She shakes her head, holds the dog a little tighter. "I don't know what happened to him." She frowns. "Or Amanda."

Then she looks me right in the eye as if trying to warn me. "She was really afraid of that house."

A chill creeps down my shoulders and settles into the small of my back. I fold my arms, shivering, and the rain comes pouring down.

"The last note she found . . ." Kay shakes her head. "It really shook her up."

"When was this?"

"A few days before she disappeared."

My skin prickles. "What did the note say?"

"She wouldn't tell me," she says. I get the feeling she's replayed this over and over. Kicked herself for not intervening. "She sat on my couch for hours. I don't think she wanted to go home. I asked her to stay here, but she wouldn't."

She stares out at the rain, frowning. "Maybe if she'd stayed with me, she'd still be here today."

"Did you go to the police?"

She opens her mouth as if she wants to say something. But she changes her mind and shakes her head. "No, I didn't."

"Why not?" My voice is harsh, judgmental. I don't mean it to be, but I'm freaking out. Kay ignores my question, stares sadly at the falling rain.

"When she got that final note and came to see you," I shout over the rain, "was that the last time you saw her?"

Something flashes in her eyes. Her teeth clamp down hard on her lower lip. "Yes, it was," she says shortly, left hand reaching for the door. "I didn't see her again after that."

I wait there on her doorstep, momentarily forgetting about the cold.

Because we both know she's lying.

Chapter 14

After Kay's, I wander the neighborhood in the drizzling rain, hands thrust into my pockets, thinking. I end up on a wet park bench, staring at the gray sky and googling **Amanda+missing+Black Wood** but coming up with nothing.

I slink back home and nod at the builders, who stand around not even trying to look busy. Half of me wants them to go home and not touch a thing here. The other half of me wants them to finish the renovations *right now*. The sooner I get them done, the sooner we can sell it. The sooner I don't have to think about the missing girl who lived here before me. Fuck. I knew that living in Black Wood was going to be creepy. Part of me was excited by it, *delighted* even. I've spent my life watching true-crime shows and reading crappy two-dollar thriller books in the darkest part of night. The prospect of living in an actual crime scene and making money off it was too good to pass up. But, God. I didn't expect this Amanda shit. Black Wood has an appalling track record with its owners. What if I'm the next person to disappear or die in this bloody house?

I walk slowly up the stairs, clutching the black banister. The first bedroom in Black Wood House is left at the top of the stairs. My room is two doors down, tucked at the end of the dark hallway to the far right.

I lean against the doorframe of the first room and peer in. The peeling wallpaper is the color of overripe apricots, and the floorboards are so dark brown they're almost black. Cobwebs hang from the ceiling like gray crepe paper, and half-hidden in the top right corner behind a thick spiderweb is a large black spider that I'm not quite sure is dead.

Silently, I step in, feeling like an intruder and batting away low-hanging cobwebs with the back of my hand. The heels of my shoes click softly across the filthy floorboards littered with mouse poo.

It's windowless, bare, and silent in here except for the hammering downstairs. And God, it's dark. The lightbulb's blown, and we haven't bothered replacing it. I eye the room critically and get the feeling it's appraising me too.

Who are you? What are you doing here? Get out.

It's like some dormant monster that hasn't been disturbed in centuries. The last time I was in this room was when we inspected the house. I stood in the center, side by side with Joe, eyeing the wallpaper critically and breathing shallowly through my mouth to avoid the sour smell.

It has that echoey, cold stillness of a garage, and I'm certain that Amanda wouldn't have chosen it for her bedroom. I creep out of the room and close the door behind me, grateful to leave.

The second bedroom is next door on the left. I turn the handle, step inside, and the first thing that hits me is the smell. Even the realtor remarked on it when he ushered us inside. He crinkled his nose, waved his hand in front of his face to waft it away, and made no attempt to hide his disgust.

"Smells like bleach in here," he muttered before quickly pointing out the built-in wardrobe and high ceilings.

I cup my hand over my nose and mouth, peer inside, and remain at the door, unwilling to go in. The second bedroom is as painfully bare as the first. There are fewer cobwebs dangling from the ceiling and no mouse poo on the splintered floorboards. Maybe the smell put the rodents off. There's a sterile clinical quality to this room. Like a laundry. I doubt Amanda would have slept here either.

I back out, shut the door, and continue down the hallway. Night or day it's dimly lit, and by the time the sun goes down, you have to keep your eyes on your feet and take small steps forward in the darkness lest you miss the staircase and tumble to your death. We really need to plug in a nightlight up here.

For now, I creep forward. I throw open the second-to-last bedroom door. This has to be where Amanda slept.

I step inside, looking for any signs of disturbance. Any sign that a young woman lived in here for a few weeks. The baseboards are faded petal pink, and the drooping wallpaper is lemony brown and hideous. Still, the smell in here is tolerable, and out of the four bedrooms, it's the obvious choice.

I roll up my sleeves. I'm going to look over every damn inch of this room for any sign of Amanda and what happened to her.

I'm gingerly pulling back a floorboard when my phone rings in my pocket. It's a number I vaguely recognize. I hesitate, afraid to answer it, afraid not to. It might be one of the builders from downstairs. Probably found a leaking pipe or some shit that'll set us back another five grand.

Warily, I answer it.

"Sarah speaking," I say brightly.

A passive-aggressive voice answers back, "Hi Sarah, just wanting to check—are you still coming in for your appointment today?"

It's a voice I've used on clients who haven't shown up. *Hi there, are you fucking coming in or not?*

I clear my throat and try to remember. What appointment? Doctor's? No. I don't need them lecturing me on drinking or gently insisting I up my meds again.

"Um . . ." I transfer my phone to my other ear. "Sorry, I can't seem to recall . . ."

On the other end of the phone is heavy, angry silence, and I drop the act and blurt out, "Sorry, but who's calling?"

A sigh. "Luxe Beauty?" I know the name. I went there weeks ago. "You made a hair appointment for today? For *twenty minutes* ago?"

I hate the woman's bitchy tone, but I hate even more that my fingers start to tremble.

"I didn't make a hair appointment for today," I say, confused. "I don't need anything done to my hair."

And I fucking don't. I got caramel highlights put in last month for that Keeping It Weird with Whitney blog.

"You called yesterday, Mrs. Slade," the woman icily insists. "You wanted a haircut. It's right here on the books."

No. No, I didn't. I'm up to my arse in renovations, arguments with Joe, and the usual bland misery of my clients. At no point did I think, *You know what I need? A haircut.*

"Look, I didn't call you yesterday, okay?" I snap. "Bye."

I end the call and shove my phone into my pocket. My hands shake, and my forehead is prickly with sweat.

You called yesterday, Mrs. Slade.

I bloody didn't! But I *have* been to Luxe Beauty before. Who else could've known where I get my hair done?

I freeze.

Everyone. That's who.

Last month, I documented the trip on Instagram. I even posed with the stylist, who flashed a peace sign for some reason.

Fuck.

I scroll through my Insta posts. There it is. I'm sitting in the black leather swivel chair, my new caramel highlights framing my smug face. The stylist, whose name I don't remember, crouches beside me, smiling, her index and middle fingers in a V.

Had such a great time with the gorgeous girls at Luxe Beauty! I'm LIVING for these caramel highlights. Use my code SARAH10 to get a discount on all hair and styling products. Don't miss out!

Oh, shit. I forgot they gave me a promo code. Quickly, I reach into my pocket for my phone and call them back. *Please pick up,* I mouth over and over. *I'm sorry,* I'll humbly say. *I've been under a lot of stress. I forgot I made the appointment. Please don't tell anyone I'm losing it.*

"Luxe Beauty?"

Thank God. "Hi! Yes, it's me again. Sarah. Slade." I'm so anxious, I fumble all my words. "Sorry about before. I—"

Click.

My heart plummets. "Hello?"

Silence.

They hung up on me. Shit. I grip my phone so tight I nearly shatter the glass. That was so stupid of me. I've gotten exactly zero sponsorships since I bought Black Wood. I'm starting to sound desperate on my Insta posts, like I'm begging for scraps from anybody who'll give me a discount code. And now I've probably gone and lost one of the only sponsorships I did have.

Why do I feel like I'm losing control of everything? Like I'm failing over and over again?

I stare silently at the floor, thinking. I can fix all this. I *can* and I *will*. I'm going to renovate this house, shove the pictures all over my shiny socials, get my greedy hands on more sponsorships, and I'm going to find out what the hell happened to Amanda. I tuck my phone into my pocket and reach for the floorboards.

I lean back on my knees, wipe the sweat from my jaw. My cream slacks are stained with cobwebs, and my nose and eyes itch from the dust. I've checked over every inch of the walls and baseboards. I peeled back one of the broken floorboards, and I swear the house yelped in pain, like I was yanking its teeth out. I quickly dropped it back into place, feeling like I should apologize or something.

It doesn't look like anyone's disturbed the room for a long time. I wait here until my legs cramp, before getting painfully to my feet. I rub the ache out of my shoulders and stare at the peeling walls.

Amanda. Amanda.

What happened to you?

I sigh heavily. The builders will be heading home soon. Thank God.

I can slink downstairs, make a coffee, grab something to eat, and go to bed. I turn slowly and stare at the dark hallway, thinking.

Which bedroom was hers? There are four upstairs.

I creep down the hallway, breathing in the sourness of the air. It takes fourteen steps from the third bedroom to reach my room. The murder room. I pause at the door, peering in, but my room is just how I left it this morning. The hummingbird quilt cover is thrown back, there's a pillow on the floor, and it's too dark out the window to see anything but the silvery outline of the graves. It smells like old cheese in here.

Surely, Amanda wouldn't have chosen this room. Even Joe doesn't step foot in here. But still . . .

I crouch and examine the baseboards, not even sure what I'm looking for. I reach up and carefully peel back the wallpaper where it hangs off in large strips like flaking skin. I run my fingers across the entire length of the back wall, stopping only once to glance at the graves out the window. There's a creak of floorboards behind me. I spin around, heart pounding. A hulking shadow stands at the door, blocking my exit, holding a hammer tight in their fist.

I stagger back, frantic with fear. "Don't!" I squeak out. "Don't!"

"Mrs. Slade?"

Warily, the man steps inside my bedroom. It's Dan, the foreman. God.

I breathe again, gulping down a rush of stale air. "I thought you were . . ." I pause. *I thought you were Bill Campbell, back from the dead and about to smash my head in.*

He stops in the middle of the room, scratching his jaw with a meaty hand. He's a short man with a thick stomach and a giant laugh. Nice enough.

"Sorry to scare ya," he says lightly, like there's nothing weird about him stalking into the murder room, carrying the death instrument. "Was just gonna say that me and the boys are knocking off for the day. Be back tomorrow mornin'."

He looks around with amusement, twirls the hammer in his palm like he's a trick shooter, and whistles. "Is this *the room*? You know, where . . ." He makes a throat-cutting motion across his thick neck.

I nod, wishing he'd hurry up and go home to his simple wife, ten children, and fridge that's probably full of beer and bloody meat. His eyes finally rest on my bed, and he raises his eyebrows. "This where you sleep?"

There's nothing sexual in his voice, more an underlying question: *Why would you choose this room? Lady, what the hell is wrong with you?*

The windowpane is cold against my back, and I wrap my arms around myself. "Would you sleep in here?" I don't know why I ask him this.

His eyes drop to the bloodstain next to my bed, and we both stare at it silently. For a long moment, he doesn't speak. When he lifts his eyes again to mine, there's a hint of sadness in them. "Nah," he says. "You couldn't pay me to."

He nods goodbye and turns around.

"Dan?"

He looks back in surprise. I don't think I've called him by name before. I clear my throat and wrap my arms tighter around myself. I'm so cold. "You've lived in Beacon for a while, right?"

He smiles. "Yeah," he says proudly. "The missus inherited the house from her dad a few years ago."

Typical.

"Do you know if anyone lived here before me?"

He twirls the hammer again like he wants to leave. "The Campbells, you mean?"

"No, not them," I say quietly, then bite my lip before adding, "Someone else. A woman. About my age."

Abruptly, he stops twirling the hammer, and it bangs against his thigh. He looks away a bit too quickly, like he's been caught out. And I have my answer.

Does everyone in this bloody town know?

I wait for him to speak, but he doesn't. He's purposefully not looking at me. His tired eyes roam the room before settling on the bloodstain again. He looks hypnotized by it. "No," he finally says, his eyes drifting back to mine. "I don't know anything about that."

For a big man he can move quickly. He's halfway to the door before I call out desperately.

"But if you did"—he pauses at the door, his back to me, and a loose floorboard groans under his weight—"would you tell me, Dan?"

Slowly, he looks over his shoulder at me. His eyes are sad. He looks at me the same way Kay Potts did. Like they have terrible news for me but they don't want me to know. I shiver at the window, rub my arms to get the chill off me. Who warned him not to speak? "Dan, you coming?" an annoyed voice calls from downstairs.

Dan steps forward, half disappearing into the dark hallway until all I see of him is the silvery hammer. Abruptly, he turns around, half-hidden in the dark. Nervously, he transfers the hammer from hand to hand. I can't see his face, only the whites of his teeth in the darkness.

"Darren Foster," he says low as if someone's eavesdropping. "Find Darren Foster. He knows about Amanda."

And before I can even open my mouth, he's gone.

Chapter 15

May 28

SarahSlays.com

HOME   ABOUT SARAH SLADE   BUY MY BOOK   CONTACT

It's Friday night, and there are three things I want you to know:

    1) I googled "Darren Foster" for hours and didn't find shit.

    2) I'm so drunk I can barely type this.

    3) I think my fucking husband's having an affair.

I chug the rest of the wine straight from the bottle. The cold liquid spills out the corners of my mouth right onto my darling pink cardigan. The same one I was wearing when Kay Potts lied to my perfectly made-up face about what happened to Amanda. The woman who . . .

a) lived here before me

b) somehow disappeared without anyone investigating or giving a shit

c) is making me wonder if I might be the next to wind up missing or
   dead in this fucked-up murder house

I slump back onto the couch like a corpse, and the blood rushes to my head, making the cold room spin. I sigh loudly, pressing my face into a couch cushion. I could bang on Kay's spotless door with my grubby wine-stained fingers and demand answers. But if I make a scene, she might call the police. And if my drunk ass gets arrested for harassing my elderly neighbor, no one's going to buy my next self-help book.

I throw the empty bottle over my shoulder, and it lands with a delightful crash. I'd throw the other bottle, but it's all the way in the kitchen, and I'm so drunk I'd have to crawl there.

I roll over slowly, the room spinning in wild circles. I breathe through my mouth and glare at my phone tucked tightly into my fist. Nobody's going to come to me for marriage counseling if they know my idiot husband is having an affair.

I swipe open the text message he sent me three hours ago. The text message that set off my two-bottle binge.

Staying at Andy's for the weekend

Liar. I drop the phone, and it lands with a heavy thud. I hope I haven't broken it. Then I burst out laughing, because it doesn't matter. Everything else in my life is irreparable. Why not my phone too? I roll over and hope I don't vomit. The words spin through my drunken mind, over and over again.

I swipe at my eyes with the back of my forearm because I'm crying and hate myself for it. Hate him. Did Joe forget I can log on to his bank account? I know every damn purchase he makes. Always have. *Controlling,* he used to spit at me during our worse fights. *You're too damn controlling.*

I'm only controlling because you lack control! I'd shoot back.

Fucking Joe. He's been so lost since we left our hometown, *someone* had to take over. *Someone* had to make plans while he stared into the distance with wet eyes and a heart crammed with regret.

I drove us all the way from Scarbour, north Queensland to New

South Wales, and then the nine hours down to Melbourne. *I* wrote up his CV, complete with two fake references because no one in our hometown would give him one. *I* sent his fake CV to Seventy-Seven, the bar he's been working at for two years, while he wept on the couch and wrote groveling letters to my sister. I read every one of them. In my quiet moments, his aching words come roaring back like I just read them yesterday.

Biggest mistake of my life.
I'm so sorry. I'm so sorry.
I hate what I've become. Hate what she made me.

Hate what she made me . . . as if he had no choice. Blame is for the woman. Always the woman. I tilt my head back and grit my teeth so hard my jaw hurts.

"Asshole!" I yell at the ceiling, and the house seems to wake up. The walls groan, and even the floorboards seem to vibrate. The house is like a slumbering monster opening an eye.

The house likes my anger. It feeds off it.

I don't know where the thought comes from, but I feel the rightness of it. The house has been asleep for years, and now it's waking up. I haul myself upright and sit on the edge of the couch, anger roaring through my blood, heating me up until I'm burning with it. I smash my fist into the couch, and upstairs, I swear I hear a door bang open.

"Asshole!" I scream it again. It roars up the stairs, bleeds under the cracks of every closed door like smoke. Like fire.

I snatch up my phone, heart racing with fury, and smash in Joe's bank details again. And there it is. At 7:51 tonight, he spent $54.75 at Chinese Palace in Ellenvale. A town forty minutes away from Andy's place. Sure, they might've gone there together. Maybe even had a few beers and bitched about me over crab cakes. I could believe that. I scroll down and nearly hiss in rage. But I doubt Joe would've spent $35 at Stalks and Stems for Andy.

"A fucking florist," I tell the house, flipping the glowing screen toward the wall so the house can read it. So it can *see* it.

I slam the phone down on the coffee table. My husband *knows* I check his bank statements. Is this his half-assed way of letting me know he's having an affair? How listless and passive-aggressive of him. He always was a coward.

My head pounds viciously, and nausea creeps up the back of my throat. But I'm too angry to care. I squeeze my eyes shut, fists planted like rocks at my sides. The house seems to hold its breath. But I know it's really waiting. The smoke is here. But the house wants the fire. *Craves* it.

I never thought Joe would cheat on me. But of course he would. You lose 'em how you get 'em.

My eyes snap open. Oh, shit. What's going to happen if he asks for a divorce? I might be an F-grade celebrity, but people know I'm married. I've kept Joe's face out of my social media posts. He's paranoid someone will recognize him from our hometown. But I doubt I could keep our divorce a secret. My heart plummets to my feet. What if people found out about his affair? After all, *I* wrote the book on marriage. Well, a few chapters on it, anyway: "The Spark and How to Keep It Alive." And "Fuck like Everyone's Watching."

Nausea creeps steadily up my throat as I imagine the comments on my feed.

If Sarah Slade can't even keep her husband, then why the hell should I buy her book??
Relationship expert, my ass!!
She should lose her license. Bitch can't even keep a man.

How dare Joe fuck this up. *How fucking dare he.*

Slowly, I stand up. The nausea retreats, and for an icy moment I am stone-cold sober. I gave up everything for Joe. He forgets that. *I* fled my hometown too. Everything I'd ever known, all for him. All for a man who never loved me. A man who let me work full time for three years while he lay on the couch, playing *Skyrim* until 3 A.M.

The house closes in around me like a warm jacket, heating me up. It's on my side. It hates Joe for doing this to me. *Hates* him. He's going to ruin everything I've worked for. And I realize with dull shock that I can't let him. I *can't*. I couldn't handle people finding out about my husband's infidelity. Couldn't handle him asking for a divorce.

I couldn't handle that at all.

BLACK WOOD SHOCK:

SECOND BODY DISCOVERED AT MURDER HOUSE

July 2

ABC News, Melbourne

The mystery of what happened at Black Wood House has deepened after police discovered a second body today. It's been two days since police found the first body. But after searching the area again, police admitted to finding a second victim early this morning.

Police have revealed the second body was discovered in an unusual part of the house but are tight-lipped about the cause of death. Rumors are swirling about the identities of the bodies, but police are remaining silent for now.

As reported earlier, Sarah Slade and her husband, Joe Cosgrove, bought the famed Black Wood House more than two months ago and have not been heard from since the first body was discovered.

"There's a lot more tests that need to be done," said Beacon police sergeant, Eddie Johnson. "Police and the coroner's office are working to identify the victims. Then we'll notify the next of kin."

But one thing is for certain: Foul play is involved.

"Due to the significant injuries sustained by both parties," Sergeant Johnson stated, "we'll now be investigating this as a double murder."

Chapter 16

May 31

SarahSlays.com

HOME   ABOUT SARAH SLADE   BUY MY BOOK   CONTACT

I keep dreaming about the forest. I dream I'm running in the cold darkness as the trees reach down and try to snatch me up into their hungry mouths. I run and run. And all I can think is, I've got to find a way out. I've got to get home. I've got to get home.

Then the realization hits me like a fist to the jaw. And I finally stop running.

I don't have a home. I've never had a home. There's nowhere to run. And there's nowhere to go.

I stand in the darkness, lost in the deepest part of the forest, and it doesn't even matter, does it?

I've always been lost.

I hit delete on everything I just wrote and nod encouragingly at my second-to-last client for the day. I have no idea what the hell Mrs. Reid is saying. Her husband, a slight man with sad eyes, didn't show today for their second appointment. I scribbled useless notes for a few minutes before giving up. I zoned out but kept my eyes on the bridge of her nose. And I saw the forest. I've been dreaming of it every night.

She's mid-fifties with over-plucked eyebrows and an air of genuine sadness. Our last session together revealed the usual bland problems of a twenty-year marriage. Trust issues, poor communication. Not enough intimacy. It's fixable, but I don't want it to be. It only highlights my own glaring failures. I want to sabotage this poor woman's happiness because I'm miserable as hell and I want someone to drown with me.

Joe finally got in late Sunday afternoon. I didn't confront him. I'm not ready for that yet. I also didn't bother going downstairs for the rest of the day, and he never once checked on me. By Sunday night I was stuffed full of rage and cold pizza, pacing the room, hoping he could hear the creaking floorboards. Hoping he'd knock on my door and deny the affair.

This morning he left early for work, and I glared at the couch where he sleeps. I picked up each pillow and sniffed them carefully, wondering if I could smell *her* on him. That's who he's made me. A pillow-sniffing crazy woman.

Damn him.

Mrs. Reid continues her word-salad marathon, and all I want to do is throw up a careless hand and roar out, *Look, love, your marriage is over. Mine too. Fancy a glass of red?*

Then Mrs. Reid and I will throw ourselves on the rug and chain-smoke until my manager fires my unstable ass. I half smile, thinking it all over. Mrs. Reid will prop herself on an unsteady elbow, brush the ash-blond hair from her eyes, and ask me questions nobody's bothered asking in years.

How'd you meet your husband?

I see myself taking a long, dramatic drag of the cigarette, then blowing the smoke softly toward the ceiling. *I stole him from someone.*

She raises her tiny eyebrows, nudges me hard in the ribs. *Do tell!*

I inhale again, long and deep until my lungs are close to bursting. Finally, I exhale. *My sister,* I tell her. *I stole Joe from my sister.*

Mrs. Reid flinches, squints at me like she's seeing a monster. *Why?*

Disgust clogs her voice. She edges away from me, sits up, and brushes herself off. She blames *me*, obviously. So did everyone else in our stifling hometown. That was why Joe and I left. Partly, anyway. Word of my betrayal spread hot and quick, and for the first time in my life, people were looking at me. Glaring and muttering loudly when I stood in line at the general store I'd been going to since I was a child. Old Mrs. Avery from next door actually marched up to me when I was hopping into my car. She wrenched the door open, thrust her head in, and yelled at me with a mouth full of yellowing teeth, "You're disgusting, you know that? What you've done to your sister . . ." She shook her head like she couldn't even get the words out and looked at me like I was an insect. "Joe was a good boy until you came along." I stared at the steering wheel, not breathing. I felt sick. "He'll figure you out soon enough." She slammed the door, left me shaking.

My sister used to take Mrs. Avery's bins up to her door every Monday morning. Nobody ever asked her to do that. But that was my sister, looking out for everyone. And when she started dating Joe, our elderly neighbors squinted at them like they wanted to commit them forever to their fading memories. Like they were the only good things in a world full of evil. My pretty, chatty sister and Joe, the football star with the smooth hair and kind eyes. Such a nice young man. Such a nice couple.

Until I came along and stole the fucker.

Immediately after, my sister stopped leaving our shared room, and Mum doubled her drinking and watched my sister fade. I started driving to parking lots after work. I'd kill the engine and sit there with a straight back, staring ahead at nothing. When it was safe and dark, I'd drive home, ready with an excuse about where I'd been, but nobody ever asked.

Then it got worse, and we *had* to leave. Joe and I stuffed my thirteen-year-old Nissan with our clothes and fled the town in darkness. I didn't drum my hands on the wheel and scream my freedom song out the open window. I didn't feel free. I felt like I was fleeing a crime scene. We drove in absolute silence. I looked over at the weeping blond boy in my passenger seat, but he wouldn't look back.

Later, we dyed his hair black in a shitty truck-stop bathroom with flickering overhead lights. He stared at himself in the mirror and wept so hard his shoulders shook. I said nothing. I stared down at my hands, stained black from the dye, and thought how fitting that was, considering all we'd done. The lives we'd ruined.

It was me who insisted that we marry. I thought it would help us. Thought we could rebuild. Turns out, we couldn't. I asked him once why he married me, and he shrugged like I'd asked him what he wanted for dinner. Then, in a voice crammed with regret, he said, "I dunno, to be honest."

I dunno. For fuck's sake, he couldn't have cut me deeper.

I rub my eyes and jot down some half-hearted notes as Mrs. Reid continues bitching about her husband. God, I'm tired. Last night I stayed awake again until 2 A.M., looking for Darren Foster. I've found twenty-three Darren Fosters on Instagram so far and sent an identical DM to each:

Hi there!
You wouldn't happen to know an Amanda by any chance? She owned a black Labrador called Winter. I'd love to interview her for my website! Thanks SO much!

I didn't tell them why I wanted to interview her, and fortunately it made no difference. So far, nine Darrens have replied in the negative, and two attached charming pictures of their penises.

I scrolled through all the probate deals in the area for the last two years and found no trace of an Amanda ever owning Black Wood. I even rang Peake Probate. But all I've gotten are annoyed receptionists who made weak excuses about why Rodney wasn't available to take my calls.

"Well . . ." I must've zoned out again, because Mrs. Reid's icy voice interrupts my thoughts. She leans forward and grips the white leather couch with tense fingers. "Looks like my time's nearly up."

She gets to her feet, loops her lime-green handbag over her shoulder, and I blink in surprise. I've never had a client abort their session like this. My eyes drift to the clock ticking silently over her head. 4:41 P.M.

I clear my throat, embarrassed that my client paid $120 for this session and wants to abandon it twenty minutes early. I gesture grandly to the couch she just vacated, in a "please sit down" motion. "Oh, there's still plenty of time left," I tell her airily, crossing my bare legs at the ankles. "So, tell me about—"

My phone beeps urgently. I whirl around, panicked. My iPhone sits faceup on my desk, screen glowing. I recognize the Instagram logo, and my heart burns with fear and expectation. Darren Foster. It's got to be him.

I turn back to Mrs. Reid, pulse leaping in my throat. She gives me a look that says, *What the hell is wrong with you?* before she grips her handbag tighter and leaves my office in a cloud of anger. She won't be back again. I've got to start paying attention before I lose more clients.

Quickly, I close the door and lock it behind me. I lean against my desk, and it digs into the small of my back as I snatch up my phone. My hands shake so badly, I have to tap my phone password in twice. Finally, Instagram opens. And there he is. I squint at the profile picture. It's a man in his mid-twenties, with thick black hair that brushes his shoulders, aviator sunglasses, and an arm slung around a golden retriever. A green circle on his profile picture says, Active Now.

Who gave you my name? His message is short, blunt.

I chew the inside of my cheek, wondering if I'll get Dan the builder in trouble if I reveal him as the source. I tap the reply, feeling guilty. Dan Martin. The builder working at my house.

Immediately, three gray dots appear as he types a reply. I inhale sharply and wait.

You bought Black Wood after Amanda.

So she *did* buy it. Then why is there no record of it? Desperation seeps from my pores, and my fingers fly over the tiny keyboard.

Yes, I did. Can you tell me anything about Amanda? What happened to her? Where is she now?

Three dots appear, then disappear. I bite hard into my cheek and wait. Finally, two messages fill the screen, and my hands go cold with fear.

Be careful.

They're watching you.

Chapter 17

I think Darren blocked me on Instagram. I can't find his account anymore, and our chat thread's disappeared. But there's no way I could forget his final words.

They're watching you.

I stare at the forest mural in my bedroom, unable to sleep. Unable to do anything at all but lie here silently for the third hour. Joe finally came home an hour ago. He's been coming home later and later. He hates Black Wood House and me and, oh, everything really. Except his new girlfriend, I guess. Today he stayed out until eight. I haven't even bothered checking the bank statements to see where he's been. For a while I listened to faint gunshots drifting upstairs from whatever game he was playing, and the *crack-hiss* of him opening another Pepsi Max. But he's quiet now.

I tap my iPhone's screen. 12:34 A.M. I roll onto my side and check Instagram again, searching for the Darren Foster with the golden retriever. But he's gone.

The bedroom lamp throws ghostly shadows over the walls, until it really is like sleeping in a forest.

They're watching you.

Unwillingly, my eyes drift up to the rotting forest, not sure what I'm looking for. A camera, maybe? A listening device? I wouldn't even know what one looked like.

I toss and turn, unable to get comfortable. Maybe it was all bullshit. Maybe this Darren Foster didn't know Amanda at all and thought he'd mess with me. The only problem is, I never said she lived at Black Wood. *He* was the one who told me that. He knows her. And he thinks I'm in danger.

My stomach clenches in fear, and my ears prick up. Suddenly, every creak of the floorboards is someone sneaking up on me. Staring at me. Watching.

Beep.

I gasp, choking on my own breath. My phone lights up: Instagram DM. Frantically, I read the name, and my heart sinks. It's not Darren Foster. It's Judy Fuller, a fan I occasionally chat with.

Hi Sarah! How's the next book going? Thought it would be out by now. Can't wait to read!

It feels like a threat. I've noticed fans are becoming more impatient for the next book, and I'm worried they'll lose interest by the time I release it.

A lump forms in my throat, and I quickly shut my phone off. How the hell am I supposed to focus on writing the next book? I sit up in bed, cradle my head in my hands, half-tempted to fire back a response.

Hi there!
The book isn't ready yet. Actually, I haven't written a word! I'm a bit behind schedule because . . .
The previous owner of my house went missing.
No one knows who the fuck she is.
My husband's cheating on me.
And ever since we moved in, my cat Reaper's been acting strange.
Oh, and also! I can't remember where the hell my anti-depressants are (like they even work, ha!). I usually keep them on my desk, but they (along with Amanda and her dog!) seem to have disappeared.

So sorry about this! Also, please don't look too closely into my past—you won't like what you find there.
Okay, super. Thanks—bye!

I stare at my desk in the half dark. I take two fifty-milligram anti-depressants at the same time each day, right when I wake up. But they're gone. I swear I had an entire box left. My doctor's voice echoes through my bedroom.

Make sure you don't run out, okay?

I rub my temples, massaging the headache away. I've had nonstop stress headaches ever since we moved in. And now I've got to find the time to go to the doctor's and get my prescription refilled.

They're watching you.

I sigh. When I raise my head, it feels heavy. My eyes fix on the family of blackbirds. They look through me like I'm not even here, and something about it chills me.

I feel so mentally exhausted, like I could sit here in my bed for weeks. A part of me still wants to run downstairs to Joe and unload all I've been carrying. But we've never had that sort of marriage. Our entire relationship, I've tried to be a team with him, but he doesn't want to be my teammate.

Makes me wonder why he hasn't cheated on me before this.

And then the thought hits me: Unless he has.

I cover my eyes with the back of my palm, but tears spill down, hot and unwelcome. I cover my face with both hands, though I don't know why. It's not like anyone's here to see me.

Or maybe there is.

They're watching you.

I sit there for the longest time, hands cupped over my face, breathing into my palms. And all I can think is, I'm going to lose it all. My marriage. My career. This house, even. If Joe and I divorce, he gets half of it, and I can't afford to buy him out. I was once so clever. I had a plan. I had direction. Now I've gone and lost it all.

The straightforward pathway had been lost.

The words fill my mind like someone's standing over me, whispering. I raise my head from my hands, startled. Where have I heard that before? Then I remember: the book in the library.

I found myself within a forest dark,
For the straightforward pathway had been lost.

It feels like it was written just for me.

I shake the thoughts off, suck in one long breath. Get it together. Come on. I chew my lip, thinking. Darren might have blocked me on Instagram, but that doesn't stop me from finding him again with a new account.

And luckily, I have one.

I turn my phone back on and sign out of my account. I enter the password for my other. The one no one knows about: Evie Langley. Evie is an ardent Sarah Slade fan who leaves simpering messages on every one of her posts. God, I'm pathetic.

I type in "Darren Foster" and search for his profile picture.

And I find him.

My breath sticks in my throat when I see the green circle on his profile pic. Active Now. Quickly, I type a DM, afraid I will lose him again. Darren, please. It's Sarah Slade.

My fingers hover over the keyboard, trembling. I wait for the three gray dots to appear, wait for him to type back or block me again. But he doesn't answer.

I type quickly:
I need to know more about Amanda. Please. Something weird is going on, and nobody will tell me the truth.

I wait again, rocking back and forth impatiently. The blackbirds eye me silently, and my stomach twists. I type again:
Am I in danger??

I wait and wait, glancing at his icon to make sure he's still online. Active Now. Please, Darren. *Please.* I bite down hard on my lip and count to one hundred, hoping that by the time I'm finished, I'll get a response.

Ninety-eight. Ninety-nine. One hundred.

I peer at the screen, not breathing. Nothing. No response at all.

I exhale finally, leaning back and closing my eyes. Then I shut the phone off, crawl under the covers, and pull them up to my chin. God, the house is quiet.

Unwillingly I stare at the forest mural again. My eyes roam over the rotting oak trees, the mottled sky, and the baby blackbirds calling out for their broken mother.

I roll over, sighing. I desperately wish I had someone to talk to. My sister and I shared a room our entire lives. Right up until I stole Joe from her. The night she found out, she threw my blankets and pillows out the window. For the first night in my life, I slept alone on the couch, aching with regret.

In the days after, I wondered if she missed me in our room. Missed the late-night conversations we'd have, propped up on our elbows, laughing in the darkness. Sometimes, if one of us couldn't sleep, we'd tiptoe to the kitchen and raid the cupboards. We'd empty our bounty onto the bedroom carpet and play endless games of Uno. When we tired of card games, we'd sprawl out on the carpet, heads close together, munching on whatever we'd found in the kitchen.

I'd ask her what it felt like to French-kiss a boy. And she'd ask me about what book I was reading, though I know she wasn't that interested. But she listened. My sister always listened to me.

I swipe at the tears, but they don't stop falling. Whenever I think back to all that Lizzy mess, I just lose it. I miss my sister. I wish she'd talk to me. Wish she'd forgive me.

I see her in my mind, all teeth and tears. She says those same three words over and over again.

How could you? How could you?

And I fall asleep with them still ringing in my ears.

* * *

I dream I'm digging a grave. I'm in the forest, standing under a giant blackwood tree, alone and afraid. It's dark and silent, and I can hardly see a thing. I dig and dig, not even stopping to wipe the muddy sweat from my cheek. A cockatoo lands on my shoulder with an ear-piercing scream. Its eyes are two black sockets, and I stumble back in horror, thrashing and yelling.

That's when I see the name on the headstone: Sarah Slade.

On the wind is my sister's voice, calling and calling, *How could you? How could you?*

I wake up screaming.

Chapter 18

I'm going to be sick.

I throw open the toilet cubicle, fall to my knees, and out it comes. Again. I've been vomiting all morning, making frantic excuses to my clients before scurrying from my office, clutching my stomach.

I wipe my mouth with the back of my hand. Shakily, I flush the toilet. I rest my back against the navy-blue cubicle wall, pulling my knees up to my chest. I take shallow breaths through my mouth, hoping I don't vomit again. I don't know what's wrong with me. I'm definitely not pregnant. But my medication . . .

Make sure you don't run out, okay?

Weakly, I reach into my pocket, pull out my phone, and google "SSRI withdrawal symptoms."

chills

dizziness

vomiting

Oh. I tuck my phone back into my pocket and breathe in the toilet smell of bleach and mint. I'll go to the pharmacy after work, I think wearily. I'll pick up more tablets. But the thought of getting up off the tiled floor is exhausting. I just want to sit here all day. I got hardly any sleep last night, and when I did, all I dreamed of was my sister.

Nausea rushes up the back of my throat, and I reach for the bowl again. I vomit so hard I see stars. My forehead is slick with sweat, and my hands are clammy. I flush the toilet, and then I cry, because it's all getting a bit too fucking much.

I stare at the toilet door, shaking my head. Lovely. The icily composed Sarah Slade is at work, sobbing on the toilet floor. If only my followers could see me now.

"Sarah?"

Oh, shit. I scramble to my knees, swipe at my mouth again, and notice my lipstick's smudged all over my hand. Emily knocks gently on the cubicle door, and I feel like an insect about to be stomped.

"I'm okay!" I call out far too brightly and wipe my mouth and eyes quickly. I crack the door open, and Emily's worried face peers in.

I smile. Of course I do. Even though my lipstick's smeared over my palms, and my mascara's probably running down my cheeks. "Bit of food poisoning, I think," I say cheerily. I'm babbling now. I know I'm making things worse, but I can't seem to stop. "I've been living off takeaways since we bought the house."

Her eyes are gentle with sympathy, and I'm so low and so gone that I'm violently grateful for it. God, Emily. You don't know what I've *done*. How many lives I've ruined to get here. How I hate myself with an *unquenchable* hatred.

Her paisley skirt swishes over her toes. "How about a nice hot cuppa?" she says, smiling. "My mum used to say, 'When all else fails, put the kettle on.'"

My mum used to say, *You're the fucking reason I drink.* And, *Ew, is that fat on your stomach?*

"Come on, lovie," she says. Gently, she pulls me to my feet, and I follow her out of the bathroom like a little child.

She ushers me to a soft gray couch that squeaks when I sit down. I shift uncomfortably as Emily hands me a steaming mug of coffee. I thank her, and she sinks into her desk chair, settles her long skirt around her sandals, and sips the tea she made for herself. Her body is languid, relaxed. And I sit there with a painfully straight back, feeling like I have to hold myself perfectly still or my entire body will shatter.

Is this how my clients feel when they come to me? The thought hits so hard, my breath catches in my throat. Do they sit there on my overpriced chair, staring at my bestselling book crowding the wall and my slimy smile plastered over my too-shiny teeth, and feel like this? *Like fucking this?*

Like there's a tidal wave of pain washing over them? Like if they don't hear a word of kindness, or encouragement, or hope, all will be even more lost?

Emily clasps her hands, the little wooden beads on her bracelet clacking softly. A framed child's painting hangs on the back wall, a mess of pink and orange stripes.

"I don't know why I'm here," I say before taking a sip of the coffee. Her couch is leather and warm under my knees. "But hi, anyway," I add awkwardly.

"Hi." She smiles widely, gives me a little wave that makes me smile. The knot of nerves in my stomach starts to unravel. She's nice, Emily. My coffee is strong, scalding, just how I like it. Her cup smells of lavender.

"This stuff tastes like perfume." Emily wrinkles her nose, staring into her cup. "Lavender tea's s'posed to detox the body and boost the immune system." She sips, shakes her head. "Tastes terrible, but it's worth it."

I *hate* tea. I'm a coffee drinker. I smile wanly, looking around. I've never been in her office before. It's orange and pink and has a child's bedroom feel about it. It feels safe in here, and my limbs slowly unclench. Emily plucks a stray hair from her skirt, and it flutters to the ground. "Dog hair," she explains, grinning. "We've got three at home."

"I have a cat," I say dumbly. "Reaper."

"Bet he's easier to look after than three slobbering mutts." She grins again and sips her lavender tea. "The kids want another, can you believe?" She shakes her head, but her eyes are shining. This is a woman who lives for her family, I can tell. A woman who goes home to a messy kitchen counter and a lounge room littered with toys, while tiny children tug at her skirt. She cooks dinner with the radio on as her oldest kids spray each other with the hose outside and her husband plops a big kiss on her forehead on his way to the fridge for a beer. It's always noisy, but she's never felt more at peace.

She plucks another hair off her skirt. "How's your week been, Sarah?"

This is exactly how I start sessions, minus the errant dog hair. I balance my yellow notepad on my left knee. *How's your week been?*

Then I scribble clinical notes as my clients howl and seethe and cry. But it's different when Emily asks. Like she actually wants to know.

I nearly snort as I consider her question. Well, let's see. I lean back on the couch, and the leather squeaks as I move my weight. My husband's cheating on me. I have nonstop, debilitating headaches. I can't sleep. My house is a nightmare, and I'm worried about my cat.

And Amanda.

"It's been a tough few months," I concede, then smile brightly. "But nothing I can't handle."

Then why were you crying on the toilet floor?

We both think it, but she's too polite to point it out. I bounce my knee, and her eyes flicker at it wordlessly. I want to get up and run from the room. I sip the coffee, not even tasting it.

"I've been sick a lot lately," I finally confess.

"How so?"

"Nausea, migraines, dizziness," I reel them off. "I nearly fainted at home the other week."

Her mouth makes a little O of surprise. "Bloody hell!" she exclaims heartily. "Sarah, why didn't you tell me?" she adds with a hint of reproach.

This throws me. She's not speaking to me like a therapist to a client. She's speaking to me like a friend. I'm so unused to it that I lean back and say nothing. Emily cradles her mug in her left palm. It's ceramic with black writing. I'M A VET NURSE. WHAT'S YOUR SUPERPOWER?

I motion to it in an attempt to change the subject. "You were a vet nurse?"

She smiles, but there's a hint of sadness in her eyes. "I was," she says lightly. "The pay's terrible, so I had to give it up after we had Archie." I raise an eyebrow, and she smiles. "My hellish second born."

"I'll get back into it when the kiddos are a bit older," she says resolutely, a faraway look in her eyes. "I love animals. Been a vegetarian for twenty years now."

Interesting.

Her eyes drift to mine again. Everything she does is so calm, so slow. It makes me want to speak softer.

"Is it possible you might be pregnant?" she asks gently.

I snort. "My husband's been sleeping on the couch for months so I doubt it."

Oh, shit. I freeze. My eyes drift guiltily up to hers, but she's remarkably impassive. I stare at the bright orange rug.

"That's hard," she says softly.

And for the first time, I have to admit to myself that she's right. It *is* hard. And it's more than just sex. I miss having someone to talk to at night. Or someone to talk to at all. I haven't had a friend since we left our hometown, except for Joe. . . . And other than him, I've never really had a friend.

Except my sister.

How could you? How could you?

"Do you *want* him back in the bedroom?"

Silence. I can't stop bouncing my damn knee. "I don't know," I admit. "I don't know how I feel about anything these days."

My mouth opens automatically to recite the poem:

> *I found myself within a forest dark,*
> *For the straightforward pathway had been lost.*

I wonder if she'll understand, and for some reason I think she will. But I keep my mouth shut all the same.

"It's hard, isn't it?" She grins knowingly, crossing her legs at the ankles. "We're used to giving the advice, not taking it."

I nod slowly, my mind elsewhere. She brings the mug to her mouth, takes a long sip, savors it. "Do you have a journal, Sarah?"

I shake my head.

"You might find one useful," she suggests, leaning back, settling the mug on her knee. "They can really help organize your thoughts."

"Well, I have a website." I tap my nail against the ceramic cup, thinking. "I use it to keep my followers updated . . . about the house, I mean." *My followers.* God, I sound like a dickhead.

She says nothing, just lets me talk. Lets me find my own answers. And I find one.

"You know," I say slowly, pressing my back against the couch, "it's funny about my website. I never seem to end up writing about the house . . ."

"What do you write about?"

The truth, Emily. I write the truth. I write about the stubborn little stains of my life, the ones I can't scrub out. But I don't tell her this.

"Just random things," I say vaguely and take a sip of the cooling coffee. "My feelings."

She nods eagerly. "That's good! That's good."

"No, it's not," I say.

"Don't be afraid of the truth," she says. "Be afraid of believing your lies."

I tear my eyes away from her and focus on the rug again. "Lies aren't so bad," I whisper.

"Have you ever heard the saying, 'You repeat what you don't repair'?"

"No."

"Well, *now* you have." She laughs. "Do you feel like it rings true to you?"

Yes, actually. I think of the dream I had about the forest. I was standing in the darkness, lost in the deepest part of the forest, and it didn't even matter.

I've always been lost.

We fall silent for a long time. Emily doesn't have a clock in her office, and there's something calming about that. Like I can take my time in here and she won't mind at all. In my own office, the wall clock ticks loudly. *Tick, tick, tick.* Time's running out, it says. *Spill your guts, and then fuck off. Tick, tick, tick.*

"When you write down your feelings on your website," she finally says, "do you ever refer back to them?"

"No," I say, horrified. "I delete them all."

"Maybe next time, don't."

Well, that sounds fucking terrifying. I shift in my seat, cradle the mug in my left hand.

"Sarah?"

Slowly, I raise my head. Emily's blond plait falls softly over her stomach. It's tied with a blueberry ribbon. It's pretty. "What really brings you here today?"

My pulse throbs in my neck. I've used this on clients before too. *Why are you really here?* Dig deep. It's never what you think it is.

I see therapy as layers of skin. The first level is what I call the epidermis-level shit. The "I'm in therapy because I hate my mum."

Below it is the dermis. The meatier level. Then it's "I hate my mum because she didn't give me enough attention."

Until, finally, we reach the subcutaneous level. The very bottom, where the truth has buried itself. Then it's "I hate *myself* because my mum made me feel worthless."

My hands are clammy, and my breathing comes too fast. But I force myself to go deeper.

Epidermis: I'm here because I'm stressed about the house, my career, my book.

Dermis: I'm stressed about the house because everything I've built feels like it's about to fall.

Subcutaneous: I constantly need to prove my worth, because my mum didn't love me and I feel so fucking guilty about my sister.

My forehead is prickly with sweat. I bring the cup to my lips, methodically swallow, and hope she doesn't notice my hands shaking.

"I'm just . . ." I squirm. My heart is burning hot. "I'm . . . I'm worried about selling the house."

It's true, but that's not the reason I can't sleep. Or eat. And Emily knows this. My breathing is too loud. It comes out in panicked gasps. My stomach is all cramped up.

"Why are you really here, Sarah?"

My heart clenches like a fist. Panicked, I stare at the door. Emily notices.

"You're safe here," she says so softly. "Whatever you tell me is in confidence."

And I want to tell. *I do. I do.* My sister's face flashes into my vision. Lizzy is the root of all my issues. Lizzy is my subcutaneous layer. The back of my throat burns with the need to spew the words out. I lick my lips, and nobody is more shocked than I am when I finally open my mouth.

"Lizzy," I choke out. "Lizzy."

As soon as the name's out of my mouth, I double over, gasping for breath. Emily's at my side in an instant. My cheek's pressed into my left knee, and Emily places a strong hand on my shoulder that says, *I'm here. I'm here. It's okay.*

I close my eyes, breathing shallowly into my kneecap. I'm nervous I'll vomit again, but other than that, I'm strangely still and calm. Emily's nice. She's safe. This is a safe place.

Slowly, I lift my head. Emily crouches at my side, her plait brushing my shoulder. "Sarah," she begins, and I actually raise my hand to stop her. My heart thumps so hard I feel it in my ears.

"I'm not Sarah," I finally say. "Sarah is my little sister's name. Sarah Harris."

Emily's hand drops from my shoulder. Is it just me, or is she staring at me uneasily? The air feels combustible, and it hurts to breathe.

From somewhere far away comes Emily's strained voice. "Who are you, then?"

My head and heart throb so loudly I can barely hear her. I have one more bombshell to drop, and it might as well be right now. I raise my head and look her right in the eye.

"Lizzy," I whisper. "My name is Lizzy."

PART TWO

Chapter 19

June 4

Dear Diary,

The first time I knew something was wrong with me was the day I lost my arms.

Okay, that sounds crazy, but hear me out. I was a teenager, lying in bed, reading a book I wasn't interested in. Dad had mercifully left us a few months earlier and not once asked for custody rights. It was hard not to take that shit personally.

Sarah walked to school at 8:30, laughing loudly with the school kids who lived on our street, and I followed numbly behind. I spent my school hours looking out the window, holding my breath and pretending I was dead. Mum would retreat to her room at 4:00 P.M. and emerge red-eyed and drowsy at 8:00 to make dinner, but mainly she didn't emerge at all.

I called them Ditto Days.

One Ditto night, Sarah snored quietly in her single bed, and absolutely everything was normal.

And then it wasn't.

I snap the diary shut and drop the pen. It rolls off my desk, falls to the floor before coming to a stop next to my big toe. My heartbeat is frantic. My hands cold and jittery. I feel like I've been caught stealing. I remind myself that this is what I wanted. This is why I bought the diary this morning on one of my rare trips to town. But it doesn't make it easier.

This time I can't just erase the words with a click of a button. This time they remain.

I lay there in the quiet dark and became intently aware of my forearms. The pale skin from wrist to elbow and everything underneath. I bolted up, heart pulsing, making noises like a panicked animal. Something was wrong with my arms. I held them out in horror and watched them disappear. It wasn't like a flickering light. It was more like someone came along and hollowed them out, removing all the pulpy flesh and blood and bone. I felt like a gutted fish. I could not feel my arms, and it was pants-shittingly scary.

Maybe I yelled to Sarah for help. I don't remember. All I know is she was suddenly there, wild-eyed and frantic at my bedside. "What's wrong? What's wrong?"

I held my arms up, teeth chattering, trying to show her that they were hollow. That they were gone.

She ran for Mum, and I bit down hard on my left wrist, hyperventilating until the room spun in dizzying circles. I bit until I drew blood. And finally, I felt it. Yes, I could feel it. My arms were still there. Then what the fuck was all that about?

Mum arrived, bleary-eyed and annoyed, at the doorway, knotting her bathrobe with a vicious twist. And I held my bleeding arms out, palms facing up like a waiter balancing plates.

Days later, it happened again.

I was sitting quietly in the passenger seat, Mum blowing cigarette smoke out her window. My right forearm lay on my thigh, and the buttery sunlight lit it up until my arm glowed golden.

But I couldn't feel a thing.

I yanked my arm back, and there it was again. That scooped-out feeling, like I'd been gutted. The panic roared again, and the next thing I remember, Mum was standing over me, smoke on her breath, hissing, "Calm down, for heaven's sake!"

It got worse. These episodes were unpredictable and resulted in public freak-outs I could not control.

Sometimes I would bite down hard on my wrist to make certain it was really there. It didn't matter if this happened during the quiet time in class or on the school bus. So, you can imagine how kind the kids at school were about it.

And the teachers. They used to shove me in the bag room when I started "acting up." I'd sit on the floor, knees pulled up to my chest, arms thrust out in front of me. I was terrified that if I placed my forearms on my knees, they would fall straight through. I would sit like that until my arms shook. Sometimes the teachers forgot I was even there.

One day, I was sitting like that in the bag room when the lunch bell rang. My teacher, Mrs. Dryley, finally wandered in and stood at the doorway, clicking her tongue. "I've called your mum," she said flatly. When Mum showed up, she and Mrs. Dryley stood at the bag room door, staring down at me like I was a pile of laundry they'd been putting off doing. They talked about me like I wasn't even there.

Don't know what's wrong with her.

Her father's no help. Her sister never gives me any trouble.

Needs to see a doctor.

Disrupting the class . . .

Mum apologized to Mrs. Dryley, promised her she'd take me to see a doctor, then yanked me to my feet. To her credit, she took an hour off work to take me to the appointment.

Depersonalization, the doctor called it, doling out this information like I had a clue what to do with it.

"You need to find something to care about very quickly," he said sternly.

"Or what?" I asked, but he didn't answer.

He tapped his pen on his thigh. "What are you interested in?"

I had no interests other than getting safely through each day until I could crawl into bed.

"Reading?" I suggested.

But he shook his head like I'd given the wrong answer.

"I think you need something a bit more social."

I thought of Sarah, the social butterfly, welcome in any house on our street. She cycled through hobbies the same way she cycled through boys. Last year she'd harassed the neighborhood kids into starting a band. She practiced piano for a week but lost interest quickly.

I was thinking of her when I said, "Maybe I'll learn piano and join a band?"

Maybe I'd become popular like my sister, and maybe Mum would look at me with something other than her usual revulsion.

He nodded like I'd finally given the right answer. "You know what?" he said approvingly. "I think that's going to be the key for you."

So, I went to the library, borrowed a stack of piano books. I studied them as if my life depended on it. And in a way, it did.

I joined a band a few months later and we jammed after school in the drummer's garage. It was a good time in my life, and the arm thing became less frequent. But the drummer joined another band, and it all fell apart after that.

Shortly after, I started biting my arms again.

I tried football next, joined an all-girls team. But quit when I started getting bullied by the fullback.

A pattern emerged. I started a new hobby, immersed myself in it until it didn't work anymore. Then I moved to something else. But they were short-term answers. And sooner or later, the arm thing came roaring back.

And then, by accident, I finally found something that worked. It wasn't hobbies I needed. It was personalities.

There was a girl in grade eight. Her hair was chin length and flame red. Katy Kelly. She wore faded denim jackets and liked the Mr. Bean show. Katy said things like, "For reals," "Slay me," and "Totes." It fascinated me, this foreign language of hers. So, I practiced saying those phrases until they settled under my tongue like I was born trying to say them. I watched Mr. Bean episodes one after another like I was studying for a test. I shoplifted a denim jacket when the store clerk wasn't looking. And one afternoon, I used the kitchen scissors to chop all my hair off until it was chin length like hers.

Turned out, I had a secret talent for borrowing people's personalities. I repurposed them, made them my own. I called them skins. Katy was my first.

Until she marched up to me on the school oval and demanded, "Why are you copying me?"

I plunged my hands into the pockets of my denim jacket, stared at her flaming hair with envy. I had plans to dye my hair red that very afternoon. I was going to take the bus to the general store and look for her exact shade. "I'm not," I said. "For reals."

She eyed me up and down, looking a bit uneasy. "Freak."

I didn't like her after that. So I abandoned her skin, gave the denim jacket to Sarah, and grew my hair out. Over the next few weeks, I felt like a crab without a shell.

My next skin was obvious.

Sarah.

She wanted to be a therapist, so I became one. She wanted Joe, so I stole him. She was quick-witted and had all the answers.

So Sarah I became.

Chapter 20

I feel like the house approves of my new diary. It loves reading all my wicked secrets. *So, this is who you really are.* The house smiles, reading each entry, its warm hand on my shoulder like an approving parent. *I knew you were ugly.*

I lean back in my desk chair, staring out my bedroom window at the night sky. Pain pulses through my head, but I'm so used to the headaches it barely registers. The sour air turns my stomach, and I wonder if I'll vomit again. I've been vomiting a lot lately. Funny thing, though: I'm back on anti-depressants. Have been for a few days now.

"If you're still nauseated in a few days, let me know," the doctor said, tearing off my prescription and passing it across his desk to me. "The headaches should stop then too."

They haven't.

I reach for my mug and swallow a mouthful of cold coffee. I've been back to see Emily twice now. I'm not her client. I don't know what I am. I lingered at her door after work today, telling myself I'd leave any minute. I'd get in my car, nod goodbye to my co-workers, and not speak a word to anyone until I saw them again the next morning. Like always. But she saw me standing there and waved me in. "Want a coffee?" she said. "I'm *dying* for a tea."

So, we sipped our drinks in her calm little room, and I found myself relaxing. When Emily speaks, the words just melt from her. She's genuine in a way I've never been. Is this why I can't seem to keep clients? Because I don't come across as though I give a shit? Because they can tell that, underneath my oily advice, I'm just as artificial as my caramel highlights and SNS nails?

I cupped my coffee, and Emily gave me a friendly, patient smile. It said, *I give a shit. I'm on your side.*

I bet I've never made a client feel like that. And the longer I sat there, the more I felt like I was on trial and about to be found guilty. I take notes in my own sessions with clients, but I've never really *listened.*

"Tell me about your sister," she finally said. "What's she like?"

"She had a giant laugh and eyes as green as olives. She was very sure of herself, and she always knew the right thing to say." I bit my lip, eyes downcast. "And she wanted to be a therapist."

"I see," she said finally, but I don't think Emily understood.

I chose to be a therapist because I wanted to *be* Sarah. I was uncomfortable in my own skin, so I borrowed hers. I couldn't tell Emily this, obviously. Even to me it sounds crazy. She doesn't know the half of it.

I sipped my coffee slowly, allowing myself to think about my sister, to dwell on her for the first time in years.

"Should I be calling you Lizzy?" Emily asked me.

"No," I said quickly. "Please don't call me that."

I bit my lip again, darting a look out her window. Our colleagues were bustling around their offices, snatching up their car keys, stopping to chat for a moment before heading home. "Whatever you tell me in here is confidential." She must've seen panic in my eyes.

"Thank you," I said simply.

Tim popped his head in, gave us a curious look. He had a sports bag slung over his shoulder, big enough to fit a small child in it. "Having a women's meeting, are we?"

Before we could even answer, he gave a military salute for some reason. "Got tennis in ten," he said. "Better be off."

I shook my head as he half jogged down the hallway. "Where *does* he get his energy?"

"I suspect he's part machine," Emily said. "But wherever he gets it"—she shifts in her seat, groaning—"I could use some. I need some up-and-go."

"No!" I protested too loudly. The word was out of my mouth before I could stop it. "I like you how you are. You're so—"

Calm. Gentle. Kind. Oh no. The blush spread down my neck like a rash. I fumbled with my mug, nearly spilling it. My hands were trembling. Fortunately, she didn't mention it.

"Does your husband call you Sarah?" she asked.

I smiled grimly. "No, he's never called me that."

He wouldn't even agree to it for the blog interview . . . and God, what a shit show that was. We'd fought in the car on the way over.

He hadn't wanted anything to do with promoting Black Wood. He was too afraid. I kept him out of the pictures, obviously. Always have. And for God's sake, we've changed our names, our appearance, and our driver's licenses. We're nothing like what we were back then.

Joe stood stiffly beside me during the entire interview, clutching my shoulder so hard it hurt. At one point the writer asked him about Black Wood, and I held my breath. "To be honest, the place gives me the creeps," the idiot said. I rolled my eyes and wondered if I could get that removed from the article.

"What does he call you?" Emily asked curiously.

I had to think about that. On the odd occasion I mixed with his friends, he called me "Hey" or the nickname Sarah gave me. I think it's his way of fucking with me. "Sometimes he calls me Lamb. It's the nickname my sister gave me. Lizzy Lamb." I half smiled, remembering. "As in 'quiet as a lamb.'"

My smile quickly faded. Nobody would suspect that quiet little Lizzy Lamb with the waist-length dirty-blond hair had evolved into me. Everyone always seemed to think there was something wrong with me. Even my mum's chatty sisters skirted uneasily around me when we were left alone together. They'd stand up too abruptly, murmuring something about needing some fresh air or another hot cuppa, even though their mugs were still half full. I made people nervous without even meaning to. Made enemies without even trying. It made *me* feel uncomfortable in my own skin and only added to my private confusion. *What's so wrong with me? What's missing in me that people see so clearly?* Sarah, meanwhile, was personable, lively, always there with a perfectly timed quip.

Emily studied me, really looked, as if seeing me for the first time. "Lizzy Lamb," she said, and for some reason I flinched.

"I didn't talk much." I gave her a wry smile. "Not back then, any-way."

"Shy?"

I sipped the coffee again, felt it burn going down. I considered her words before finally shaking my head. "No. Just lost."

"A lot of kids feel the same way," she said, shifting in her seat.

"Not Sarah," I said quickly.

"And you envied that."

Yes, I did envy that. So much.

"Were you ever diagnosed with anything?" Emily prodded. "By a psychologist, maybe?"

Another small sip. "Why?"

"Just curious!" she said chirpily.

My heart fell a bit. I didn't want Emily to think badly about me, so I paused for a moment before smiling cheerfully back.

"No," I lied, still smiling. "I was never diagnosed with anything."

Chapter 21

The vet wrenches open Reaper's mouth and peers down his throat. "How long's he been acting strange?"

I swallow nervously, tucking a strand of hair behind my ear. Poor Reaper wriggles violently like a fish being dragged to shore. I cup my hand at the back of his neck, feeling the tremors ripple through his small body.

"A few weeks, I think." I bite my lip and feel horribly guilty for dragging Reaper here. The vet shines a torch into Reaper's eyes, and he howls his rage. The vet doesn't even flinch. She's mid-twenties with severe eyebrows and brassy red-brown hair, and I've forgotten her name already. It took half an hour this morning to wrangle Reaper into his kitty carrier. He howled the entire drive here, and by the time the vet opened the door and smiled, I felt like screaming.

"We just moved into a new house, and I thought maybe that's why he's been acting up," I say helplessly.

The vet's eyes flick up to mine, but she keeps shining the torch into Reaper's. "Black Wood, you mean?"

I freeze. Reaper tries to swipe her, but she dodges him expertly, clicks off the torch, and walks to her upright desk in the corner.

"How'd you know that?" I ask a bit stiffly as she busies herself at her workstation.

"News travels fast in small towns," she says, her back to me. She types something into her computer, pauses. "You said he was vomiting all last night?"

"Yeah," I say grimly, remembering the piles of watery vomit I discovered on the couch an hour ago. "He's been missing for a day or two, but he finally came home yesterday arvo."

I was so relieved to see him there on the doorstep, yowling and indignant. I wrenched the door open in relief, bent down to pick him up, but he darted inside and ran straight for the water bowl in the kitchen. He gulped for an entire minute, and I hovered behind him, chewing my lip. He went straight to the couch, perched on the armrest, and I left him sleeping there. It was 9 A.M. when I got downstairs and saw the puddles of vomit. There was a bit of blood in one, right on the cushion. It scared me enough to google the closest emergency vet and rush him here.

I pet Reaper over and over, trying to calm him, trying to calm myself too. The vet clicks away at her keyboard, and I peer at the screen, trying to see what she's writing. She turns around, reaches for him again, and rubs both sides of his stomach, a faraway look on her face.

"I can't find any foreign bodies in him," she finally says. "You said you hadn't seen him for a few days?"

I nod eagerly. "Yeah, he didn't eat any of the food I left out for him. Maybe he was hungry and ate something he shouldn't have?"

"Maybe," she says, letting him go. "I'll give him an anti-nausea injection for now. Keep an eye on him over the next few days, and if he gets worse, just bring him back in."

"I will, thanks."

She looks him over, clicking her tongue. "What've you been eating, buddy? Hey? Don't scare your mummy like that."

Yes, I want to say out loud. *Stop scaring me, Reaper.*

I've got enough to be frightened of right now.

*   *   *

I load Reaper's kitty carrier into the passenger seat, and he howls and spits at me through the wire cage. The vet said it should take an hour for the anti-nausea injection to kick in, but for now he's an asshole. I shut the door firmly and lean against it. I'm so mentally exhausted that for a few moments all I can do is stare down the street, watching the people of Beacon go about their Sunday routine. The general store is packed with people sitting outside, sipping flat whites and calling out friendly hellos to passersby. It must be a nice feeling to be so settled. So communal. They speak the same language, share the same history.

Overhead, a flock of black cockatoos screech through the sky, their red tails shining like a warning. I shove my hands in my pockets and watch them. My dad used to say that when cockatoos started screeching like that, it meant a storm was coming. But the sun's as full as an egg yolk, and the sky is burning blue, so maybe the cockatoos got it wrong. Or most likely, my dad was just full of shit.

I chew my lip and wonder if I could take Reaper with me to the general store. We could sit in the sun for a while and drink coffee. I'd smile at the dog walkers, read my newspaper, and pretend I belonged.

But I don't. Never will. I'm the outsider with nothing to offer this million-dollar town but my horrific family history and brilliant lies. Maybe they can even see the two-bedroom flat I was raised in with its moldy ceiling, rusted taps, and corroded pipes spewing out muddy bathwater.

And is it just me, or are people starting to look my way? I glance at the general store, feeling someone's eyes on me. An elderly woman holds a coffee mug to her lips and blatantly studies me. I rarely come into town, and I think my reputation precedes me.

I drop my gaze, and a teenage girl jogs by with a golden retriever, frowning at me. I shove my hands deeper into my jean pockets. Forget the coffee. I hurry to the driver's side door and wrench it open.

"Nice day, isn't it?"

I whirl around. The guy is around my age with a giant forehead, bulky teeth, and hairy forearms. He's smiling, though.

"Haven't seen *you* for a while!" he says eagerly, folding his arms across a violet T-shirt. "Where've you been hiding yourself, then?"

I pause. I've never seen this guy before. I'd remember his gigantic forehead. I glance over my shoulder at the general store, feeling someone's eyes on me again. A young waiter carries a black serving tray with three white mugs, and she must feel my eyes on her, because she glances at me. And freezes. Her mouth falls open, and the serving tray drops to the ground. Someone cries out when the mugs shatter, spilling coffee and thick slices of porcelain everywhere. Coffee splashes all over her smart black shoes, but she doesn't even flinch. Her eyes never leave mine. A moment later, the entire general store falls silent. My skin prickles as a dozen pairs of eyes fall on me.

The forehead guy slings a forearm up, shielding his eyes from the sun. We both stare at the waiter as she says something to a black-haired woman with a pixie cut, who nods grimly. When the guy turns back around, he studies me. He sucks in a breath, holds it.

"I'm so sorry," he stammers, red-faced. "I thought you were . . ."

Amanda.

I clutch my car keys. "Who did you think I was?" My voice comes out unnaturally high.

But he mumbles something into his chest and scurries away, half running now.

"Wait!" I yell it too loud, and even the dog walkers look up with interest. "Who did you think I was?"

He tucks his head low and keeps going, leaving me all alone. My palms itch with sweat, and nobody even has the decency to look away. They study me silently, eyes cold and mean. They know who Amanda is. Everyone in this damn town is keeping secrets from me.

The street that was bustling only moments ago falls into a hushed silence. Even the birds seem to be holding their breath. Sweat gathers at the back of my knees. This is a fucking nightmare.

Panicked, I fling the car door open and jump in. Reaper's frantic and anxious in the front seat, clawing at the wire, pupils wide and dark. I fumble with the keys, heart pounding as I start the engine up.

My tires squeal as I race out of the parking lot. I keep my eyes on the road as I drive past the general store, but it makes no difference.

Darren's words race through my mind.

They're watching you.

CLEAR, CRASS, AND OUT OF CONTROL:

BEACON RESIDENTS TELL OF UGLY INCIDENT INVOLVING SARAH SLADE

July 3

ABC News, Melbourne

It's been less than 24 hours since the discovery of a second body at Black Wood House. Police are still tight-lipped on the identities, admitting, "We're having trouble locating the families."

But it's becoming more and more likely that they may belong to current owners, Sarah Slade and husband, Joe Cosgrove. According to colleagues, Cosgrove hasn't shown up to his bartending job at Seventy-Seven pub since last week.

Mercy Community, where Slade works as a self-development therapist, hasn't responded for comment.

Friends describe Slade as "ambitious" and Cosgrove as "a humble guy, with a kind word for everyone."

But in new developments, it seems that neither Cosgrove nor his famous wife was very popular with Beacon residents, a close-knit, exclusive community in rural Victoria.

In fact, Beacon residents have described an ugly incident involving Slade at a town meeting, just two weeks before the first body was discovered.

"She showed up to the meeting, drunk," a resident revealed. "She absolutely lost it and started screaming her head off at everyone."

"She was making horrible accusations," another resident said, "accusing one of her neighbors of harassment and poisoning her cat."

It's believed Slade was particularly angry with one longtime resident who has not been named.

"She said he'd broken into her house."

It's believed that Slade was then escorted out and told she was banned from attending any further town meetings. The first body was discovered at her property two weeks later.

But before she was escorted out of the meeting, she apparently made a chilling statement.

"She said he was going to pay for what happened to her cat. She was mad enough to kill someone."

Chapter 22

I think I'm about to lose my job. I text my boss, Adria, another bullshit excuse about why I won't be at work today, and thirty seconds after I send it, she rings. I cringe when I see her number, and I swear the black-birds on the wallpaper cringe too.

"Hello?" I croak, making sure to sniffle loudly.

"Sarah?"

I sit up in bed, squeezing the bridge of my nose. Truthfully, I *am* sick. I was feverish all night, stripped off all my clothes, and lay on top of the bed, sweating. I got up weakly for some water, and on the way back to bed, I nearly passed out. But that's not why I'm calling in sick. I've got a plan for today, something I have to do, and I can't exactly tell my boss what it is.

"I got your text," she says tiredly. "I take it you're not coming into work again?"

Oh, piss off, Adria.

"Yeah." I squeeze the bridge of my nose tighter.

"May I ask why?"

I pull the phone away from my ear and swear softly. *I'm going for the trifecta, Adria. I've lost my sister, my husband. Why not my job too?*

"I've got the flu, I think. I've been under the weather lately. You can ask Emily."

"Have you messaged your clients to let them know, at least?"

I wince at that. "Yeah, I've let them all know."

Actually, I had only one client booked for today at 11 A.M. I'm losing clients at an alarming rate, and even my regulars are conspicuously quiet. A sharp pain seizes my skull, and I bite my lip to keep from yelling. "I'll be in tomorrow for sure. Thanks, Adria."

"Okay," she says unwillingly. "But this can't keep happening, all right? Mercy Community prides itself on . . ."

I pull the phone away again because she's making my headache worse. I reach for my bedside table, pop three painkillers, and fumble with the new box of my SSRIs.

"No problem." I throw back my anti-depressants, swallow them down dry. "Thanks for being understanding. See you tomorrow."

I end the call, swing out of bed, and throw some clothes on. I button my shirt and stare out the window as a lone cockatoo picks at the dirt of Susan's grave.

I stop buttoning my shirt and let my arms fall to my sides. What made Bill Campbell murder his wife? By all accounts he was a loner, not well liked, but people say they had a solid marriage. And what made Amanda buy this house and then disappear? If Black Wood could talk, what would it tell me?

Where are you, Amanda?

Where are you, Janet?

I wait. I listen. But all I hear is that familiar cry.

Don't kill me. Don't kill me. Don't kill me.

If the house can't give me answers, maybe the neighbors can. I pick up my Friendly Neighbor Sarah cardigan, slacks, and gold necklace, but a wave of exhaustion hits me. It didn't work last time on Kay Potts, and I'm too tired to try again with her.

I throw on the closest pair of tracksuit pants, my eyes on the twin graves. Today I'm going from door to door of this damn street, and I'm going to find out what happened to Amanda.

* * *

The sky is dove gray, and frail sunlight sneaks through gaps in the clouds. Of the five houses on the quiet street, only one door was answered. Mark O'Donnell is two doors down from me, mid-sixties and somber as hell when he realized who I was. I didn't even get through half my spiel: *Hi! I'm your new neighbor, Sarah. I live at Black Wood House. I was just wondering about the young woman who lived there before me? I think her name was—*

Bang.

I flinched as he slammed the heavy oak door, feeling the vibration in my teeth. Dazed, I walked to the next house, a $1.1 million beauty with a four-car garage. But the owners, the Charleses, didn't answer. I thought I saw the lounge room curtains flutter as if someone was peeking out through them. I left, dejected, and stood on the bitumen road in the weak sunlight, thinking that I shouldn't have bothered taking the day off. The Whitmans weren't home, and Kay Potts didn't answer, either, though her little dog barked furiously behind the door.

That leaves the last house, and I really don't have a good feeling about this one. I stuff my hands into my pockets and stroll farther down the road. The first house on the street is a colonial, sitting on three golden acres of land. Native plants provide brilliant splashes of color against the blue stone walls: rows of sun-bright daffodils, and sprays of blood-orange Grevillea.

I stop at the mailbox, watching the pale corellas feed in noisy flocks on the manicured ground. The nicest house on the block. Currently owned by Jeff Johnson, who inherited it from his late mother last year. I hesitate, chewing my lip and wondering if this will end with another heavy door slammed in my face.

I walk to his front door and marvel at the stained glass spraying red-gold light over my shirt. God, even his front door is glorious. I knock softly, two self-conscious raps that not even the birds hear. But Jeff Johnson does because he barks, "Just a minute!" so viciously, that I already want to apologize. I wait, rocking back and forth on my heels, desperately nervous with a heavy foreboding that this is not going to go well.

Jeff Johnson's the current chairman of the board of the town meetings. He's actively campaigned to get Black Wood bulldozed.

He flings the door open. My mouth slackens in surprise.

"What do you want?"

Jeff Johnson is mid-thirties, rugged in that "I spend all my time at the gym" way. But there's something vicious about him. I open my mouth to answer, but it's not quick enough, apparently.

"Well?" He raises an eyebrow. I hate that I wipe my sweaty palms on my tracksuit pants before answering.

"Hi, I'm—"

"Sarah," he says impatiently, looking over my shoulder as if he's bored of me already. "Yeah, I know who you are. What do you want?"

"I bought Black Wood House in April." He makes me so uneasy that I start to babble. "Was just wondering if you knew the lady who bought it before me—"

"I don't know anything about that," he says sternly, starting to close the door. "You can get off my property now."

I poke my toe forward so he can't shut the door. "How could you not know anything? Nobody's lived at Black Wood since the eighties, and you're telling me you didn't notice her moving in?"

He eyes me with disappointment like I'm a slovenly teen. My toe is still firmly wedged in his door. He opens it wider, and I wonder if it's to show off the spectacular scene behind him: marble tile floors and an impressive vaulted foyer lit by two stunning chandeliers. The walls are rose pink, and the L-shaped couch is butter yellow. The house has a decidedly mumsy feel, and I don't see much of the man standing before me in it.

I think of Black Wood with its Formica floor and blank, soulless bedrooms with flaking paint. It really is a monstrosity compared to the rest of the street, and with its gruesome history, God, no wonder they all want it bulldozed. I realize I've been staring wide-eyed at the gleaming marble floors, and when I straighten up and compose myself, I can tell he hasn't missed my reaction. He gives me a smug asshole smile, one that says, *Yes, this is my house. Nicer than yours, isn't it?*

But it's not his house. He didn't work for this. Probably never worked hard a day in his life. He has that cozy assurance of someone who grew up rich. Someone who never dreaded an aching tooth because there's no way in hell they could afford a dentist. Whose mum never served the same damn cheese and tomato toasted sandwiches every night for a month, until she couldn't even be bothered to do that anymore.

I force myself to lean in. "But if you *did* know something . . ."

He doesn't even blink, just runs a casual hand through his thick blond hair. He's dressed nicely—indigo jeans, black bomber jacket that brings out the blue in his eyes. I wonder why he isn't at work, and then I wonder if he even *has* a job.

"Amanda disappeared from Black Wood," I tell him, though of course he already knows this. "No one's seen her since."

He just stands there looking like he doesn't give a shit. I'm shocked when he raises his chin and demands, "Who says she disappeared?"

I open my mouth.

"There's no evidence she disappeared," he says, beating me to it. "She probably left Black Wood because she was afraid."

I freeze. "Afraid of what?"

He shrugs, leans against the doorframe, like he's got all day to talk. "It's a dangerous place, Black Wood," he says meaningfully. "You never know what could happen there."

I step back, sweat gathering on my forehead.

"What do you mean by that?" I ask him shakily.

Silence. The hairs on my forearms stand up, and the primal part of my brain is telling me to run. Just how dangerous *is* this man?

A cruel grin tugs at the corner of his mouth, and it turns my blood cold. "It's no place for a woman alone at night," he says coolly, eyes lingering on me. "But then, you're not alone at night, are you? Got your cat with you. And your husband. Though"—he gives me a mocking smile—"I notice his car's never in the driveway. I guess he doesn't sleep there much."

I don't even care about the slight about my marriage. Reaper. How does he know about Reaper? I swallow. "How'd you know I have a cat?"

He waves my question away like a fly. "Someone musta told me."

Bullshit. No one could have told him about Reaper. Only Emily knows about him. I bite my lip, wondering how I can call him out on this obvious lie when I notice his eyes darkening. "I hate cats."

I want to go now. I really want to go. I turn around, nervous that my back is to him. What if he were to drag me inside? Nobody knows I'm here. Is that what happened to Amanda? Did he pull her into his house, murder her? Dump her body somewhere? My eyes drift to Black Wood Forest, just down the road. God. What a perfect place to dump a body . . .

I stagger away, hands and legs shaking. I mutter a quick goodbye and hope my voice doesn't tremble. What if he sees my fear? What if he sees I'm onto him?

"See ya, Amanda!" he calls out chirpily.

My back stiffens. I'm so shocked it paralyzes my fear. I whirl around, breathless. "What?"

He's still leaning against the doorframe. He makes a show of furrowing his brow, as if confused. Fucker.

"You just called me Amanda," I say hotly.

"No," he says firmly, but there's a cruel half smile on his lips. "I didn't."

My fists clench. I shake with anger. With fear. "Yes, you did."

He smiles wider.

Trembling, I look behind me, studying the bright lawn and the corellas chittering in the low branches of the gum trees. I swallow hard. "This house was recently valued at 1.1 million, yeah?" I begin. "You'd think a place like this would be worth more."

His eyes turn cold. He can't say anything, because he knows I'm right. I will my voice to be calm. Controlled.

"The Fitzgeralds sold theirs last year for 1.25 million. And it's no-where near as nice as this one."

I don't need to tell him that the Fitzgeralds' is only two streets away. Or that it's only a three-bedroom, one-bathroom on less than an acre. Nothing as nice as his five-bedroom, two-bathroom, three-acre beauty. He knows that. And it pisses him off.

"Location, location, location," I tell him. "I'm guessing that living down the road from Black Wood isn't very appealing to new buyers." I look carefully at him. "Might drive the asking price of your house down too."

He tilts his head, blond hair falling over his shoulder. "What exactly are you trying to say?"

"Did you put something in my mailbox?"

That smile again. "Like what?"

"Like a dead rat?"

He shrugs. "My uncle's the town cop," he says slowly. "Did you know that?"

My shoulders slump, and he smiles in that "I've got you" way. "Tight-knit community, as you know," he adds smugly.

"And you hate it, don't you?" I ask, breathlessly. "You hate it because you live four doors down from a murder scene and it doesn't exactly fit in with the Beacon image, does it?"

"I don't give a shit about Beacon," he says sharply. The smile's gone and the rage shines through.

"You're trying to drive me out," I tell him, stepping back. "Just like you drove Amanda out."

"Prove it."

He slams the door, and the corellas stop squabbling. They watch me as I stagger down his driveway, shaking. He did something to Amanda. I know he did.

And I think I might be next.

POLICE REVEAL CAUSE OF DEATH IN BLACK WOOD CASE

July 4

ABC News, Melbourne

An autopsy has revealed that one of the people found in Black Wood House died from blunt-force trauma to the head.

Emergency services were first called to the house after reports that a body had been found at the infamous property. The body was lying face-down with critical injuries on the morning of June 30 and looked like it had been there for some time.

Police are appealing for help from the public as they continue to investigate the suspicious death. "It's a particularly violent injury that led to the death," they said. "We've obtained a number of statements from people in the neighborhood, but at this time we're appealing to members of the public that may have been in the area."

Slade and her husband lived at Black Wood House for two months. Residents admitted Slade argued with a neighbor at a town meeting two weeks before her disappearance. The neighbor's identity has not been revealed. Slade and her husband, Joe Cosgrove, are still missing.

Chapter 23

The coffee room terrifies me. It's too communal. My colleagues gather there in little flocks, chirping animatedly, even at 8:30 A.M. It's bright and cool, holding little but a microwave, sandwich press, kettle, and motivational poster hanging crookedly in a cheap frame: SEVEN RULES OF LIFE. Many times, I've waited for the kettle to boil and read them all, eyes darting to the door, anxious and jittery that someone will come in and start a conversation. God, it's exhausting being sociable.

This morning, Benita cradles a coffee mug, and Tim gulps his protein drink, while Emily chews on a piece of toast. The room smells of strong coffee and melted cheese, and instantly my stomach recoils like it's been punched. I freeze at the door, terrified I'll vomit all over the clean tiles. Only Emily seems to notice.

She calls out, "You okay?"

At the same moment Tim bellows out, "Ah, look what the cat dragged in!"

Piss off, Tim. Shakily, I step inside. I've got to go back to the doctor's, I scold myself. I'm sick of being sick.

"Morning." I try to smile, but it comes out a grimace. I walk stiffly to the kettle, my heels clacking on the tiles. Their watchful eyes burn into my blouse, and I hope they don't notice that it's the same one I wore yesterday. I've been slack on clothes washing lately—and any other duty that doesn't involve puking or drinking. I flip the kettle on with trembling hands, plaster a careful smile onto my face, and turn around.

SEVEN RULES OF LIFE

1. STAND UP STRAIGHT WITH YOUR SHOULDERS BACK.

I instantly straighten my spine. "I hate Wednesdays," Tim calls out like a shrieking cockatoo who's not getting enough attention. Benita quietly brings her mug to her pink-frosted lips. Her hair is shoulder length and shiny, her blouse the color of an overripe peach. She's the receptionist for Mercy Community, and I've always had the feeling she doesn't like me. She sets her mug down in the sink, gives it a quick rinse.

"Wash up after yourselves, please," Benita says, wiping down the counter with a damp sponge. "We're struggling to find new cleaners." She throws the sponge in the sink like she's mad at it. "The last guy quit after three days."

"Three days!" Tim whistles. "That's a new record."

Benita stretches, rubs the back of her neck. "Adria only hired him 'cause he's Jeff's cousin," she says darkly.

A warning goes off in my brain. I fumble with the hot kettle, narrowly avoid spilling boiling water over my forearm. Behind me, Benita says a quick goodbye, and she's halfway out the door when I call out desperately, "Benita!"

She spins around in surprise, and when she realizes it's me who called out, she gives me an annoyed look that says, *Oh God, not you.*

"Do you mean Jeff Johnson?" My voice comes out high and nervous, and even Tim watches me carefully.

She shifts in her spot, glances at Emily and Tim like she's asking them to bail her out of this. Tim's interested in that "ooh, what's going on here?" kind of way, and Emily taps her fingernail nervously against the mug handle.

When Benita realizes the others aren't going to help, she gives me a withering look. "Yeah. He's old friends with Adria. He asked if his cousin Chris could get a job cleaning the offices."

My knees weaken, and blood pounds in my ears. "His cousin." I lick my lips. "What does he look like?"

She sighs impatiently. "I dunno. Mid-twenties, tall." She chews her lip. "He had a really dumb haircut."

That's him. The guy who was in my office and lied about it. That's the guy who wouldn't give me his name.

She eyes me suspiciously as if I've done something wrong. "Why?"

"Nothing."

I say a shaky goodbye to my bewildered colleagues and brush past Benita at the door. Emily calls out, but I walk to my office and close the door.

Oh my God.

I slump into my chair, thinking hard. I try to remember everything about my skirmish with the cleaning guy.

Emily raps on the door, pokes her head in. "Hey, lovie, you okay?" She peers at me like a worried mother. "You've gone a bit pale."

Not too long ago people used to ask me, *Where'd you get your highlights done?* Or, *Love your nails. SNS, yeah?*

Now it's *Are you okay? You sure?*

"I'm okay," I tell her shakily, gripping the desk tight enough to splinter it.

I can tell she doesn't believe me, but she brushes a few stray blond hairs out of her eyes and says, "Let's talk later, okay?"

I nod, and she swishes away in her long paisley skirt. I think of the cleaner again. He could've been sneaking around my office, rifling through my drawers, for all I know. I was blind drunk at the time. He could've looked through my purse. Taken photos of my fraudulent driver's license. Seen my near-empty SSRIs.

Don't forget your anti-depressants!

The note on my laptop. The cleaner must have seen that my meds were nearly empty. Did he tell Jeff? Did Jeff sneak into my house and write that note to fuck with me? Did he find out about my sister and send me that damn DVD?

Uneasily, I wonder what else the cleaner found out about me when he rifled through my office. I've got so much dirt on me. I'm *filthy* with it.

What was he looking for? And did he find it?

I rub my temples with clammy hands. My head is killing me. For the first time in years, I consider fleeing. I've done it before. I know how to do it. I could pack a suitcase, grab Reaper, empty my bank account. I know how to start over. I know how to disappear.

But then what? Build a new life and hope the new one doesn't fall? The idea of packing it all up exhausts me to the bone. I can barely get through the day without vomiting. I honestly think I would rather die than start over again.

A soft beep interrupts my thoughts. I grab for my mobile lying face-down on my desk. Instagram DM from . . .

I gasp. Darren Foster. The man the builder told me to get in touch with. The man who knew Amanda. He responded to my fake Evie Langley profile.

Quickly, I read his message. **Do you still want to talk?**

I type back with shaking hands. **Yes. I'm free now, call me.**

My hands are cold, and my heart's in my throat. I'm finally going to find out what happened to Amanda.

But he doesn't ring. He types, **Meet me instead.**

I chew my lip, anxiety rising. I don't want to meet this stranger. The whole thing is creepy enough as it is. **Why can't you ring me?**

A pause.

Your phone might be compromised.

I blink at the phone. What the hell does that even mean? Compromised? Hacked? He messages again. **I shouldn't even be texting you. Delete this conversation when we're finished.**

God, too much is happening too quickly. I sit on the edge of my chair, gripping my phone as he types.

Meet me tonight. 11 P.M. at the Cooma pub parking lot.

The first thing I think is, the town of Cooma is a half-hour drive away. The second is, God, should I really do this? But I want to know about Amanda. I have to know.

Okay. I type slowly. I'll be there.

Don't tell anyone.

Tough shit, I think. I'm telling Emily, just in case. I place the phone on my desk, feeling sick with nerves. I rest my cheek on my knee, arms folded protectively around my body. It'll be okay, I reassure myself. It'll be fine.

But he messages one last time, and when I grab the phone and read it, my stomach drops to my feet.

Come alone.

Chapter 24

Well, this is clever. Why the hell did I agree to meet a strange man in a pub parking lot? Especially one that's dark and empty. I tap my fingers on the wheel and check my phone again. 11:26 P.M. He's half an hour late and hasn't messaged. I don't have his phone number, only his Instagram account, and I'm too scared to message him after what he said.

Your phone might be compromised.

How? And by whom, exactly?

I'm so nervous my stomach's cramping. I squirm in the driver's seat, watching the Cooma pub. It's silent except for the occasional shout of laughter from inside. My car window is cracked an inch, letting in icy air tinged with cigarette smoke. I haven't smoked in years, but I suddenly crave one. I'm jittery as hell, freezing cold, and my hands are restless and trembling.

I press my forehead against the wheel, staring down at my feet. Out of the corner of my eye, something moves. A shadow in the dark. I freeze as a man strides to my car window. Darren?

In the dim glow of the lone streetlight, he looks nothing like his profile picture. The guy in the picture looked clean-cut and harmless, arm slung companionably around his dog.

This guy raises a fist, tattoos marking each knuckle, but it's too dark to read what they say. Oh God, he taps on the window, and my pulse speeds up. My eyes flicker to the car keys still in the ignition. Shit. Is it even him? What if this is a hoax? A holdup? He leans down, eyes level with mine, and he looks just as uncertain as I am.

"Sarah?"

His voice is soft, shy almost. But he sure as hell doesn't look harmless. He's got the heavily muscled forearms of a tradie, a mullet haircut, a tattoo of the Southern Cross under his throat. Clear skin and cool green eyes. Hot, to be honest. Someone the good, clean folks of Beacon would refer to as a bogan. The type who makes old ladies wince and young ladies lose their good sense for a twenty-minute tumble in the back of his car.

He motions for me to wind the window down farther, and I notice the tattoo on the underside of his forearm. A flying dove with a name across its breast.

AMANDA.

I unlock the doors, point to the passenger seat. He shoves his hands deep into his pockets, crosses in front of the car. I grip the wheel and try to steady my breathing. Too late to change my mind now.

He opens the door, and a blast of cold air hits me in the face. He shuts it quickly, stares straight ahead, and for a moment, neither of us speaks. I've never exactly met up with a stranger in a deserted parking lot before.

Nervously, I face him, my right hand cradling my phone. Before I left work, I told Emily about him. She's calling me in ten minutes, and if I don't answer, she's going to drive here. There's a lot wrong with my plan. Like the fact that Emily's forty minutes from here. Plenty of time for this nice, hot stranger to strangle me to death.

I clear my throat, not even sure how the hell to start this. The pub door bursts open, and a man staggers out, yelling and pointing at someone still inside. We watch him silently as he stumbles off the curb, muttering to himself.

"We used to come here," Darren says softly, staring up at the pub. "Me and Amanda."

He reaches into his pocket, and I freeze. Oh God. Oh God. He pulls out a pack of cigarettes, sticks one between his teeth. "Mind if I smoke?"

It's the first time he's looked at me since he got in. Now that I'm inches away from his face, I can see bits and pieces of the guy from the Insta photo. But there's been a change in him since, an undercurrent of grief and anger, and I wonder if that change is Amanda.

"That's fine," I tell him, and he winds his window down. His hands are covered in tattoos, and I read the words across his knuckles. LIVE FREE.

"Can I have one?" I ask.

Wordlessly, he passes me a cigarette, and when he leans forward and lights it for me, I don't know where to look. My skin feels uncomfortably hot. He smells like mown grass, sweat, tobacco, and unwashed hair, and it's not unpleasant. My life is so wretched that sitting here with a hot stranger who may have bad intentions barely matters. Is my life even worth saving anymore? Was it ever?

We sit and smoke, eyes straight ahead. The silence isn't so loaded now, but it's not comfortable either. He scrunches his shorts in his tattooed palm. He's keyed up and anxious.

I inhale slowly. "How long did you know Amanda for?"

He winces as if it's physically painful to hear her name. He slumps a little, and I wonder if he loved her. Everyone said she looks like me. Does he notice? Do I want him to?

I lean back, and my limp ponytail digs into the headrest. A shout of laughter echoes through the parking lot, and I tap my cigarette against the glass, watch the ash fall away. Everything feels strangely perverse, and I kind of like it. Is this how Joe feels when he meets up with his girlfriend or whatever?

"Only a few weeks." He blows smoke out the window. "Met her here at the pub last October.

"She was from South Australia, I think, but she didn't say what town." He flicks ash out the window. "I got the feeling something bad happened there. She had a lot of secrets, Amanda." He hesitates before adding, "To be honest, I don't even know if 'Amanda' was her real name."

Well, that would explain why she's been so hard to trace. I watch the smoke float into the dark night. "What was she doing in Beacon?"

He shakes his head. "I never asked. I think she just wanted to get away from her family. Her mum especially."

"They didn't get along?"

A young couple exit the pub, laughing loudly, their breath steaming in the cold air. Darren watches them silently, eyes pained like he's been cheated of something.

"Nah," he says finally. "She didn't keep in touch with anyone. Didn't have many friends here either." His eyes turn hard, and I nervously inhale a lungful of smoke, waiting. "Not that you can make friends in Beacon," he says bitterly. "Think they're too good for everyone."

I raise an eyebrow, nod in agreement, but he's not looking at me. "People like that"—he shakes his head, smokes moodily—"they make their own rules."

"Tell me about it," I mutter, stubbing the cigarette out on the window frame.

He turns to me, elbow on the armrest. "She hated that house, you know." His mouth purses, and it looks like he's dying to spit. "Hated that fucking town."

"Did she own the house?"

He inhales deeply, sucking it in and nodding at the same time. "Yeah, she bought it for cheap and was gonna renovate it. She started with the kitchen, but something went wrong."

My ears prick up. I think of the plumber who tried to fix the shower, holding his bloodied skull and muttering, *I knew I shouldn'ta come to this house.*

"By the end, she was counting down the days till she was out." He stares off into the darkness. "'Course, it was too late by then."

The distant echo of drunken laughter seems to set him on edge. He finishes his cigarette, flicks it out the window, and immediately lights another. He speaks in short, clipped sentences now. "Nobody wanted her in Black Wood House. She had problems the minute she moved in."

He inhales rapidly, starts bobbing his leg up and down. There's a tattoo of a skull on the kneecap, and as his leg shakes, the skull looks like it's laughing.

"The neighbors?"

"Yeah." His lip curls. "All of 'em. I offered to go round and sort 'em out." He shakes his head ruefully, puffs on the cigarette like he's mad at it. "She wouldn't let me."

I ask the question I've been putting off.

"What did she look like?"

He goes still for a second. Slowly, he brings the cigarette back to his lips and inhales. Without looking at me he says, "She looked like you."

He pulls out a battered iPhone, and the cracked screen shows a picture of a golden retriever. The same one from his Insta profile. He smokes quietly, flipping through the phone before turning it to face me.

I squint at the picture in the semi-dark.

My God. She *does* look like me.

The young woman in the photo leans against the trunk of a black-wood tree. She's barefaced, freckled, and flushed with exercise. Her soft brown hair is tied in a high pony, and she's smiling uncomfortably in that "hurry up and take the picture already" way. Her arms are crossed protectively over her chest, and there's something in her eyes that makes me feel like she wouldn't want me looking. She seems like the sort of person who'd look down to avoid your eyes, and if you called out hello, she'd give a tight, reluctant smile.

A black Labrador sits adoringly at her feet, pink tongue lolling out its mouth. "That's Winter," Darren says with obvious fondness. "We used to take our dogs to Black Wood Forest." He clicks the screen off. "They loved it there."

"Did she ever take you to Black Wood House?"

"No." He frowns, takes a quick drag. "Not that I wanted to go." He turns to me then as if the thought just occurred to him. "You don't live there alone, do you?"

I have to think about this for a second. My husband's vanishing from my life inch by passive inch. He didn't stay at the house last night again. I wind the window down farther, let the cold air blast me in the face. "No," I say. "My husband lives there too."

"And he's home at night?"

I hesitate, thrown by the question. It's one thing to ask if I live alone. Another to ask when and what times. I nod carefully, eyes stinging from the cold wind.

He's silent again except for a slow exhale of the cigarette. It strikes me again that this is a bad idea. What do I know about the man in my car? Nothing, that's what. I flick the butt of my smoke with my thumb and try to make my voice as casual as possible. "Do you live in Beacon?"

I glance at him from the corner of my eye, try to gauge if he's wary of the question. But he's staring straight ahead at the pub, his green eyes glowing like an angry cat's. "Nah," he says bitterly. "I live in Red Hill with the rest of the bogans."

He shifts in his seat. "Plus . . . I can't go back to Beacon."

I stop breathing. "Why?"

"One of Amanda's neighbors," he says and puffs away angrily. "The Johnson guy who lives in the first house on the street."

I exhale loudly, throat burning, and Darren hesitates. "He took a restraining order out against me."

I flinch. I'm glad I'm staring out the window so he can't see my horrified face. I'm wondering how to ask him how the restraining order came about, and I'm relieved when he offers it up.

"I went looking for Amanda," he explains softly. "She stopped answering my texts. I didn't know what was goin' on."

"So . . ." I turn slowly to him. "What did you do?"

"Knocked on all her neighbors' doors and asked 'em if they'd seen her." He rubs his left palm over his knee in a self-soothing motion. "But they wouldn't tell me shit." He straightens up as if jolted awake. "One of 'em even said Amanda never lived there. Can you believe it? Buncha bullshit liars."

He didn't answer my question, and the omission makes my palms sweat. "What happened then?" I ask carefully.

"Nothin'!" he says, throwing up his tattooed hands. But he's more frustrated than angry. "The Johnson guy, he told me to get off his property."

"And?"

"I didn't."

A loaded silence. A car pulls into the parking lot, headlights off. It parks near the pub door, waits.

"I didn't hurt him," Darren says darkly. He turns to me, looks me right in the eye. "No matter what he says."

I believe him. I settle back in my seat.

"But he got his fuckin' uncle involved, didn't he?" He keeps puffing on the smoke. "Uncle's the Beacon police sergeant."

The pub door snaps open, and an elderly man with a black trucker's cap stumbles out. The driver of the car reaches over, opens the passenger door, and the man collapses inside. We watch the car drive off, and I try to organize my thoughts.

"Are you certain that Amanda wouldn't just up and leave?"

My eyes are still on the pub, but I know he's shaking his head. "She wouldn't just ghost me like that."

"Are you sure she wouldn't?" I ask it gently, and he gives me a reproachful look. "I mean, she left South Australia, yeah? And you said she wasn't good about keeping in touch with her family. Maybe . . ."

I let it hang there, but he's shaking his head. He scratches the back of his neck. "No. She wouldn't leave without telling me."

I'm about to speak when he beats me to it. "They bugged your house."

I blink, and he stares into my eyes as if trying to make me understand. "Amanda," he says simply, "she found a bug in her bedroom."

My heart squeezes. "Which bedroom?"

He pauses, considers this. "I never went there." He scratches his chin and looks away, embarrassed. "We always went to my place."

"Was it the murder room?" I prompt, breathless. "The main bedroom?"

"Knowing Amanda," he says, eyes soft and sad, "it probably was."

I feel like I've been punched. I grip the seat, breathing so fast I'm almost panting. "That's *my* bedroom," I say faintly. I stare straight ahead at the pub, not even seeing it. "God." I shiver. "What if they've been watching me all along?"

Darren eyes me grimly. "It wouldn't surprise me," he says.

I think of all the times I undressed before bed and slipped naked between the sheets. I feel sick at the thought. I wrap my arms across my chest. "Who's watching me, then?" I ask nervously. "Jeff Johnson?"

"I think so," Darren mutters, bunching his tattooed hands into fists. "He's a sick bastard. I wouldn't put it past him to spy on Amanda—or you."

I wind the window down all the way, let the cold air come flooding in. It's freezing, but it makes me feel better. Cleaner.

"Where'd she find the bug?" I finally ask. "Did she show it to you?"

"No." He shakes his head and takes a quick drag. "I never saw it. She found it in the wallpaper, I think." He turns to me. "It's a mural, yeah?"

The forest wallpaper. I shut my eyes. God, all those times I felt like the birds were watching me. And maybe they were.

"She wanted to confront Johnson about it."

I raise my head.

"Really?" I breathe, heart rattling. "Did she?"

Silence. He stares moodily through the windshield, like he's forgotten he even spoke. I want to reach out and pull on his sleeve. *Tell me. Please.*

"Darren?"

He brushes a fist across his cheek, and I realize he's crying. His chest heaves, like he's trying hard to hold it all in.

"I shoulda done somethin'," he says through angry tears. I'm about to speak when he lurches forward, smashes a fist against the dashboard. I let out a startled yelp, and he leans back against his seat, tears dripping freely.

For a long time, we say nothing. He lights up another smoke, and I notice his hands are trembling. He takes a short puff, dangles the cigarette out the window.

"She told her neighbor about the bug," he says softly.

"Jeff Johnson?"

"Nah," he says. "A different neighbor. The lady who lives down the street from Black Wood." He frowns, remembering, "She had a little yappy dog, a pug or something."

I sit perfectly still, heart pounding in my ears. No. No.

"Amanda used to go over to her house for coffee," he says, flicking the butt of the glowing cigarette. "Can't remember her name."

"Kay," I say quietly. "Her name's Kay Potts."

"Yeah." He nods and puffs. "That's her."

I shut my eyes. So, Kay knew there was a bug in my house, and she never told me. I rub my forehead, slump down in my seat. I don't want to go back to Black Wood House with its secrets and bugs and lies. I stare out the window, cold air blasting me right in the face.

"The last time I saw Amanda," Darren says shakily, "we were drinking at *this* pub." He nods ahead. His breath catches in his throat, and I wait for him to continue. "She'd found the bug the day before." He puffs anxiously. "And she was all nervous and crazy 'cause the next day she was gonna confront Johnson at Kay's place."

I stop breathing. The wind chills my blood, and goosebumps shoot up and down my forearms.

"I asked her if she wanted me to come, but she said she'd be okay. She just wanted it over. She was gonna confront Johnson about the bug, and Kay was gonna back her up." He stubs the cigarette out, the red glow of the embers fading to ash. "I kissed her goodbye, and she said she'd call me tomorrow."

"And?"

He looks me dead in the eye. "I never heard from her again."

Chapter 25

Kay Potts is a bloody liar. I turn the radio on just for the noise and drive silently down the dark streets of Beacon. I think I hate this place. Do they even know about Amanda? Would they even care? Or is the whole bloody town covering for Jeff Fucking Johnson? I want to wind the window all the way down, stick my head out, and scream, "Fuck you all." Fuck you and your indoor pools. Fuck you and your secrets.

I drive slowly past Kay's house, my headlights illuminating the orange tree in her front yard. Part of me wants to spill out of my seat, pound on her door, and ask why the hell she's covering for Johnson. But it's not the time.

Not yet. But it's coming. I feel it.

I pull into my driveway, drive slowly up the bumpy road. It's a starless night, and a sliver of moon offers up weak and murky light. My headlights flash over the dead, quiet land, and a cockatoo glares at me from the blackwood tree. Joe's car isn't here, and I haven't gotten a text from him. I messaged Emily as soon as Darren hopped out of my car and disappeared into the night. He didn't look back, and I don't think I'll see him again.

Emily rang less than ten seconds after I sent the text. "My God, lovie, are you okay? Is he really gone?" Her usually calm voice was strained. She'd hesitated before dropping her voice to a whisper. "If he's still there, press a number on the keypad, and I'll call the cops."

I laughed because the night was finally over and I'd survived it. And . . . it was nice to know that she cared enough about me to wait for my text. "He's gone," I told her. "It's over."

But it's not over, is it? It's barely begun.

I park the car and switch off the engine. The silence is deafening.

She was gonna confront Johnson at Kay's place.

I never heard from her again.

I climb out of the car into the freezing night air and wrap my arms around myself. I burst gratefully into the house, but it's just as cold in here. I breathe in the stale air, hating it. I rest my back against the front door, exhausted from the strange night. The house is totally dark except for the moonlight shining through the grimy lounge window. Everywhere I look, there's destruction. Doors hanging limply from their hinges, floorboards missing like gaping teeth. The half-built walls are littered with holes, wires poking through them like little snakes.

I'm about to head upstairs when I catch a glimpse of something out the window. Just a flicker of movement as something creeps past. I freeze. Reaper? I open the door a crack, and the cold wind stings my face. We don't have any porch lights yet, and I can barely see the outline of my car in the weak moonlight.

"Reaper," I call out into the night. "Reaper?"

Silence. A chill creeps down my spine, settles in the small of my back.

Meowwww.

I gasp, whirling around to face the staircase. Reaper is perched atop the couch, watching me. He's been inside the whole time. Then what did I see outside? My heart's in my throat as I quickly shut the door and lock it behind me. I scoop Reaper up, and as we half run up the staircase, I can't shake the feeling that someone's out there, watching. And worse . . . I think of the bug that Amanda found in the walls. God, there's no escaping it. Everywhere I go, they're watching me.

* * *

Hours later, Reaper wakes me up. He kneads the bedcovers, howling and howling. He slinks off my bed and walks to the open door. He turns around, meows. His tail flicks back and forth, and it strikes me that he's nervous. Joe would laugh at me, but I know Reaper's moods. And there's something uneasy about the way Reaper watches me, as if waiting for me to follow him.

My stomach tightens. Shit. Not again. The last time he did this, he planted himself under the attic steps and waited for me to go up there. I stare Reaper down. I've scanned the attic twice since last time and found nothing. I really don't want to go up to the attic in the dead of night.

I roll over, pull the covers over my head.

Meowwwwwwwwwwww.

Sighing, I throw the covers off and follow him to the door, my bare feet cold on the floorboards. As soon as I've caught up to him, he turns and heads down the dark hallway. I stop, chewing my lip, before ducking back into my room and retrieving my phone. I flick the small torch on, and there he is. Reaper's waiting in the middle of the hallway, exactly where he was last time, right under the attic. His tail flicks anxiously. I shine the light haphazardly at the walls. I don't want to go up there, dammit. Why the hell am I doing this? Bloody cat. My skin's prickling, and my hands tremble when I reach up to pull on the cord.

The staircase drops down with a loud creak, and I wrinkle my nose as the smell comes rushing down. God, the attic stinks. I've been up there only a few times. There wasn't much to see except the brick chimney, an old cradle covered in dust, and a handful of decomposing leaves that crunched like old bones when I stepped on them. The walls were covered in brownish-yellow stains like nicotine, and the smell was worse than any other room in the house. Joe muttered something about the insulation, and I peered into the cradle silently. Had it belonged to Janet when she was a baby? I wondered. Was she rocked to sleep by her adoring parents before one of them tried to murder her?

Reaper howls again, a sound that screams, *Come on. You need to see what's up there.* He leaps up the staircase soundlessly, and I watch him disappear into the gaping dark. I climb up the arthritic steps. "What's wrong, mate?"

I hold my phone out in front of me, follow the weak beam of light up the stairs, and they groan under my weight like they're mad at me. I clutch the banister with my free hand, and it's like holding on to a brittle tree branch. I mentally add it to the growing list of renovations and duck my head as I enter the attic.

I pause at the top of the stairs, shining the torch around the room, illuminating the falling dust. God, it's bad in here. It's like standing in a little snowstorm. I pull the collar of my nightshirt over my mouth and breathe through that. The attic is windowless, and I ache to let some fresh air in. The brick chimney leans dangerously to one side, like it's had too much to drink, and smells of soot and smoke.

Reaper's still hissing somewhere up there, and I shine the light around, wondering if he's found a dead possum or something. He does that sometimes—brings me to his little kills and probably wonders why I scream. I bought him a bell collar, but it doesn't seem to make a difference.

But when I shine the light on Reaper, he's not standing in front of an animal at all. He's standing in front of the cradle like he's guarding it. His tail flicks back and forth like a windshield wiper, and he does that weird howl/scream thing that he did when he jumped on my bed and terrified me. My pulse jumps, and my stomach tightens. I really don't want to walk any closer. I wait there in the attic, the silence growing heavier and heavier.

I shine the torch at the cradle, not moving from my spot. It would've been beautiful back in the day, smooth redwood with twelve ornate bars. But the longer I look, the more dangerous it seems. The spacing between each bar is too large, wide enough to trap a child's head. And it's missing four bars. A soiled blanket lies in a tangled mess over a yellowing mattress. It's creepy, but it doesn't seem worth a look.

But Reaper won't move, and I have to see what he's guarding.

I take a small step forward, shining the torch at the ground.

I freeze.

What the hell? What the hell? Reaper watches me silently, gives me a steady look that says, *See? I told you.*

I stagger back, hand over my mouth. Right there in the dust at the foot of the cradle is a pair of footprints. It's as if the person was standing over it, looking down. My hands are jittery, and my breath comes in panicked bursts. What the hell is in that cradle? I swallow hard and step forward.

I'm careful to avoid stepping on the footprints, treading lightly around them. They're larger than mine. A man's, definitely. Joe's, maybe? But then, I don't remember him going anywhere near the cradle when we last came up here. He hovered in the doorway, grimacing the entire time.

I stop at the cradle, torch in hand, terrified to shine the light down on it. Terrified not to. Reaper waits silently at my left foot.

I sweep the torch over the cradle, holding my breath. But there's nothing there. Only the blanket and mattress. It looks like it hasn't been disturbed in decades. The blanket is disgusting, speckled with mold. I give Reaper a quizzical look, but he's still not moving. I crouch on my haunches, Reaper's hot breath on my knee, then shine the light inside the cradle, peering through the gap in the bars.

And then I see it.

Tucked under the moldy blanket is a note.

My heart slams hard against my chest. Part of me wants to run back down the stairs and forget everything that happened tonight. Part of me has to know what the note says.

Slowly, I reach between the bars and pick it up. I take a deep breath and read.

Hi Sarah Slade!

Is that the name you're going by these days? Would be a shame if people found out who you really are. . . .

Wouldn't it?

BREAKING NEWS: POLICE REVEAL IDENTITY OF ONE OF THE BODIES FOUND AT BLACK WOOD

July 4

ABC News, Melbourne

Victorian police have released the identity of the second body discovered at Black Wood House.

The woman has been identified as 25-year-old Amanda Vale. Vale, an administrative assistant from Port Murphy, South Australia, went missing seven months ago.

It's understood she moved from her hometown to the infamous Black Wood House in September of last year. It's believed she lived there for only a few weeks. Surprisingly little is known about her time in Beacon, southeast of Melbourne.

Her devastated mother, Linda Vale, wasn't even aware her daughter had lived at Black Wood.

"I knew she was living in Victoria, but she moved a lot and wasn't good about keeping in touch. It wasn't unusual to go weeks, even months, without hearing from her. But when I didn't hear from her at Christmas, I went to the police."

Amanda Vale had been declared missing for seven months before the shocking discovery of her body at Black Wood House.

The body, too decomposed to immediately gauge its height, weight, or race, was taken to the Victorian coroner's office. The identification was made this morning, but police are still tight-lipped about the cause of death.

The identity of the first body found at Black Wood is still unknown.

Chapter 26

Someone is saying my name. My real name. "Lizzy. Lizzy, what's wrong?"

I try to open my eyes, but it's surprisingly difficult. The person shakes my shoulder, their voice rising with anxiety. "Lizzy, wake up."

My eyes flutter open. Joe peers down at me, eyes wide with concern. He's wearing his bartender uniform—black jeans, crisp white T-shirt. I sit up in bed, groggy, head aching. I've no idea what time it is or why my husband is up here in my bedroom when he hasn't stepped foot in here for . . . I shake my head. I can't remember how long we've been in this house. Can't even remember what day it is.

"What time is it?" I ask, eyes blurry, tongue thick in my mouth. What the hell is wrong with me?

"It's midday," he says uneasily, shoving his hands in his pockets. "Shouldn't you be at work?"

Oh, shit. My phone's buried under my pillow. I grab for it and click it on. Three missed calls from Adria, three from Emily. Four text messages also from Emily:

You coming in to work today?
Is everything okay?
Please call me when you get this.
Lovie??

Shit, shit, shit.

I bolt out of bed, or try to anyway, but as soon as my legs hit the floor, they crumble. Joe calls out, and I wave him away when he reaches for me. I grasp the corner of my bedside table, my face sweating, my hands clammy. I get slowly to my feet, head spinning. Am I hungover? I don't remember drinking last night.

"Are you sick?" Joe calls from far away. His voice rolls in and out of my ears. *Are you sick? Are you sick? Are you—*

I swallow down a wave of nausea and step into a pencil skirt that has a jam stain on it. I zip it up, feeling slightly breathless. Something tugs at my mind, something important about last night. I throw a work blouse around my shoulders and fumble with the buttons, trying to remember. I feel more asleep than awake, and I give my stomach a sharp pinch as I dress, making certain I'm not still dreaming.

Then I remember. My hands drop to my sides.

Hi Sarah Slade!

Is that the name you're going by these days?

Oh God. Oh God. That wasn't a dream. I step into my work shoes, grasp the ornate bedpost to keep myself from toppling over. I lace up a camel boot, try to act normal. "Did you sleep here last night?"

Silence. I look up at him, tying my boot with a sharp knot. He scratches the back of his neck with restless hands and looks longingly at the door. I bet he wishes he hadn't come in. I'm sure he won't make that mistake again. "No," he says finally. "I didn't. Haven't been here for a few days . . ."

"Well, where the fuck have you been, then?"

Silence.

He doesn't look guilty, and I wonder if I've got it all wrong. Maybe he's been working late. Maybe he's been sleeping at Andy's.

"Joe?" I demand.

My phone goes off. I glance at the caller ID: Emily. Joe snatches the moment to leave the room.

"Wait," I call, trying to tie my boot and answer the phone at the same time. "Joe," I yell, but he's already gone. Shit. I answer the call and shove the phone to my ear. "I'm coming, Emily," I tell her, throwing my jacket on. "I'm coming."

I burst into the Mercy Community office, fumbling with my jacket and smoothing my hair at the same time. I knock on Adria's door, my mouth crammed with apologies. But no one answers. Shakily, I walk down the navy hallway, reaching out to steady myself against the wall. I breathe hard, sweat dripping down my nose.

I stagger into the coffee room. It smells like melted cheese in here, and my stomach heaves. I press a clammy palm against my stomach. Tim's stirring sweetener into his coffee mug, the one that says, I NEVER ASKED TO BE THE WORLD'S BEST ATHLETE, BUT HERE I AM, ABSOLUTELY CRUSHING IT. Emily cradles her vet nurse mug in her left hand and nibbles on a piece of toast held in her right.

"Hey," I murmur weakly.

"Well, look who finally decided to show up for work!" Tim bellows.

Emily cries, "Lovie! My God, I've been trying to ring you for days!"

I wipe my forehead with the back of my jacket sleeve. "Is Adria in?" I ask breathlessly.

"Lucky for you, no." Tim smirks, placing a dripping teaspoon on the counter. Emily points to the kettle, raises an eyebrow. I nod gratefully, and she pulls another mug out of the cupboard, starts making me a coffee.

"I'm in the shit, aren't I?" I groan, leaning against the doorframe. "I slept in this morning. Didn't mean to get here so late."

Tim gulps the coffee like it's a tequila shot. "And what's your excuse for yesterday, then?"

I narrow my eyes at him. My mind is unfocused, blurry. But fragments of yesterday come back to me. I was here in the coffee room yesterday morning with Tim, Benita, and Emily. I went to my office, and Darren messaged me, telling me to meet him outside the pub. And later that night . . . I wince at the memory. Later that night, I found the note in the attic.

"Yesterday?" I ask Tim. "I was here yesterday."

Silence. Emily's busy pouring milk into my mug, but she gives me a strange look out of the corner of her eye. I breathe shallowly through my mouth. No one's talking, and my stomach twists with nausea and nerves.

Tim gives me a sideways glance that says, *Are you pulling my leg?* For the first time since I've known him, he looks unsure of himself.

"You weren't here yesterday," he says finally, giving me a quizzical look, like he's still not sure if I'm joking. "Adria was pissed, to be honest."

My stomach churns like I'm making butter in there. I frantically sort through my memories of yesterday, but my mind's working so slowly. I was here, in this kitchen with them and Benita. I'm sure of it. I asked Benita about the cleaner, and then I met up with a strange man in a pub parking lot and went home to a note in my attic.

Hi Sarah Slade!

Is that the name you're going by these days?

I shudder. God, too much is happening too quickly.

"It's Thursday," I say slowly. "Yesterday was Wednesday."

Now it's Tim's turn to look confused. He gives Emily a look that says, *Is she for real?* Emily places my mug on the counter very gently. She chews her lip anxiously, eyes on me.

I'm so nervous I could vomit. It's not time for one of Tim's jokes. Not when I'm already losing it. But when I look desperately to Emily—safe, calm Emily—for answers, it's clear something's horribly wrong. She fidgets with her wooden bracelet, playing with a pea-sized bead.

"Emily . . ." I swallow, sweat beading my forehead. "It's Thursday, right?"

She presses her lips together like she doesn't want to answer. "No, lovie," she says gently. "It's Friday."

I step forward, my knees wobbling. "You were standing *right there* yesterday morning," I tell Tim. My voice is too high, frantic. I've lost it now. "You were drinking your protein shake, and you said, 'I hate Wednesdays.'"

He blinks slowly. Emily studies me silently.

"That was two days ago," Tim says finally and looks to Emily for confirmation. He scratches the back of his neck uncomfortably. "Yesterday was Thursday, and you didn't show up for work."

My head spins. He's joking. He must be. I take a step back. "Then where the hell was I yesterday?"

"Sarah . . ." Emily steps forward, her paisley skirt swishing across the cool tiles. She's at my elbow, softly patting my shoulder. "You're going through a lot right now," she says in her therapist voice. My eyes dart to Tim, and I hope she doesn't say anything about me meeting Darren. I got in bed at 1 A.M. and slept hard until Reaper woke me up. The note in the attic. I remember that.

I lick my lips. They're flaky and dry. My head throbs so hard I wonder if Emily can hear it. Think, I tell myself. What happened after I found the note? I search my mind, but I just can't remember. I awoke today in my bed . . . so I must have slept through the entire day and night. But how? I don't feel hungry, only desperately thirsty.

But then I remember something from Wednesday night. I saw a flash of something out the lounge room window. Jeff Johnson. He planted that note. What else did he do while he was inside my house?

My legs tremble violently, and I find myself slumping to the floor. I can't hold my head up. I rest it on my forearm, and my heart pumps weakly like it's dying to stop.

Around me is a flurry of activity, panicked footsteps, someone tugging at my shoulder, trying to get me to my feet. I think I hear Emily say, "I'm calling the doctor," before she rushes from the room.

Tim's at my side, telling me to breathe in a surprisingly panicked voice. Footsteps come rushing up the hallway. Office doors snap open and colleagues call out, "What's going on?"

I want to get to my feet and tell everyone to relax. But I can't seem to move. I reach blindly for Tim, wrap a clammy hand around his fore-arm. "How well do you know Jeff Johnson?"

"Don't try to talk," he cautions quite gently.

"Tell me." I breathe into my lap.

"He's bad news, Sarah," Tim says gravely. "Why? What's wrong?"

I inhale shakily, wiping my palms on my skirt. I raise my head, and Tim's worried face flickers in and out of my vision. "Because," I say, "I think he's trying to kill me."

Chapter 27

I stagger through my front door, dripping sweat. Reaper glances up from the couch cushion with interest. *What are you doing home so early? And why are you sweating like a mad lady?*

"They're calling it a panic attack," I tell my cat. "Adria sent me home early."

I lurch to the stairs and grip the banister firmly. My legs are weak, and it's hard to catch my breath as I climb. Behind me, Reaper drops from the couch and follows me up the stairs. So, I continue my conversation. With my cat. I don't care if that sounds crazy.

"Adria's pretty pissed at me," I say, pausing to wipe my forehead. "*Really* pissed, actually."

She called me into her office and said brusquely, "Go home, okay? You're looking very pale. We'll discuss a few things on Monday . . ."

My head spins. I grip the banister with both hands now, afraid I'll fall. I rest my head on my sweating forearm, breathing hard. Reaper leans against my leg, meowing anxiously.

We'll discuss a few things on Monday . . .

Don't kill me.

They're watching you.

Jeff Johnson was here last night, or was it the night before? I'm losing track of time. I'm losing everything. Maybe I'm even losing my damn mind.

Did Jeff creep into my room as I slept? There's a water bottle on my bedside table. Did he spike it? Is he trying to kill me? Are there cameras in my bloody bedroom? It's too much. All of it.

Reaper meows louder. *Get yourself together, woman.*

Slowly, I raise my head. Reaper bounds up the stairs and sits at the top, swishing his tail, waiting. I surge forward without stopping. We reach my bedroom at the same time and hover outside it, peering in.

My room looks unchanged since I left it. The bed is messy, pillows everywhere, even the floor. My water bottle sits harmlessly on my bedside table. Everything looks normal, but now it all feels so threatening.

They're watching you.

I step inside, my entire body trembling. Reaper jumps noiselessly onto my bed. I stand very still, looking up at the wallpaper. At the eerie forest. The blackbirds stare back with their hollow eye sockets.

They're watching . . .

With a cry, I lunge forward, throwing myself at the damn wallpaper and those bloody blackbirds. I tear at one with my fingernails, scratching at the wall, feeling for anything that shouldn't be there. Like a secret camera that's been watching me all along. I poke my finger into their eye sockets until my nail bends all the way back and cracks in half, and even that's not enough. Panting, I run from wall to wall, tearing and scratching at the blackbirds with clawed hands. Reaper meows, drops to the floor, and spins in a frenzied circle. I'm scaring him, and I can't stop. Can't stop. I tear at the blackbirds until all my fingers bleed.

I gulp the rest of my wine, and watch the roaring flames in the fireplace. The house is unnervingly silent, and outside, a quiet electrical storm rages on and on. The air feels charged. I'm so jumpy that when Reaper sprang onto the couch beside me, I screamed. He fled under the couch, fur all puffed out, teeth bared at me and maybe the storm too.

We're all on edge tonight.

My fingers are throbbing, the nails all broken down to the quick. I found nothing in the wallpaper. No cameras. No listening devices. Nothing.

I reach painfully for my laptop and google Jeff Johnson's cousin. The cleaner who quit shortly after starting work at Mercy Community. Chris. That's what Benita said his name was. It doesn't take long to find him.

I peer at his Facebook photo, and the hairs on my arms stand up. Mid-twenties, smug eyes, black cap on sideways. That's him. Chris Macon Johnson. I stare uneasily at his Facebook banner, a quote written in dripping red ink. THE VIOLENT TAKE IT BY FORCE.

I pour another glass with an unsteady hand and sip it, staring at Chris Johnson's face. He lasted three days at Mercy before he quit. But he made damn sure to get into my office, even unlocking the door while I was sleeping. I grip the stem of the glass. I bet the only reason he started working at Mercy was to get dirt on me. That's why he wouldn't answer when I asked his name.

Watta's it matter what me name is?

I type **Chris Macon Johnson+Beacon** into Google, my fingers fumbling over the keys. I'm a bit drunk. More hits. A Twitter account. Same profile photo as Facebook but a different banner this time. BORN WITH HORNS.

I click on Facebook again and scan the About section to see if there's a phone number listed. And there it is. I hesitate before pulling my phone out of my pocket, chewing my lip. So what if I ring him? What can he do?

I type in his number and stop breathing when it rings. I fumble with the wine bottle, pouring it into the glass with my shaking right hand. I've filled the glass almost to the top when someone answers.

"Yo, who dis?"

I almost drop the bottle. I press the phone to my ear. In the background is thumping music and laughter. "Another round, boys?" someone calls out. I wonder if he's down at the Beacon pub, the bastard.

I swallow the lump in my throat. "Hi, it's . . ."

My mind blanks. Shit. What's my name again? Sarah Slade?

"Who?" He has to yell it over the music.

"You worked at Mercy Community?" He doesn't answer. I swallow hard. "I work there. I'm one of the therapists. Sarah Slade."

More laughter in the background. The beat is constant. *Boom boom, pop. Boom boom, pop.*

"Yeah? Whattya want? I don't work there no more."

"Uh, that's why I'm calling." I transfer the phone to my other ear. "I don't know if you remember me, but . . ."

"Lady," he says impatiently, "is this about the key thing?"

The key thing? I chug the wine, and it dribbles down the side of my mouth. I swipe at it. "Yeah," I lie. "It's about that."

Boom boom, pop. God, the music is terrible.

"Well, I didn't do it," he says with a violent edge to his voice. "Told them that already."

I rack my brain for what he might be talking about. I swirl the wine in my glass as if looking for clues. The wind slams against the front door, and the doorknob rattles like someone's trying to open it. And then I realize what he means, and my stomach drops to my feet.

"You were fired," I say slowly, piecing it together, "because someone accused you of making copies of the keys."

He says nothing. I set the glass down firmly on the coffee table, anger roaring through my blood. "You were in my office. You stole my keys while I was . . . asleep," I say. "Didn't you?"

He snorts. "Shots! Shots! Shots!" someone calls out in the background.

I wait for him to answer, but he doesn't. I press my palm to my forehead. It's sweaty and hot. I shouldn't have lit the bloody fire. I'm burning up without it, thanks to this fucking illness that won't cease. Here comes another feverish night of twisting sheets and early-morning vomiting.

I get the feeling he's enjoying this. Enjoying his power over me. The only kicks he probably gets now is spitting in burgers at whatever fast-food restaurant he works at.

"Your cousin got you the job at Mercy, didn't he? Jeff Johnson?"

"Why?"

"Did he ask you to search my office?"

Boom boom, pop. The noise is deafening. I have to pull the phone away from my ear. And then. He laughs. It's low and cruel and makes my stomach cramp in fear. The wind surges against the house like it's trying to push it over, and I really wish I wasn't alone.

"Lady," he says coldly, "why don't you ask *him*?"

"I'm asking you."

The music grows more distant, as if he's walking away from it. I pull the phone closer, holding it painfully tight against my ear. On the other end of the phone, there's a soft click of something, a lighter maybe. He breathes in raggedly, and I know he's smoking.

"Maybe he was looking for something," he says softly. "Maybe he checked you out, Sarah Slade. Maybe there's no record of you before 2015." He exhales loudly as if he's blowing smoke into the phone. "Why is that?"

Mind your own fucking business, I want to say. But I'm scared now because they know something's up. So, why hasn't Jeff played his hand yet? Why hasn't he confronted me with this?

I rub my temples. Because he's waiting, that's why. He's going to dig right down into the dirt of my past, and when he finds out about my sister, it's over. All of it. He'll threaten me. He'll say, *If you don't get out of Black Wood House, I'll go public with what happened to your sister.* And I'll leave. I'll have to.

I rest my forehead against my knee, wishing I could break down like a little child. Then I remember the note upstairs in the attic, and I raise my head. "Did you make a copy of my house keys?" I demand, wondering what I'll do if he says yes.

He snorts into the phone, sounding like a pissed-off horse. He doesn't answer. Instead, he takes a long drag. "Been lovely chatting," he says. "Stay safe, yeah?"

But before I can answer he adds threateningly, "If you can."

He hangs up. For a long time I stare at the phone, listening to the wind scream outside. Reaper jumps into my lap, and I clutch him tight, but it makes no difference. I've never felt so alone.

I call Joe. Why not? The phone rings, and my stomach tenses. *Ring, ring.* Pick up, Joe, you coward. *Ring, ring.*

Voicemail. "Hi, this is Joe Cosgrove. Please—"

I don't leave a message. Instead, I hang up and immediately call again. *Ring, ring.* I grip the phone so tight it hurts. *Ring, ring.*

Voicemail again.

Fuck this.

"Please leave a message, and I'll get back to you!" His voice drips with politeness. Like he just *can't wait* to return your phone call and he feels *so bad* that he wasn't there to take it. Dickhead.

Beep.

A rumble of thunder rolls by, and I feel it deep in my bones. The phone is silent, waiting. What to say? What to say? Five years together, three of them as man and wife. This is how it ends.

"I know you're having an affair, you dickhead."

For a long time, I'm silent. Tired. Done.

"She would've dumped you, eventually," I tell him, surprising even myself. "My sister, I mean. You would never have been enough for her."

Out the window, a flash of lightning illuminates the blackwood tree. "You know what the problem is with you, Joe?" I get to my feet and start pacing. "You never wanted to go forward, only backward." The floorboards whine, and the sound merges with the thunder until it feels like the storm is inside the house, not out.

"I tried to save us," I say flatly, and the rain pours down like it will never end. "I was sorry, Joe. Sorry for what happened. All I wanted to do was build a life for us to make up for the one we lost." I swipe angrily at the tears streaming down my stupid face. "I told myself that I didn't care if you worked or not. That it didn't matter that every time I reached for you, you flinched. But it did. *It really fucking did.*"

Back and forth, I pace. Back and forth. The floorboards are shrieking now, and they don't seem angry. It's like they're joining in the fight and they're on my side.

"All my life I felt like an exile," I tell him. "Except for when I met you. You were like me. We could've been exiles together, Joe. I could've loved you deeply if you'd *only let me*."

I stare out the window crying and not quite ready to end the call. If I could say one last thing to my husband, what would it be?

I open my mouth and tears drip onto my tongue. They taste like failure.

"I loved you. You broke me."

I end the call. I say one final thing, and I'm glad he can't hear it.

"Now you've gone and fucked it all, Joe. And I can't let you get away with that."

Chapter 28

Hi!! It's me again! Lizzy. Sarah. Katy. Sabrina. Gina. Mrs. Short, your friendly, nosy neighbor. Take your bloody pick!

Want to fix your shit life? I can help!

Want a healthy body? Try my weight-loss gummies! Hopefully they won't give you diarrhea like they did me!

Care for a scone, deary?

Stand up straight with your shoulders back.

For reals.

I stare out my bedroom window, breath caught in my throat. The sky is heavy with rain, and the wind shrieks against the glass. But there's something else out there. I can feel it.

I drop the pen and shut my notebook with a snap. Slowly, I crouch and crawl across the floorboards. I hover below the window, holding my breath. I wait and listen.

I count to ten before easing myself up and peering through the grimy glass. At first, I don't see it. But then a flicker of movement behind the graveyard. It's large and crouched low to the ground. An animal, I think. But then it stands up, and my heart squeezes.

Because it's not an animal at all.

It's a man.

It happens quickly. The man sprints past the graves and disappears around the side of the house. It could be anyone. But I know it's not. It's Jeff Johnson.

I stumble back, hands freezing cold and shaking now. I look desperately around for clothes, but all I find is my bathrobe. I fling it on, fasten it tight around my waist. My mind is frantic; it's hard to think straight. I lunge for my bedside lamp and flick it off. Joe. Ring Joe. I reach for my phone, but I'm shaking so hard, I type the wrong passcode in. Shit. Shit.

The phone finally unlocks. I ring Joe, press the phone to my ear, and peer outside, fear flooding my veins. The phone rings once. "Hello, the number you have called has been disconnected," an automated voice tells me.

What the hell? I stare at the phone, swearing under my breath, but it's definitely Joe's number. He's the only number listed in the Favorites section. Plus, I called him only a few hours ago and left him that message . . .

I check the number again and press redial. "Hello, the number you have called—"

I hit the end-call button. Wow. I bet he's already changed numbers after the charming message I left him. I'm momentarily distracted, raging at my husband, when I hear it. I lift my head and freeze. Downstairs, a door creaks open, and the raging wind shrieks in. The front door. It's the front door.

My hand slackens, and the phone drops to the floor. I'm too scared to breathe.

My pulse thunders in my wrist. Do something. But I can't move. The only ways out of the house are the front and back doors, and both are downstairs. Hide under the bed, then? Or in the cupboard? Shit, shit, shit. I search frantically for an escape. The bedroom window! The damn fixed window. It can't be opened. But if I smashed it, surely I could crawl out onto the roof? But they'd hear that, and they'd surely come running.

The wind is still roaring in, and the walls rattle and moan. Why haven't they closed the door? Why don't they care about the noise they're making? And the answer hits me like a blow to the head: Maybe it's because I won't be around to tell anyone.

I stand perfectly still. The lights are all off, except for the blue glow from the phone charger. Slowly, I creep to the door. I open it as quietly as I can and peer into the blackness. How many fucking times did I tell myself to install a hallway light? I can't see shit out here. But I hear it.

Click.

Silence. The wind stops abruptly. They've closed the door. Downstairs, the floorboards creak, creak, creak, like someone's tiptoeing. I shake at the thought of someone creeping around my house in the darkness. My blood drums in my ears. I wait there, hand on the doorknob, desperate for them to leave. Should I call out? Tell them the police are coming? That my husband's home? But we don't have a garage. And the only car parked outside is mine.

They know I'm here. They know I'm alone.

And they're coming straight for me.

Creak, creak, creak. I stumble back. They're coming up the stairs. I rush to the bedside table, rip the lamp cord from the socket, and wrap my hand around the base of the lamp. It's not even heavy, but it's the best chance I've got. I run to the door, not even caring about the noise I'm making.

"Hey!" I call out, hysteria gripping my voice.

A stair groans in response. I want to run screaming from the house. But if they're on the stairs, then I'm blocked in. There's nowhere to go. Nowhere to run.

I grip the lamp tighter. "Get out! Get the fuck outta my house!"

God, I wish Joe was here. Or Reaper. I flatten myself against the door, panting with terror. Silence. They move like a sleepwalker, and somehow that's more terrifying. For a disorienting moment, I think it's Bill Campbell's ghost.

They're walking *right down* the hallway. A few more steps, and they'll be at my bedroom door. I grasp the handle, locking it in place, heart thumping, thumping, thumping.

"Jeff?" I call out desperately.

A floorboard groans, and the creaking stops. It's him. It's him. I know it is.

I can't breathe. I press my ear to the door, gripping the doorknob so hard it hurts. I'm about to twist it open when the footsteps retreat, thundering back down the hallway. I wrench the door open and step out into the dark. The intruder flees down the stairs, making no attempt to be quiet. I make it to the top of the stairs and squint down at the lounge room.

There! I see a faint outline in the dark as he throws the front door open. I hover there at the top of the stairs, heart in my mouth, as he flings himself out the door and slams it shut.

Fuck this. Jeff Johnson might have Beacon in his big, dinner-plate hands. He might have the town cop in his back pocket, but he doesn't own everything. And everyone. The next closest town is Wilora, fifteen minutes away. I quickly google the police station number, dial it, and hold the phone to my ear. As it rings, I mouth over and over, "Fuck Jeff Johnson. Fuck him."

The young man's voice is brisk, efficient, "Wilora Police Station?"

I clear my throat. I have a sudden desire to burst out laughing. The pressure's getting to me, and I feel a bit unhinged. Even more so than usual, I mean.

"Hi," I begin awkwardly. "A man just broke into my house." I'm speaking too fast. I'm nervous as hell and shaking with adrenaline. "I know who it was. My neighbor Jeff Johnson. He lives at One—"

"Mrs. Slade?"

I hesitate, heart hammering, stomach twisting. I never told him my name. It catches me so off guard that my mouth drops open for one long second.

"Yes?"

He clears his throat and speaks warily. "Mrs. Slade . . ." He sounds young. Mid-twenties, maybe. "You say the man broke into your house?"

"Yes! He broke in downstairs. I called out his name, and he . . ." I pace, irritated, swearing under my breath. "Well, he . . ."

"And did you get a good look at the man?"

No. I didn't.

"It was dark," I admit. "But I called out Jeff's name, and he . . . well, he stopped."

"So, you saw his face?"

No. I didn't.

I exhale impatiently, swatting my hair away from my face. "He stopped when I called his name, okay? He's the same height as Jeff." I'm breathless now, frantic. I have to make him understand. "He's mad that I bought my house. He wants me out. He—"

"Mrs. Slade." The young man sighs. I can see him sitting at his cramped desk strewn with manila folders and a stapler he never uses. He's rubbing his head with his fingertips, wishing someone else had answered my call.

"Mr. Johnson says you've been harassing him."

I'm so stunned that I stumble over my feet. "What?"

"He says you went to his house this week, uninvited." He pauses, then asks gently, "Is that true?"

I fumble for words, outraged. Why the hell am *I* the bad one here?

"Yeah, I went there," I say hotly. "But I—"

"He said you were harassing him," he continues in his gentle, persuasive voice. "That he asked you to leave but you refused."

No. No, this is all wrong. I sit down heavily, elbows on my knees, tears springing into my eyes. God, I'm tired. I'm so tired of this shit. "I was *not* harassing him. I—"

"What were you doing there, then?"

I was accusing him of murder, actually. "I just . . ." I stare out the window, eyes on Susan's grave. A black cockatoo's perched on her headstone like a terrible omen. "I was just introducing myself," I murmur.

Silence. My lie lingers, and it's loud.

"He said he asked you to leave," the cop says bluntly, firmer this time.

"I *did* leave."

"Only after he ordered you, *several times,* off his property."

That's bullshit. I press my palm to my forehead. They're both clammy, sticky.

"He's not pressing charges," the policeman says.

"He was in my *house* tonight," I say tiredly.

"And did you see the man's face?"

"No," I choke out. "I didn't. But I *know* it was him. And my cat, Reaper." I breathe in sharply. "He threatened my cat."

"What did he say?"

I want to reach through the phone and grab this guy by the collar. Make him understand. "He told me he can't stand cats," I say, realizing how weak it sounds. "You have to believe me. He needs me out of Black Wood so he can get it bulldozed. Ask anyone," I say, voice rising. "He did something to the last owner too."

"The previous owner of Black Wood?"

"Yes," I gabble. "Her name was Amanda, and she went missing. You can look her up, can't you?"

"What was her last name?"

"I don't know," I say, quickly changing the subject, "but she lived at Black Wood last year."

Over the phone, I can hear the rustling of papers. "Are you sure that was her name?"

My heart sinks. I remember smoking in the parking lot with Amanda's boyfriend. He'd said, *I don't even know if "Amanda" was her real name.*

"No."

"Okay, well," the cop says slowly, "I'll fill out a break-in report for you."

I grip the phone helplessly. "Forget it."

I hang up.

Chapter 29

Adria's office smells like vanilla and fear. I settle awkwardly into the chair opposite her, pulling my smart black jacket tighter, and place my hands demurely in my lap so she doesn't see them tremble. Keep it together, I tell myself. Don't let her see how crazy you are.

The last time I was in here, Adria was grasping my hand like she didn't want to let me go. Now she smiles grimly at me from across her desk, like I'm a problem she wants solved *right now*. She's a small woman, all delicate bones and tiny hands. Nestled between her collarbones is a golden heart-shaped pendant. When she shifts in her seat, the light catches it, and it glints like a mirror.

Or a knife.

Adria clears her throat, and I hold my breath.

"Sarah," she begins, clasping her tiny hands on the desk, "I'd like to—"

"Am I being fired?" I blurt out.

Silence. I sit on my hands, willing them to stop trembling.

Adria leans back in her chair. Here it comes. Benita strolls past the office window, carrying a stack of envelopes. She raises a hand to knock on Adria's door but Adria frowns and shakes her head. We watch Benita shuffle away, no doubt to tell my colleagues that I've been called into the boss's office.

"I think it would be a good idea for you to"—she pauses—"have a bit of a break."

"I'm fine," I protest.

Silence again. God, I wish she'd speak. I exhale slowly, a headache pinching my skull.

"You've been under a lot of stress," Adria says calmly. "I think a break would be good for you."

I don't. I need this paycheck. How the hell am I supposed to make the mortgage payments without an income?

I press my lips together so she can't see them shaking. I lean forward. "I know I've missed a few days lately—"

"You've missed *fourteen* in the last three months," she says stiffly.

Wow, that *is* a lot. My skull throbs. I press my palm against my temple, willing the headache to go away. "Please," I begin nervously, "I really—"

Knock, knock.

I jump in my seat, letting out a startled cry. Adria notices, her eyes never leaving mine.

"Come back later!" She almost yells it, and I jump again. I feel like I'm about to burst out of my skin.

My knee bobs up and down. "Maybe I can come back when I'm . . ." I falter. "Rested."

She presses her lips into a line. "We'll see, shall we?"

She stands up, and I know it's time to leave. But if I'm about to be fired, then I have to know one thing before I go. I stay in my seat, and she hovers above me, impatient and disapproving.

"The cleaner," I begin, and she raises an eyebrow. "Jeff Johnson's cousin . . ." I don't know how to put this delicately, and her stare is making me nervous. So, I just blurt it out. "Was he fired for making copies of the office keys?" I lick my lips, thinking about the note in the attic. "And maybe house keys too?"

But she's already shaking her head. The little heart pendant glints, and something about it makes me nervous.

"Why was he fired, then?" I ask bluntly.

She sighs impatiently, gives me an annoyed look like she's completely done with me. "I can't answer that, Sarah."

I stumble to my feet, open my mouth to ask more questions, but she's already ushering me out.

"You take care now," she says, distracted, and closes the door in my face.

I don't remember driving home. But I do remember sitting in my car, staring up at Black Wood like I was in a trance, my seatbelt strapped firmly across my chest.

Fired. I've been fired.

For the first time in a long while, I thought of my mother. She worked odd jobs throughout my childhood. House cleaner. Kitchen hand. Grocery store clerk. She hated them all, and when she got the sack, she used to celebrate. But I don't feel like celebrating.

I slump in my seat, eyes on the blackwood tree. A cockatoo shrieks on a bony branch.

My mother died two years ago, an overdose. She was forty-six, far too young. I don't know where my dad is. He's dead to me, and I to him. I have no family but Joe and my cat. I hang my head, press my forehead to the steering wheel.

What have I done? What have I fucking done?

If I could take it all back, I would. God, I would.

I look down at my left arm resting on my thigh. I can't feel it. I can't feel my arm. I shriek so loud the cockatoos in the blackwood tree stare. My breathing is frantic. I bring my hand up to my mouth and bite down hard. Bones. I can feel bones under my teeth. It's okay. It's okay. I'm here.

I take my hand out of my mouth, place it in my lap. Help. I need help. Reflexively, I grab my phone with my right hand, open Instagram, and hatefully scroll through. Look at all these shiny, pretty people on my feed.

Now look at me, breathless and frantic and *fired*.

I start a new post. I don't even know what the hell I'm saying.

Gloomy day here at Black Wood House!! But just because the sun isn't shining doesn't mean it isn't there! #bestrong #murderhouse

I hit post and wait for people to comment and like and fill my hollow arms with flesh.

Come on. Come on.

Heal me. Fill me. Or *fucking kill me.*

Nothing.

No likes. No love.

Fuck.

I undo my seatbelt and fling the car door open. I have no idea what I'm supposed to do for the rest of the day. And for all the days to come. I hadn't anticipated being suddenly unemployed. But I shove that thought away too.

Dazed, I open the front door and freeze.

I let out a gasp of horror. I cup my hand over my mouth as waves of nausea roll through my stomach and leave a burning trail up the back of my throat.

Oh my God. Oh my God.

I stagger to the couch, heart wrenching in pain. Reaper is lying in a heap beside the couch. His mouth is open, eyes wide and unblinking. I drop to my knees, shrieking his name, hands all over him, but he doesn't respond. And when I lift my hands to my face, they're covered in blood.

I sit quietly on the hard-backed chair, bent forward, cheek pressed against my knee. The teenage receptionist taps away at her keyboard, and though I can't see her, I feel her eyes on me. I haven't moved since a vet nurse dashed out, grabbed Reaper from my shaking arms, and disappeared with him behind the gray door. I slumped on the chair, shaking uncontrollably, and the receptionist came over, squeezed my shoulder, and offered me a tissue. I didn't realize I was crying.

It feels like hours since I discovered Reaper lying still beside the couch. His mouth and neck were stained with blood, and his eyes were glassy and still. For a horrifying moment I thought he was dead, but I felt a weak pulse beating fitfully. I scooped him up and sped to the emergency vet. I burst through the door, screaming, "Help! Please!"

Reaper. I cry into my lap. Reaper. My baby. The only remnant of my life before I was Sarah Slade, other than my cheating husband.

Memories of our five years together drift through my head. Me, dressing Reaper up for his birthdays in pirate costumes, and him, hating every minute of it. That time when Joe's drinking buddy, Andy, patted him and he whirled around and bit him. That shitty first Christmas when I cooked a chicken and he snatched it off the table and bared his claws when I tried to make him give it back.

My angry, vengeful, beautiful boy. God, I love that cat.

My head's still in my lap when I hear the door swing open. Brisk footsteps stop just short of me, and a harried voice calls out, "Sarah?"

Weakly, I glance up. The vet is dressed in sky-blue scrubs, her hair in a messy bun, mouth tight and grim. Oh God.

"Is he okay?" I croak out. Amazing how powerless hospital waiting rooms can make you feel.

She hesitates, and I swear to God my lips go numb.

"It looks quite serious," she says carefully, but my heart lurches in relief. He's alive. He's alive.

But a moment later she asks, "Has he ingested anything he shouldn't have?"

I stand up, knees and hands trembling. "I don't know. I brought him here a few weeks ago," I babble, swiping at my eyes with the cuff of my jacket. "Or was it last week? I can't remember."

I'm so distracted by the timeline that at first I miss the importance of her question. Has he ingested anything he shouldn't have?"

I narrow my eyes, blood going cold. "Why?"

She presses her lips together, shuffles in her spot. "Because," she finally says, "I think he's been poisoned."

* * *

I drive home without Reaper. I sit stiffly on my couch, flick on the TV, without Reaper. I walk to the kitchen and fill a shot glass with whiskey, without Reaper. I drink it all in one gulp and feel the pleasant burn all the way down to my toes. I pour another before carrying it back to the couch. I sit stiffly on the edge of the seat, right where I found Reaper all those hours ago. I stare at the silently flickering TV, thinking only of him.

I brought Reaper to Black Wood House. I didn't know the danger he'd be in. Didn't know how crazy the neighbors were. Didn't know that someone would be so evil as to poison him. But I brought him here. *I* did.

The thought hits me like a fist to the jaw. Oh my God. What if the poison was intended for me? Not Reaper? My baby. My poor baby.

If we'd never bought this house, he wouldn't be dying.

I think he's been poisoned.

I think he's been poisoned.

I think he's been—

I hurl the glass at the wall, and even before it shatters, I stand up, wild-eyed and woozy. Fuck this. Fuck Beacon. They think they can bully me out of this place like they did Amanda? They think I'm going to let them get away with this?

I grab my keys, stomp to the kitchen, and take another shot until my blood feels uncomfortably hot. Around me, the walls of the house seem to vibrate like they're shouting encouragement.

Yes! That's it, Lizzy. Get them. Get them. Make them pay.

My blood pumps loud in my ears. But I can still hear the hissing of the house, over and over, like a sick nursery rhyme.

Get them.

Get them.

Make them pay!

Chapter 30

The bi-weekly town meeting is a banal affair held in the historic community center. It seats eighty, sits in a dozy street, and hosts a shitload of community services. The Whitmans show up every Monday morning for the popular beekeeping workshop. Kay Potts attends Wednesday morning Gentle Exercise for Mature Ages. And Emily volunteers most Sunday afternoons to teach Computers for Beginners.

The meeting is held every second Monday night, at 6:30 P.M. sharp, and attended by the same core group of busybodies in desperate need of authority and something to bitch about for four hours a month.

And by the time I reach the parking lot at 7:20, I'm crying and absolutely shit-faced. Watch me give them something to talk about for decades to come.

I burst into the room like a bomb and stand with my back to the only exit, blocking the bastards in. I flatten my back against the wooden door, and the knob sticks uncomfortably into the small of my back. Everybody in the room looks up. Some gasp; some step back, hands over their hearts like I've given them an almighty scare. Just wait, I think. *Just wait.*

Dimly, I register how beautiful it is in here. Dark wood and soft lights. It's pretty enough to hold a wedding. An expensive redwood table sits to my right, covered with plates of biscuits and sandwiches cut into charming triangles. It smells like coffee and polished wood. The attendees have already drained their coffee cups, and they stand in groups of three or four, watching me uneasily.

Every time I blink, I see Reaper. I see him wide-eyed and bloody. Gasping for breath. I am raging mad, half-drunk, and ready to make someone pay.

And I find him.

Tears drip freely down my cheeks. I raise my hand, and it shakes so badly I have to support it with my other arm. Jeff Johnson stands in a pack of three, hands tucked into his jeans' pockets. He looks completely unconcerned, even amused.

"You."

Nobody moves. You'd think I was holding a gun on them. Mr. Whitman places a calming hand on the shoulder of the woman beside him. She has close-cropped hair and red-brown lipstick, and she looks like she wants to get the hell away from me.

"What did you do to my cat?" I choke out. I can't get enough air in. Can't breathe. Can't breathe.

Jeff steps forward, raises an eyebrow. He's dressed smart—camel suede sneakers, thigh-length wool coat the color of ash. I see myself in the bookcase door and flinch. Streams of mascara run down my face and neck. My hair's in a messy bun, bits of hair sticking up like chicken feathers. My face is sweating and red, and I'm missing a shoe.

I look crazy.

But I'm not. I'm not.

"My cat," I say through gritted teeth, stepping forward. "He's fighting for his life, you absolute fuck."

An elderly woman with a pixie cut flinches when I swear, making me want to say it again.

"Sorry to hear it," he says flatly. Mr. and Mrs. Whitman peer at me from behind him, saying nothing. The rest of the residents look desperately uncomfortable, eyes flicking to the door or to Jeff. Like he's their attack dog and they're the cowardly sheep in need of protection.

From me.

I'm struck again by how young he is. He's half the age of everyone else in here, and yet he commands the room. And they *let him*.

The Johnsons run this town.

"You poisoned him," I roar, and someone gasps. I step forward, my stomach cramping with rage and nerves. "You poisoned my cat."

"Hold on, there!" he says sternly, palms up. "I didn't even know you *had* a cat." He gives the other attendees a conspiratorial look that says, *This woman's crazy, isn't she?*

"Yes, you did! You *did*!" I yell it so loud that Mrs. Whitman clamps her hands over her ears and cowers. "You came to my house. You saw Reaper!"

"I never went to that godforsaken house," he says. "Why would I?" And he raises his voice a little louder for their benefit, "Black Wood should be destroyed."

Some of the residents mutter their quiet agreement. Others stare at the floor, nodding sadly.

"Yeah, you'd love that, wouldn't you?" I say shakily. "Been campaigning to get rid of my house since you moved back here."

"We all have," he says coolly. "And it's *not* your house."

Slowly, Mrs. Whitman lowers her hands.

"It belonged to *Susan*," Jeff says firmly and looks behind him for confirmation, like he's rallying a crew. "And to Janet." His eyes are wet with tears. He's faking it. He doesn't give a shit about them, not the way the Whitmans did.

But the residents are nodding. They're agreeing with the bastard. The sides have been drawn if they weren't already.

Jeff Johnson gives me a smug look only I can see.

"Susan is dead, and Janet probably is too." I try to say this tactfully, but it comes out blunt. Harsh. I clear my throat. "I'm sorry for what happened to them. I know some of you knew them both."

But I can see it in their eyes. They don't want my apologies. They just want me out. I exhale painfully. I'm so tired. So tired.

"I never meant any harm in buying the house," I tell them finally. I look up and catch Mr. Whitman's eye. "All my money's gone into it," I reveal. His eyes soften a touch, but not much. "Once the renovations are finished, I'll be gone."

"You shouldn't have bought it in the first place," he says gruffly.

"Well, I'm not the first," I say slowly, scanning each face. "Am I?"

Mr. Whitman stares me down. They must know about Amanda. They must.

"He's trying to drive me out of Black Wood House," I declare, glancing wildly at all the faces, trying to make them understand. I'm not the crazy one. He is. He is. He is.

"He poisoned my cat, Reaper," I choke out, tears stinging my eyes. Behind Jeff, Mrs. Whitman looks at me like I'm a wounded animal, like she wants to help me but she's afraid to come close.

"Reaper's been sick ever since we moved in," I explain desperately. I want to sit down on these glorious hardwood floors and cry my eyes out. "Jeff Johnson's been leaving me threatening notes. The bastard even left a dead rat in my mailbox."

Mrs. Whitman's eyes flick to Jeff, and for the briefest moment, a look of distrust creeps into her eyes. Does she finally believe me? God, I hope so.

"I think he did the same to Amanda," I tell them shakily. "And now she's gone. Disappeared."

Nothing. Mrs. Whitman looks purposefully at the floor, and my heart sinks. No one cares. No one's going to help me. Maybe they were complicit in driving me out . . .

"My God," I stammer, hand on the doorknob, sweat breaking out above my lip. "You're all involved, aren't you?"

My skin is uncomfortably hot. I feel like a goat among wolves. I take a small step back toward the door. God, I thought I was safe coming here. What if I'm not? What if Amanda thought the same?

She's gone. I'm next.

These people. They're dangerous.

I scramble backward, heart leaping into my throat. Mr. Whitman steps forward, and I shoot my hand out. "Back the fuck up!"

I scream it because I'm frightened. Because I'm losing all control and the room is spinning in nightmarish circles. Behind me, the door springs open. My throat closes up, and I feel like I can't breathe. I whirl around and come face-to-face with a man in his fifties, clean-shaven and calm. He gives me a once-over, winces. He's wearing a short-sleeved navy-blue shirt. A badge on the arm says VICTORIA POLICE.

Relief floods through me. I grab the crook of his arm. "Please," I beg, voice cracking. "This man here"—I point shakily at Jeff Johnson—"he broke into my house, and he poisoned my cat." I gulp in air, crying noisily.

"Mrs. Slade"—the policeman speaks in low, gentle tones, eyes flicking to the silent residents—"why don't you step outside for a minute?"

I ignore him. "Please." I'm fucking sobbing now. I swipe at my tears, and Mrs. Whitman looks away. I feel like the roof is about to crash down on me. God, I just want my cat to be okay. I can't change anything about what happened with my sister. But I can change this. Reaper. Reaper. Reaper.

"Have you been drinking, Mrs. Slade?" the cop asks brusquely, wrinkling his nose.

"Ask him about Amanda!" I yell. "Ask him what he did to her!"

My eyes find Mr. Whitman's. His lips move silently, like he's saying a prayer. He knows something. They all do.

"The woman who bought Black Wood before me," I choke out. "She's disappeared. And no one will speak of her."

Mrs. Whitman turns sharply away. She swipes at her eyes with her sleeve. I pull at the cop's sleeve. "They know something about Amanda! They all do."

I'm waiting for the cop to start asking questions. To do something. But he gives me a look that stops me cold.

"I think it's time to go home, Mrs. Slade," he says gravely. Behind him, Jeff Johnson doesn't even try to hide his smile.

My uncle's the town cop.

I drop his arm. Of course. He's not on my side at all. It's me against them.

"Come on." The cop tries to usher me out the door.

I pull away, blood boiling. "Why?" I spit out. "So your shithead nephew can poison my cat again?"

Someone gasps. The room spins wildly, and I can't get enough air in.

"Time to go now," he insists angrily, reaching for my arm.

Blood pounds in my ears. I wrench away. "Don't touch me!"

I'm screaming now. Screaming in this beautiful two-hundred-year-old room with the soft golden lights and golden people. I'll scream the stained-glass windows apart, shatter the pieces like rain until I learn the truth.

I point at Jeff Johnson. "You broke into my house!"

"That true, Jeff?" the cop says over his shoulder.

Jeff waves his hand dismissively. "Of course not. She's crazy."

"Bullshit!" I explode. I'm running now, running on stumbling feet, my hands hooked into claws, ready to spring on him like a feral cat. Behind me, the cop yells, and a woman shrieks in surprise. But I'm already on Jeff, my fingers digging into his skin. When the cop pulls me back, I'm screaming.

"You son of a bitch! You son of a bitch!" Spittle flies out of my mouth. "You're going to pay for Reaper."

The cop drags me toward the exit, kicking and spitting. He yanks the door open, throws me out, and before it closes, I scream a final warning.

"I'll fucking kill you, Jeff!"

Chapter 31

June 19, I think

Dear Diary,

  Hi, it's me again. Sarah Slade. Lizzy Harris. Joe's wife, or soon-to-be ex-wife. My husband. Or wasband. I dunno yet. I dunno anything anymore.

I pour another glass of red with a shaky hand. Some of it sploshes down the side of the glass and stains my pajama pants. I take a long gulp, eyes on the forest mural.

I really shouldn't be drinking on my medication. I think I've told you that before.

I hesitate, tapping the pen once, twice against the page.

I was "let go" from work a few days ago. I'm not earning any money, so I can't afford to continue with the renovations. I've got no sponsorships left. My engagement on socials is terrible. Nobody gives a shit about me anymore. But don't worry! Filling my days is easy. I wake up, drink. Ring the vet for an update on Reaper and drink. Fall asleep, wake up, drink, drink, drink.

Outside, the cockatoos squabble in the graveyard. They sound like angry children. I hate them. I'm sick of their unending screeching. I hear it night and day, and early in the morning.

May I tell you something? I'm starting to forget things. Sometimes I find myself in the laundry, staring at the washing machine, with no memory of what the hell I'm doing there. Sometimes I'm sitting on the couch, staring at nothing. Yesterday I found myself at the back porch door, staring off into the forest.

I bite my lip, run my thumb over the back of the pen. My hands are shaking, and my palms itch with sweat. I want to drop the pen, shove the diary in the drawer, and snap it shut. I want to fly down the stairs, out the front door, and run, run, run because I don't want to admit this next bit.

This might not seem odd, but I was holding something in my hand. A TV remote. I don't remember picking it up.

I drop the pen like it's a hot stone. My pulse leaps in my throat. The cockatoos' screeching sets my teeth on edge. I cover my ears, but I can still hear them. I'm losing it. I'm losing it.

With a cry, I grab for the pen. I scribble the last part, my hand trembling and frantic. I'm gasping for breath when I finish the entry.

Dear Diary,
  I lied about that last part.
  It's true that I was standing at the back door, staring off into the forest.
  But I wasn't holding a TV remote.
  I was holding a hammer.

June 19 night, I think

Dear Diary,
  I got a missed call from a number I didn't recognize. I called them back, and they said, "Who am I speaking to, please?"
  I opened my mouth and realized I had no answer.
  "My name is Lizzy," I finally said. But it didn't feel right, so I quickly added, "Oh, wait, no. Sarah, I mean."

But that wasn't right either. All I could think about was that girl I told you about. The redhead with the chin-length hair and denim jackets. Katy Kelly.

"Katy Kelly," I said. "Yeah, my name is Katy Kelly. For reals."

"The fuck is wrong with you?" the caller said before hanging up.

Hang on. Someone's at the door—

I trip over my legs when I stand up. My clothes are thrown carelessly over my bed and cover every inch of the floorboards. I blink at the mess. I don't remember making it. My stomach howls. I don't remember the last time I ate either.

I'm holding the doorknob when the thought finally hits me. Why the hell is someone knocking on my bedroom door? The builders haven't been here in days. And I haven't seen my husband for God knows how long.

"Lizzy?"

I throw the door open.

Well, well. Look who's come crawling home. My darling husband.

He shoves his hands deep into his jeans' pockets. New jeans. Expensive. He's freshly shaved, had a recent haircut. He smells like mint and betrayal.

I reach out and steady myself against the doorframe. He raises an eyebrow, and it seems to say, *God, you're a mess.*

So are you, Joe, I think. But lucky for you, *I've* always been here to clean up your messes. The night we left our hometown, *I* packed his bag while he curled into a ball at the foot of his bed, staring at his AFL posters with red eyes. Joe played football every Saturday morning. The entire town was his devoted fan club. People clapped and whistled when he kicked a goal. Now they looked at him and saw me. Now when he stepped out onto the oval, the town went still and horribly silent, thinking only of my sister and how we betrayed her.

I tried to save us. I tried to build a life to make up for the one we lost.

I shouldn't have fucking bothered.

"I'm going away for a while," he says carefully. His eyes are wide, uneasy. "Camping in the bush."

I blink at him. "You hate camping."

He looks down, examines the floorboards. I grip the doorframe tight enough to shatter it. "Who are you going with?"

Pause.

"A friend," he says simply.

"A girlfriend?" I grit my teeth.

For a long time he doesn't answer. He looks past me, eyes searching for something. He takes in the messy floor, the empty wine glasses on my desk. I think he's looking for Reaper. God, I realize, he doesn't even know Reaper was poisoned.

"Yeah," Joe says, and I look up, confused for a moment. He straightens his back, but his eyes are scared. "I've been seeing someone else."

I shut my eyes tight. A girlfriend. My husband has a girlfriend. Even though I knew it was coming, I'm still surprised by it. My husband has a girlfriend. My *husband* has a *girlfriend*.

"You fucking asshole," I say.

Joe steps back, making himself as small as possible. It only pisses me off more. Out the window, the cockatoos are screeching, and even Joe winces.

I lean against the door. "Did you get my voicemail?"

Joe stares at the floorboards. "Yeah."

I throw up my hands. "And?"

The damn cockatoos keep screeching and screeching. I want to throw something at them. Or him. Yeah, just him.

My husband asks in a tired voice, "You know what, Lizzy?"

"What, Liam?"

He doesn't even flinch when I say his real name. Instead, he straightens his back, looks me in the eyes and says, "Go fuck yourself."

Screech. Screech. Screech.

Go fuck yourself. My husband just told me to go fuck myself. My *husband* who has a *girlfriend* just told me to go fuck myself. Laughter starts bubbling up my throat. I double over, holding my stomach because I'm laughing so hard.

Joe eyes me nervously. "There's something wrong with you," he says, stepping back. "Seriously."

I stop laughing.

It's dead silent now. Even the cockatoos are quiet.

"You're right," I finally tell him. I even shrug. "There *is* something wrong with me."

Joe backs away like he just can't wait to leave me.

"But you know what?" I ask quietly. "There's something *really fucking wrong* with you too."

Joe raises both hands like he's telling me to stop. "I'm moving out, all right? I'm gonna pack up all my things tonight," he says very slowly. "I'll be gone by morning."

My blood heats to boiling point.

Very softly I ask, "What makes you think you'll be safe here tonight?"

He stares at me in shock. I stare back.

I slam the door shut, feeling completely unhinged. Joe has pulled on the final thread holding my sanity in place. I grip the wine bottle in both hands and gulp it all down. It takes a while. But I'm game. I smack my lips when I'm finished. Cheerily, I grip the pen.

Okay, welcome to my breaking point! So my husband just confessed to cheating on me. I've lost my job and my marriage this week. Wooooooo.

I catch a glimpse of myself in the grimy reflection of the vanity mirror. I must've spilled wine down my pajama top. It's bright red and soaked. I look like I'm covered in blood. I wish it was Joe's blood. The cheating bastard. I built him a good life, and all he saw were the cracks.

I lunge clumsily for the diary. Before I even know what I'm writing, out it comes in one long furious scribble, like I was born trying to say it.

I find myself within a forest dark,
  For the straightforward pathway has been lost.

No one understands how this feels. How lonely it is. But Bill Campbell did. Maybe Susan was a cheating scumbag, and Bill did everything he could to make their life work. Maybe Bill worked a job he didn't like, fled his fucking hometown, and built a life Susan wasn't even grateful for.

I bolt up, blood pumping hot and fast. I grab the mug and hurl it against the wall, feeling like I'm about to fucking explode. I stomp over to the diary and scribble one last thought.

Maybe Susan died because he just couldn't fucking take it any longer.

Teehee.

Hi Andy! It's me (Joe's bitch wife).

I hiccup into my knee and fumble for more wine.

Did you know that Joe isn't his real name? Did you know he used to have shiny blond hair before we dyed it black and chopped it off in a nasty truck-stop bathroom?

Teehee. It takes me a while to tap the message into my phone. The letters are like naughty children who won't sit still. I hiccup again. What was it Emily said about the truth? Something, something. *Don't be afraid of the truth. . . . Be afraid of believing your lies.*

Well, this is the truth. The hideous, filthy truth. Out it finally comes. Wheeeeeeeeeeeee.

Maybe you don't believe me, Andy. I know you don't like me. None of Joe's friends have ever liked me. I'm not perfect. I know that. And my darling black-haired husband? Well, he's not so perfect, either . . . or nice.
Want to know why, Andy?

I sit up straight and listen. The house is silent and still, waiting, waiting, waiting. Joe is downstairs packing his shit and probably bitching about me to *his new girlfriend* while I'm up here unraveling all his filthy secrets. Teehee.

My marriage is done. It's over.

But not quite.

Finish it off, Lizzy, the house urges me.

So I do.

Joe left my little sister, Sarah, for me.

I hesitate, holding my phone in the palm of my hand as the walls and floors begin to tremble. The house is stirring. The house is angry on my behalf. It hates Joe. *Hates him.*

Get him. Get him, the house roars. *Make him pay!*

I tap the final words out and hit send.

And ten days later, I think he killed her.

Chapter 32

Dear Andy,

I chew my lip as the pen hovers over the blank page. I'm going to send this letter to him soon but not tonight. Tonight, it's enough to just write it all down. Cathartic, even.

Joe sank into an almost catatonic depression after my sister's death. To this day, I can't speak about her without him going into a very still and very silent rage. For years, I put it down to grief.

But was *it grief?*

Or was it guilt?

Because, you see, there are a few things that make no fucking sense about my sister's death. And all of them involve Joe.

Reasons I think my husband might be a killer:

The Book.

A few months ago, I had an interesting case at work. A woman in her twenties, pale and painfully thin, reeking of panic. I prodded her gently for two one-hour sessions, but she gave me nothing. In our third session, she finally broke down and confessed. Years before, she'd been driving home from a housewarming party. "I'd had a bit to drink," she confessed, trembling. "I shouldn't have been driving. I know that. I know."

She looked up at me with pained eyes and whispered brokenly, "I never even saw the boy."

She ran a stop sign and plowed into a child riding a bike. "I pulled the car over," she told me in a dead voice. "I looked in my rearview mirror and saw him. He was lying in the middle of the road . . . just a child. Just a little kid."

She drove off, never told a soul, and somehow I was supposed to put all her broken pieces back together. But I didn't know how. In a half-hearted attempt to cover my ass, I bought a $4.99 book on Amazon titled Let Go of Guilt. I spent hours reading it, and something about it just set my teeth on edge. Excessive guilt can open the door to a host of problems. It can lead to anxiety, extreme weight loss, rage, preoccupation with past mistakes, regret, self-defeating behavior.

One night, I was sitting on my bed, wrapped in a blanket, reading this, and it hit me: My husband ticked off all these boxes.

I stared at the wall for hours, thinking. Well, of course he felt guilty. We were the reason my sister killed herself. But I just couldn't let it go. Something had always felt off about the way he grieved my sister. It was obsessive. Fanatical. Personal.

God, I finally thought, you'd think he was the one who actually killed her . . .

The Lie.

My sister hanged herself in our garage on August 5, 2015. Mum found her. It wasn't hard to believe she killed herself. She'd always suffered from dark moods, and when she found out I'd slept with Joe, she plunged headfirst into the worst dark mood I'd ever seen. She spat; she howled; she ripped off the posters over my bed and defaced my side of the wall with thick black marker. HOW COULD YOU? HOW COULD YOU?

Her dark moods rarely lasted longer than three days. This one lasted ten days and nights. Then it came to a gut-wrenching, screaming halt on August 5.

Joe was inconsolable, lost. But one thing stood out. In the blur following her death, I do remember him telling someone, a friend maybe, that he hadn't seen Sarah since she found out about us.

But that wasn't quite true. The truth was, he'd been showing up at our house for days, desperate to get back with her. Sometimes he'd park on our street late at night and stare at our house. Sarah even confronted him once—stormed out onto the street, stuck her head in the car window—and I heard his whiny cries about how much he missed her, how sorry he was. That was only two days before she died.

I guess he didn't want people knowing he'd been borderline stalking her. So, it made sense that he kept it to himself. But what didn't make sense was the ring.

The Ring.

My sister always wore the same ring on her left index finger. She slept in it, showered in it, never took it off. It was cheap stainless steel with a black spiderweb on it. The last time I saw her, the day before she died, I'm certain she was wearing it.

How do you think I felt, then, when I found that same damn ring in my husband's possession?

I did all the packing when we moved here to Black Wood, while Joe sat listlessly on the couch. I was on my knees, reaching under the spare bed, pulling out empty Pepsi Max cans, shoving them into a garbage bag, and hating him for not helping. Then I peered under the bed and saw the box. It was palm sized, made clumsily out of balsa wood. It looked homemade. Sentimental. Odd.

Something about it made me stand up and silently close the door. I sat heavily on the bed, stomach churning, and opened it. And that's when I found her ring. The spiderweb ring that belonged to my dead sister. What. The. Fuck.

I closed my fist around it, thinking. Then I slowly put the ring back in the box and shoved it under the bed.

For months now, all I've been thinking is, Did Sarah kill herself? Or did Joe go to our house, beg her to take him back, and she refused? And then . . . did he snap? Stage her suicide? *I don't know, Andy. I don't know. I don't know.*

What I do know is that if I hadn't gone after Joe, my sister would still be alive. My sister with her answers and drive and passions. What a terrible waste to lose her so young. The world never even got to know her, Andy. Please look into this. Please. *And Andy . . . if something happens to me . . . Joe did it. He's not who you think he is.*

I don't write this next bit. Andy doesn't need to know this: But what if they could? What if my sister could live on through me? I could become what she wanted to be—a therapist who has all the answers. I could even have the boy she loved right by my side while I did it.

Some people might think that's messed up.

But I am not some people.

My eyes drift to my bedroom door. Downstairs, Joe is probably sexting his girlfriend in between packing up his shit. I sit up, and my head spins. Then I get slowly to my feet.

Dear Diary,
I'm so confused all the time. I know I'm forgetting things,
but I can't remember what.

Dear Diary,
I think Amanda is trying to tell me something, but I don't
know what. Amanda. Amanda.

Dear Diary,
Today I crawled around on all fours because I thought I
was Reaper. I lay in a ball under my bed, purring. It was
really nice. But then I remembered that I'm not a cat. I
remembered that I'm Lizzy Harris, and my sister is
dead. And I cried and cried and cried.

Dear Diary,
It's happening again. I'm losing my arms.
I'm scared. I'm scared. I'm scared. I'm scared.

~~I am not crazy. I am not crazy. I am not crazy. I am not
crazy. I am not crazy. I am not crazy. I am not crazy. I
am not crazy. I am not crazy. I am not crazy. I am not
crazy.~~

Dear Diary,
Sarah came over today. It was so nice to see her. We
stayed up all night talking, and we laughed and laughed
just like we used to. But then she reached up and pulled
her head off, and I couldn't stop screaming.
Don't kill me. Don't kill me. Don't kill me.
All my life I've been told,
You need to see a doctor.
The fuck is wrong with you?

You're strange. You're broken. You're not one of us.
Maybe I'm sick of people trying to fix me. Maybe I don't
want to be fixed, just like the house. We're dirty and
hideous, and we love it. We have blended our ugliness into
one whole pure thing.

Dear Diary,
Where the hell is Joe?
And why the fuck am I holding a bloodstained hammer?

Chapter 33

June 25

I'm vomiting in the downstairs toilet when the car pulls up. Wearily, I lift my head, swipe at my mouth, and listen. I haven't had a visitor in . . . I can't remember when. The last guests were the builders, and shit. I think I might have fired them. . . . That was days ago, wasn't it?

The car tires rumble smoothly over the dirt, and the noise is so startling, so loud, because other than the drone of the TV, the house has been silent for days and days. I flush the toilet and tighten my robe, then stumble to the couch and steady myself against it. Weakly, Reaper looks up from the cushion. *Are you okay?* he seems to ask. No, I think, and neither are you. It's touch and go with Reaper. I got him back from the vet's yesterday. I carried him to the couch, propped him up on the nicest cushion, and watched him sleep. He's eating out of my hand now, and I bring him a bowl of water so often he's probably sick of it. Sometimes I'm shaking so hard the water bowl's empty by the time I've carried it to him.

Car headlights light up the house, and I freeze, squinting out the window. Joe? But no, it's not my adulterous husband. The car pulls up, and I study it for clues. This van is muddy white, missing its driver's side hubcap. A functional, family-friendly car, probably strewn with fast-food wrappers and children's car seats. I'm surprised to see that the sun is setting. I blink, wondering where the hell the day went. I don't have a single memory of what I did today.

The headlights flick off, and the driver steps out.

Emily.

Shit. I look guiltily at the mess in the lounge room—empty wine bottles, a carton of milk souring next to the couch. Oh God, I'm not ready to be normal.

Her paisley skirt is wood brown and purple and swishes when she walks. She pulls her mid-thigh-length coat tighter, its camel color bringing out the warm brown tones in her sandals. Once upon a time I gave a shit about those details. Now I slop around in my bathrobe and cat slippers and wonder what's become of me.

Emily peers in through the window, and I'm too stupid to move. She spots me standing there, hesitates. I'm wearing my worst bathrobe and nothing underneath. It's an ill-fitting terry cloth that reveals a scandalous amount of my tits. I pull the robe tighter, but the deep V of the chest doesn't budge. She points to the front door, motions for me to open it. I shuffle forward, try to cover my chest with my left forearm while opening the door.

Emily smells like lavender and toast.

"Hi there, lovie." She gives me a tight, worried smile and a tight, worried hug, and God, I want to press my face into her camel coat and weep into her beautiful blond plait.

I hug her longer than I should. I stare over her shoulder at my vacant, desolate land, my arms wrapped around her like a child. It's comforting. But I don't want to be comforted. I want to be the *comforter*. I want to say, "Hi there, lovie," while smelling of lavender and toast and driving home to my noisy children in my functional, cheerful van.

She pulls back, studies me. "How are you feeling?"

I shake uncontrollably, tremors shooting up and down my arms and legs like someone's holding a cattle prod to them. It's the cold wind and the fever I can't get rid of.

"Oh dear," she says, guiding me back through the doorway like I'm a little chicken and she's the mother hen. "Come on, lovie. Let's get you inside."

Reaper's sleeping when Emily half carries me to the couch and gently pushes aside half-eaten containers of microwaved risotto. I collapse heavily, careful not to disturb my cat, who sleeps on peacefully. I'm breathing hard, sweat breaking out on my forehead and under my arms. The walk to the front door and back was exhausting.

Emily stands over me, clicking her tongue. Her blond plait dangles in my face, and I want to reach out and playfully bat it away like a kitten with a feather toy. My head spins, and I shut my eyes tight.

"Would you like a lavender tea?" I ask Emily, eyes still closed.

She places a hand on my forehead. "Bloody hell, you're burning up," she frets. "Have you seen a doctor yet?"

"Yep," I lie. "Got the flu again."

She sighs heavily, and when I open my eyes, it's like I'm looking at her underwater. She's a blurry mess of camel-brown shoes, paisley skirt, and blueberry hair tie.

I swipe at the sweat above my lip, try to stand. "I'll get you that tea," I slur, pulling the robe tight as my knees go wobbly. Emily catches me just as my legs give way. She cries out, holds me in her arms. "My mum used to say, 'When all else fails, put the kettle on,'" I mumble under her chin.

"That's uncanny," she says, sitting me down on the couch and propping a cushion behind my head. "That's what *my* mum used to say."

Later, she brings me Vegemite toast and a steaming mug of coffee. By the time I've finished it, I'm no longer shaking. Even Reaper seems a bit better. He meowed softly, and Emily brought him a bowl of water. He drank a little, and I felt myself relax. He'll make it, I tell myself. He'll make it. We both will.

Emily nods approvingly when I sit up. "You've got your color back," she says brightly. "Good thing too." She settles back into the recliner, crossing her ankles. "I was about to drag your butt down to the doctor's."

Her eyes flick discreetly to my feet, and I don't even blush when I realize I'm wearing avocado socks. How the mighty have fallen.

She glances around the room. Hesitates. "Is your husband home?"

I narrow my eyes, staring at the coffee table, thinking hard. Joe. Where is Joe? And why does the thought of him fill me with dread? My hands start to shake, and I tuck them between my knees.

"You okay, lovie?" Emily asks.

"I'm fine, thanks," I tell her, but my voice wobbles. I'm not fine. The headaches are constant. They make me want to rip my own brain from my head. And Joe. I swallow hard. I don't want to talk about Joe. I don't think I want to talk about him *ever* again.

"Remember how I told you about the girl who lived in this house before me?" I find Emily's eyes. "Her name was Amanda, and she disappeared."

Emily nods sadly and waits for me to continue. I look out the lounge window, eyes on the setting sun. "I *feel* her in this house sometimes."

She cocks her head, and her long plait swishes to her shoulder. "And what's she saying?"

"She's telling me to keep searching. That she has something to show me."

"Like what, do you think?" Emily speaks again very, very softly. Her voice is almost dreamlike. Lovely Emily.

I've barely spoken in days, and I'm nervous and jumpy, and my words come out in a long, crazy babble. "She wants to tell me what happened to her. Why she disappeared."

She scrunches her face up, like she's thinking hard. But I get the feeling she's doing it only for my benefit. Uneasily, I wonder if she believes me at all. God, what if she was sent here by Jeff? My heart feels like a rock. I couldn't handle Emily betraying me. Not Emily.

I place the mug firmly on the coffee table, and Reaper stirs in his sleep. "Did anybody send you here?"

She doesn't react. "Why would someone send me here?" That soft voice again.

She answered my question with one of her own, and it's making me paranoid. I pull the robe tight again.

"Sarah," she says gently, crossing her legs, "do you still think someone's after you?"

"Someone's *always* after me," I say flatly. I sink into the couch, suddenly exhausted. God, the house is deathly quiet. "Ever since my sister . . ." I swallow hard. "I've been hunted ever since."

A flock of corellas bicker in the blackwood tree. They're like a bunch of little kids. Emily and I watch them, and for a long time we sit in silence. I stroke Reaper, gently scratching behind his ear.

"Nobody sent me," she finally says. "Nobody even knows I'm here. My hubby took the kids to Canberra. His dad lives there. The kids love their grandpa."

There's something calm about the way she says it. She glows with the security that comes from a stable family, stable marriage. It must be nice.

"Do you think you'll get back into vet nursing?" I ask.

She raises one eyebrow, a neat little trick that I ache to have. Maybe after she's gone, I'll practice it in the mirror.

"Did I tell you about that?" She smiles quizzically. "I will. One day." She straightens up as if she remembered something. "Are you doing better now? You've been so sick."

My heart warms to her sympathy. I need it. Crave it. "I'm worse, actually." My voice comes out a bit too eager.

She narrows her eyes. "Headaches and nausea?"

I sip from the water bottle beside the couch, and some of it dribbles down my lip. I didn't realize how thirsty I was. "And dizziness," I add. "Sometimes I . . ."

Um, maybe it's not a good idea to admit this next bit. But Emily won't judge me. Lovely Emily.

"Sometimes," I confess, "I forget where I am."

I don't tell her that I was standing at the back door with a bloody hammer in my hand. Or that sometimes I wake up under my bedroom window, curled into a ball like a cat.

A phone rings sharply, a crescendo of notes that makes me jump. "Sorry," she says, rummaging inside her chunky purple handbag. I wonder what's inside it. Probably kids' cough drops, permission slips, and tissues. Lots of tissues.

"Hi, lovie!" Emily says.

A stab of jealousy shoots through me. I thought she called only *me* that.

"How are the kids?" she asks, transferring the phone to her other ear. I notice she has a little crescent moon earring. It's silver and hideous. But I think I want one.

She covers the phone with her palm, gives me an apologetic "I'll be just one second" look. Frankly, it disappoints me.

"Yeah, I'm at home." She bites her lip, obviously guilty. This is not a woman who is used to lying. It cheers me up, though, that she's willing to lie for me.

"I promise I won't," she says, smiling. "Say hi to the kiddos for me. Love you too. Byeeee!"

She ends the call. "Sorry," she says again, tucking her phone back into her bag, where it can't bother us.

"What did you promise?" I ask.

She smiles. "I promised not to call every five minutes. In fact, my husband's banned me from calling until they get back to Melbourne."

I stare at the corellas again, at their murky white feathers and fleshy blue eye rings that make them look like they've been punched. They're not as pretty as the cockatoos. I wonder if they wish they were. I wonder if they compare themselves with other birds and find themselves lacking.

"What's your husband's name?" I ask absently.

"Gabriel," she says, and even though I'm not looking at her, I can tell she's smiling. "Gabriel, like the angel."

"Nice name," I say.

More to myself I add, "Emily's a nice name too."

I'm halfway through my second cup of coffee when I ask Emily if she wants to see the attic.

"The attic?" She raises an eyebrow. "What's up there?"

I place my mug at my feet. "It's where I hear the footsteps."

Emily goes very still. "What footsteps?"

I open my mouth to answer, but a wave of nausea stops me. It rumbles through my stomach and starts creeping up my throat. I clutch the edge of the couch, bending forward. Reaper wakes up, meows.

"You okay, lovie?" Emily's voice seems to come from far away.

Sweat gathers on my forehead. My face is burning hot. Emily's standing over me now, her palm on my left shoulder. I reach up and cling to it, squeezing tight as another wave of nausea roars through me.

"Bloody hell, you're in bad shape, aren't you?" Emily says. "Sarah, we need to get you to the doctor's. I don't think you have the flu."

Her lovely voice fades in and out. I catch only a word here and there. When the nausea finally passes, I look up weakly. My face feels sunburned.

"There's something in the attic," I breathe. "Ever since I moved in, I've heard things up there."

She believes me, I can tell. Her soft brown eyes widen, and she looks over her shoulder like someone's about to come running down from the attic with a hammer or something.

"Have you gone up there?" she asks tentatively, removing her hand from my shoulder.

"Not for a while," I admit. I stand up slowly. My knees wobble, but they hold me up. I chew the inside of my cheek, my eyes on the top of the stairs. "I found something up there once . . ."

Again her voice fades in and out like a flickering light. I have to concentrate hard to hear. "Like what?" she asks. "I hate attics. They make me claustrophobic."

I tear my eyes away from the stairs and focus on Emily. It strikes me that she reminds me of a Jersey cow. She's all docile and calm, with big, soft eyes.

"I found a note in the attic," I tell her, remembering the terrifying night I discovered the note in the cradle.

To her credit, she doesn't even flinch. "What did it say?"

"It was a threat." I close my eyes. "It said, 'Hi Sarah Slade! Is that the name you're going by these days? Would be a shame if people found out who you really were. Wouldn't it?'"

"My God, lovie!" Emily cries, gripping my forearm. "Why didn't you tell me?"

"That's not the only note I've found."

She grips my arm tighter, leans in. "Tell me."

So I do. I tell her about the note on my laptop, the one about the cat food and anti-depressants. And I tell her about the strange phone call with the hairdresser. The appointment I didn't make. The DVD. The note on my car.

But I sure as hell don't tell her about the bloodstained hammer. Or that I hid it under the cradle in the attic. Joe . . . God, where is Joe? My brain throbs like it's trying to expel the memory of him. Don't go there, I tell myself. Don't go there. I'm sure Joe's fine. He's fine.

I turn to Emily instead. "Please," I breathe. "I need to check the attic again. I'm too scared to go up there alone."

She bites her lip. She doesn't want to go up there. But I get the feeling that she wants to help me. Like a good therapist, she wants me to confront my fear, and she's willing to do it with me. Lovely Emily.

She straightens up, nods reluctantly. "Okay," she says grimly. "Let's go."

* * *

I climb the attic stairs, gripping the banister weakly. It's only seven steps, but my legs shake alarmingly. I have to pause for breath at the fifth step. I wipe sweat from my forehead. My heart pounds, and I see stars. My left knee gives out and hits the wooden step hard. Pain shoots all the way up my leg. My head droops. It's so hard to look up. Behind me, Emily gasps. I keep my eyes shut, but I feel her at my elbow, the heat of her hand at the back of my neck like a hot-water bottle. I thrash out, pushing her hand off me. I'm so hot, too hot. I try to stand, but she holds my shoulders, preventing me from moving. "Don't get up too quickly," she cautions. "Just wait. Just breathe."

So we wait. And we breathe in the musty attic air.

Finally, she speaks. "It stinks like hell up here."

"You get used to it," I tell her.

I heave myself up.

"Go slow," Emily cautions.

So we do. We climb the last two steps, and I duck my head before stepping into the darkness. Behind me, Emily starts gagging. "God!" She presses her sleeve over her mouth and nose. "What on earth is that smell?" She squints at something, leaning forward. "And what the bloody hell is on that wall?"

I don't answer. I pull my phone out of my pocket, flick the torch on, and freeze.

Emily finally stops gagging and creeps over to me. "What's wrong?" she whispers through her sleeve.

The hairs on my arms shoot up. I stand very still at the top of the stairs, heart thudding. "Look!" I shine the weak light at the floorboards.

"Oh my God." Her fingers dig into my shoulder. There in the dust are footprints. *Dozens* of them. It looks like someone's been pacing in here. Pacing in frenzied circles, back and forth, back and forth, like a crazy person.

"We should get out of here," Emily hisses, grabbing my hand.

I pull away, shuffling forward. I lift my hand and direct the beam toward the back of the attic, where the cradle sits.

Oh my God. Shakily, I raise a finger and point to the cradle. Tacked to the headboard is another damn note.

"Stop!" Emily grabs my hand desperately, but I march forward, heart lurching. I bend down, rip the note from the headboard, and shine the torch on it.

Emily scurries over. "What does it say?"

The words are small and scribbled like the person who wrote it was in a hurry.

My name is Amanda Vale.
There's something wrong with this house. No one believes me.
They come at night.

SHOCKING TWIST IN BLACK WOOD CASE:

JOE COSGROVE FOUND ALIVE

July 5

ABC News, Melbourne

Joe Cosgrove, husband of author Sarah Slade, has been found alive. The twenty-three-year-old Beacon resident was presumed dead by the public after two bodies were found at Black Wood House. The bartender had not been seen or heard from in over two weeks.

But in a shocking twist, Cosgrove has turned up in Beacon, alive and well after camping in a remote part of Victoria.

Beacon residents aren't convinced. "It's a bit convenient, isn't it? Who suddenly decides to go camping before two bodies are found in your own house?"

"I don't trust him," said another resident. "There's something about him that rubs me the wrong way."

"Now that a next of kin has been found," a source said, "police can finally tell us whether the body is Sarah Slade's."

Chapter 34

EMILY

The note makes no sense. I got home from Sarah's a few hours ago, but it's impossible to sleep. Not after all that mess at her place. I roll over, staring at the empty spot where Gabe sleeps. He took the kids to his dad's, finally. I've been asking for months. I love the kids, but God, they wear me out. And lately . . . I stare at the flaking paint on the ceiling and add it to my endless to-do list. . . . Lately, I feel like I give so much to everyone else that there's nothing left for me.

"Now don't be callin' us every hour asking how we are." Gabe grinned as he waved goodbye from the driver's seat, and I felt so guilty because I hadn't planned on calling at all. Archie was already in a scrap with his sister, sneakily pulling her hair, while Riley wound down the back window, stuck his head out, and yelled cheekily, "Got somethin' for you, Mum!" and burped.

I smiled, waved goodbye, and blew kisses until my wrist ached. I hate admitting this, but the moment the van was out of sight, my limbs loosened, and I leaned against the mailbox and just soaked up the blessed quiet. I've taken some annual leave at work. Lord knows I've got enough. I already told Adria and Tim that if they call, I'm not answering. I'm going to have an entire week of "me time."

I bustled around the empty house, not knowing what to do with myself. Gabe dropped the dogs off at a sitter's this morning. I had a long soak in the tub, then drove to Sarah's.

Something's seriously wrong with Sarah. I've known it for a while. They did the wrong thing by firing her. It's been terrible for her mental health.

Tim and Benita are glad to see the back of her. *Thinks she's too good for the likes of us.* But I don't think that at all. Poor dear's got no family, and no friends that I can tell of. She rubs people the wrong way, Sarah. Or Lizzy, I s'pose I should call her. God, that one threw me for a six! I about dropped my mug of tea when she told me all that stuff about her sister. I hope she didn't notice my reaction. I felt guilty about it for days. Here's this poor girl showing me all her wounds, and I just sat there like a stunned mullet.

I pull a pillow to my chest. I can't settle tonight. God, that note.

My name is Amanda Vale.

There's something wrong with this house. No one believes me.

They come at night.

There's been no news coverage about Amanda's disappearance. No missing-person posters. It's like she's been swept under Beacon's rug. Imagine! A young woman going missing in this town. We knew about the tragedy of Black Wood House, but that was forty years ago.

Amanda's disappearance really rattled me. I banned the kids from walking home from school for a few weeks. But you can't keep them wrapped in cotton wool, can you?

They come at night.

I sigh heavily, staring at the ceiling. There's something off about that note. I can't put my finger on it.

I hope Sarah's okay. She was pretty shaken up, but she wouldn't come back to my place. And I feel a bit guilty about this, but I just couldn't stay at her house a *minute* longer. That house gives me the shivers. And the attic . . . I really didn't want to go up there, but she was so insistent. Poor girl. If Gabe were here, he'd poke me in the ribs. "Old Mother

Hen," he'd tease me, eyes sparkling. "Can't stand to see anyone suffer-
ing."

They come at night.

I won't sleep now. I know it. Maybe I should pop over to the pub,
have a stiff drink. Calm my nerves. But I've been doing that a bit too
often lately. Gabe's had a few words with me about it. And anyway, I
can't shake the thought that I'm missing something. Something *really*
important.

I bite my lip, thinking hard. The attic really unsettled me. And it
wasn't just the darkness, the note, and the smell. It was something else.
I close my eyes, heart thudding. Remember, I tell myself sternly. Remember. I followed Sarah up those creaky steps, wishing she'd change
her mind so we could go back downstairs. She went ahead of me, shining her phone at the cradle. That's when she found the note.

My name is Amanda Vale . . .

I roll over, frustrated. It's not so much the note that bothers me. It's
everything else. I really don't believe Amanda wrote that note. I don't
believe Sarah wrote it either. I saw the look on her face when she found
it. Saw the way she nearly fell to the floor, her palm covering her mouth
in shock.

So, who wrote it? God. I rub my temple, feel a headache coming.

Headaches . . .

I go very still. Sarah's complained nonstop about her damn headaches. Honestly, we were all sick of hearing about them. *Bloody drama
queen,* Benita called Sarah behind her back. I swallow uneasily. Think,
think. I lie on my side, my whole body trembling. Then I remember. Just
before Sarah discovered the note, I saw something on the attic wall.

God, my heart is beating so damn fast. I cover it with my palm, thinking, thinking. I called out to Sarah. I said, *What the bloody hell is on that
wall?*

I can't even breathe now. I'm shaking so hard it's rattling the bed.
Think, Em! What was it about the wall that made you call out? I close

my eyes, picturing it. In the dimness of Sarah's torch, the wall was illuminated, but only for a second. I stopped and stared. Why? Because all over the attic walls were putrid brown smears that looked like nicotine. Like . . .

I bolt upright.

Oh God. Oh God.

I grab for my phone and frantically call Sarah. Please pick up! Please pick up! Voicemail. Shit! I throw the covers off, lunge for my clothes, heart hammering. I call her again, praying she'll answer.

"Hi, it's Sarah Slade! Please leave a message after the beep."

Beep.

"Sarah!" I grab my jumper off the bedpost and rush out the door. "Don't go into the attic!"

I snatch up my car keys and throw the front door open as I scream into the phone. "Sarah! Get out of the house! Run! Don't go into that attic!"

I hang up and immediately call back. Pick up! Pick up! I jump in the car, throw the phone on the passenger seat as it goes straight to voicemail again. I shove the key in the engine and scream another warning. "Sarah, get out of the house! *Don't go into the attic!*"

The tires shriek; I gun the engine. I pray I make it to her in time.

Chapter 35

S A R A H

June 26

Dear Diary,

Emily left a few hours ago. She wanted me to go home with her, but I felt like Amanda wanted me to stay at Black Wood. She left me that note. She must have been sleeping in the attic the whole time I've been here.

The note really freaked Emily out. She ran down the attic stairs, almost tripping over her skirt. "Call the police," she'd insisted. "What police?" I'd asked. "They're on the town's side. They don't care about Amanda. They never did."

"I'll call you tomorrow morning," I'd promised. She hugged me in a cloud of lavender perfume and said, "Go to bed. Call me as soon as you wake up."

I watched her car disappear down the long driveway, and the second it was gone, I went straight back to the attic.

And waited.

I bolt awake. The hairs on my forearms shoot up. Something's wrong. Something's wrong. The attic is pitch black and so very cold. The stairs are raised and I don't remember raising them. I squint in the darkness, my pulse skyrocketing. My vision swims, and my skull feels like someone's crushing it. The diary's still open in my lap. Slowly, I reach for it and hold it close to my face to make out the words.

Dear Diary,
   Emily left a few hours ago. She wanted me to go home with her . . .

I remember writing this. I must've fallen asleep soon after. I scan the rest of the passage, and there at the very bottom are three words that I *did not write.*
   I go very still as I re-read the last line.
   Lizzy, I'm here.
   Behind me, someone coughs.

Chapter 36

EMILY

I throw the car door open, bolt to her front door. It's so dark. So dark. The sky is starless, murky with rain clouds. I don't even know what time it is. I grab the door handle and rattle it. Locked. Shit!

"Sarah!" I scream, kicking the door, pounding it with my fists. I'm shaking with cold and terror, and I just have to reach her before it's too late. "Sarah!"

Nothing.

No, no, no. With a cry, I rush to the lounge window. I tear at it, looking for an opening. "Sarah!" I keep screaming over and over until the back of my throat aches. I drop to my knees and claw at the ground until my right hand brushes something solid. I grasp it, bring it close to my face, and my heart lurches in relief. It's half a brick, heavy as hell. I get to my feet, hurl it with all my might at the window, and it smashes through in a hail of shattered glass. I don't hesitate. I plunge through the smashed window, ducking my head. Strands of my hair catch on the glass, and when I wrench my head away, my phone falls out of my coat pocket and skitters across the floor into the dark. I yell in pain as hair is ripped from my skull, but I'm finally inside Black Wood House.

My sandals crunch over the shards as I step forward in total darkness. "Sarah!" I crouch and fumble in the dark for my phone, trying not to cut myself. Where the heck is my phone? Where the hell is a light switch?

"Sarah!"

No answer. God, what if she's unconscious? I debate for half a second and quickly get to my feet. There's no time left. I'll get Sarah, and then I'll come back for my phone. I can do this. I pick up the hem of my skirt and inch forward, feeling my way, praying it's not too late to save her.

Chapter 37

SARAH

I get slowly to my feet. It's so dark I can't even see my shoes. I turn around, head spinning, facing the back wall where the cradle is. I squint. I can't make out anything at all, only shapes in the darkness. But I know someone's there. I know it. I hear them breathing.

My voice comes out in a dry whisper, "Who's there?"

Silence. Desperately, I glance behind me to the attic stairs buried somewhere in the darkness. If I ran for it . . . would I make it?

"Who's there?" I whisper again, louder this time.

I wait there, my entire body trembling.

Creeeeeeak.

I let out a cry of horror. Someone's at the back of the room, near the cradle. My heart is about to burst with terror. But I have to know. I have to know who it is. I have to know who's been tormenting me.

I creep forward, biting my lip so I won't scream. My hands are out in front of my face, shielding me. My head throbs as I step closer, closer until I make out a tall shape in the dark. I freeze.

Someone is standing over the cradle. A filthy nightgown falls past their toes, and their long hair is matted.

I hold my breath, watching. I lick my lips. "Amanda?"

The girl raises her head, stands perfectly still. I stop breathing. Slowly, she turns around.

The girl's eyes seem to glow in the dark. I blink, wondering if I'm seeing things. I blink again. Her eyes are as green as olives.

The girl is Sarah.

My heart lurches. My sister. My baby sister is standing in my attic.

"Sarah?" My voice cracks. "Is it really you?"

I don't wait for her to answer. I lurch forward with a cry. My fingers close around her wrist. She's cold, but she's real. This isn't a dream. Right there above her left eyebrow is the small scar I gave her when we were playing Ninja Turtles when she was five and I was seven. I throw my arms around her neck and sob noisily into her shoulder. For a long, horrible moment, I think she's not going to hug me back. But finally, she lifts her arms and wraps them around my shoulders.

"Sarah!" I sob, "How are you alive? I—"

Uneasily, I drop my arms. The last time I saw Sarah . . .

She tightens her grip on me. Her breath is stinking hot against my ear, but her arms are freezing cold around my shoulders. "Sarah . . ." I try to pull away. And then in one quick movement, she slides both hands up to my throat.

I lash out wildly as she squeezes tight, choking me of air. I tear at her hands, fighting hard to pull them off. But she squeezes tighter and tighter, her face contorted in fury.

"How could you!" she hisses. "How could you!"

"Sarah . . ." I choke out as spots appear in my vision. "Sarah . . ."

The world goes black and I stop thrashing. My knees buckle.

And that's when she finally releases me.

I collapse on the ground, gasping for air. My sister crouches beside me, eerily calm. For a long time, neither of us speaks. I lie still, breathing noisily and gazing into her face. People used to say we looked alike. But we don't anymore. Her hair is ash blonde, like mine used to be before I dyed it caramel brown. We're both short-sighted, but I wear contacts now, and Sarah's still wearing her tortoiseshell glasses. But we both still have the same terrible teeth, all crooked at the bottom, the front two over-lapping. It's the strangest feeling to be all alone for years and finally see bits and pieces of yourself in someone else.

How could you . . .

"I'm sorry about Joe," I finally whisper. My throat feels like a giant bruise. It hurts to speak. But I need to say this. I've wanted to say it for years. "I'm sorry I stole him from you."

She raises an eyebrow, waiting.

I gently rub my neck. *How could you. How could you.* Those three words have haunted me. But the truth is, they were never about me stealing Joe. It was about the *other* thing I did to my sister.

Slowly, I sit up. I look into her eyes and say, "I'm sorry I killed you."

Sarah found out about Joe and me, and we had screaming fights about him for weeks. She turned the *whole town* against us. I'd never exactly been liked in our hometown, but this was different. I was *hated* now. Even Gina Hampton, the nice lady I worked with at Kmart, was cold with me.

That afternoon on August 5, 2015 . . . I'd just wanted to knock some sense into Sarah. She had no clue what it was like to be despised. If she'd just *fucking get over it*, we could all move the hell on. But no.

Mum was at work. Joe was at home. Sarah and I were yelling at each other in our garage. And all I could think about was how *nice* it must be to be Sarah. How *nice* to have the whole town adore you. How nice to have Mum always on your side. How nice that even our aunties adored you and your brilliant one-liners and your answers and . . .

I don't know how it happened. I think Sarah actually struck me first. And then I was on top of her, my hands around her neck, squeezing, squeezing, squeezing.

I staged her suicide. Joe and I left town.

I hear a faint crashing noise coming from downstairs. It sounds like breaking glass. I lift my head briefly, wondering if I misheard it, but I don't care enough about anything else right now except my baby sister. Truthfully, I've missed her so much. Bloody Joe wasn't worth it at all. Men never are. And now, she's back from the dead. How?

"You're the one who's been leaving the notes."

I swallow hard, remembering them all. *Don't forget to take your meds. Would be a shame if someone found out who you really were . . .*

"Sarah . . ." I begin uneasily, "Have you been in the house all along?"

She opens her mouth to say something but freezes instead. I'm about to ask what's wrong, when I hear it, too. There's a creaking sound coming from downstairs.

"Lizzy," she says, "I didn't write those notes."

Creak, creak, creak. My stomach ties itself in anxious knots and my head pounds harder. I have no idea what's going on, but I know it's bad.

Urgently, she says, "They're coming . . ."

The note.

My name is Amanda Vale.

There's something wrong with this house. No one believes me . . .

Oh God. I grab Sarah hard.

They come at night . . .

"Who comes at night?" I ask frantically, eyes darting behind me. I grip her hand tighter, whispering urgently, "Who's been tormenting me?"

But my sister purses her lips into a severe line and backs away with scared, wide eyes. I freeze, and she clasps my hand. We both hear it. Footsteps underneath the attic. Whoever it is, they know we're up here.

She whispers, "Someone's coming, Lizzy. They're coming for you. For us."

No, no, no. I'm not losing my sister again. I drag Sarah to the back of the room. "Wait here," I whisper, leaning down, fumbling in the dark.

Creaaaak. God. I glance over my shoulder, frozen in horror. Someone's opening the attic pulley. The stairs unfold, emitting a strangled sound. For a long, heart-stopping moment, we wait. The pounding in my head is so bad now. It feels like someone's slamming it against a door over and over.

Then, someone calls, "Sarah? I'm coming for you."

Behind me, Sarah gasps. The whites of her eyes shine in the dark, and I stare helplessly as the person begins climbing the attic stairs.

"Lizzy," my sister cries, reaching for my hand, "help me!"

Help me. Help me. I will. I will this time. I failed my sister once. I will not fail her again. With a desperate cry, I drop to my knees. The edge of Sarah's nightgown brushes my face as I thrust my hand under the cradle.

"Hurry, hurry," Sarah whispers, clutching at my shoulder. "Please, Lizzy, they're coming!"

The footsteps grow louder up the stairs. They're about to burst into the attic and take my sister away from me. Rage and pain cloud my thoughts. My head hurts, God it fucking hurts so bad. My fingers reach desperately until they brush cool metal, and I nearly cry with relief. I grasp the hammer in my fist, get quickly to my knees. Too fast. Too fast. My vision swims, my head pulses, I choke back a cry of pain. My fist clenches around the weapon, and all I want to do is bash my own damn skull with it. Anything to get rid of this *fucking* pain.

I reach blindly for my little sister, shielding her body with mine.

"It's okay, it's okay," I whisper, oddly calm now. "I'm not losing you again."

Chapter 38

EMILY

The entire house is so damn *dark*. It's 2 or 3 A.M., the darkest part of night, and Black Wood is as dark and silent and claustrophobic as a coffin. I have to feel my way along the narrow hallway with my hands. My boot knocks something. I can't see what. I check the first two bedrooms and call out for Sarah, but she doesn't call back. She's in the attic. I know it.

I inch forward, trying not to remember the ghastly history of Black Wood. Like Susan Campbell lying in her bed with a bashed-in skull . . . or Bill Campbell slumped dead on the bathroom floor.

I *hate* this house. I reach what I think could be the middle of the hallway and raise my arms above my head, searching for the little cord connected to the attic stairs. I must look like an idiot, hands waving around like I'm shooing flies. My right hand knocks something, and I grab it. The cord! I yank on it and give a cry of relief as the staircase creaks down. I wait at the bottom stair, peering up into the darkness. It's deathly silent up there, and somehow that's worse. I clear my throat. "Sarah? I'm coming for you."

Hearing nothing, I suck in a breath, pick up the hem of my skirt, and climb the seven stairs to the attic.

I hover at the entrance, peering into the dark. "Sarah . . . oh!"

I jump back in fright, hand clutching my chest. Someone is standing at the cradle, looking down. They're still and silent, and creepy as hell. I take a small step forward, squinting.

"Sarah?"

A gruff voice yells out, "Stay the fuck away from her!" I let out a startled cry as the person charges forward. "Get out! Get the fuck away from her!"

I'm so confused that I stand there frozen. Finally, the person steps closer, until they're right in my face, panting hard like an animal. The whites of their eyes glow eerily in the dark, like two floating eye sockets.

But I'm sure of it now. The wild-eyed person standing in front of me is my co-worker. Sarah. Only . . . God, she looks awful. She's wearing a filthy nightgown, her pupils are fully dilated, and her face is sweaty and cherry red. I left her only a few hours ago. The change in her is shocking.

"Lovie." I gently reach out for her, but she jerks away, eyes darting back and forth like a feral cat's. "Lovie," I say again, trying to get her attention. She takes a small step back and looks at me like she doesn't even know me. Shit. "You need to get out of this attic," I tell her. "Right now."

She bares her teeth. "No! You're the one who needs to get out of this attic."

I hang back, unsure how to handle this. I hadn't anticipated how hard this would be. Gabe found a feral cat in our garage once. Its front leg was clearly broken, and he spent an hour trying to corner it. The kids were excited, asking me if we could keep it, but I'd seen the look in the cat's eyes. It was too far gone. For the entire hour, it scratched and hissed and bit Gabe when he got too close. Eventually, he gave up, and I drove him to the doctor's for a tetanus injection.

Anxiously, I chew my lip. Right now, Sarah is that cat, and I'm hoping I don't get bitten. Her eyes glow dully. Her face is dripping sweat. I have to get her out of here before it's too late.

"Lovie," I say gently but firmly. "You're burning up. You keep getting sick." I step a little closer. "Sarah, I think I know what's wrong with you."

She's not even listening to me. She's in constant motion, rocking on the balls of her feet, eyes flicking behind her to the cradle.

"Lovie"—I try to take her hand, but she wrenches away—"I think you're being poisoned."

She bares her teeth again, steps forward menacingly. "I know that! It's Jeff Johnson," she says through clenched teeth. "He poisoned my cat. He wants me out of this house. He wants—"

I hold up a hand to stop her. "It's not Jeff who's poisoning you." I yell now, desperate for her to understand. "It's the attic."

She doesn't react. She's too far gone to listen to me. But I speak anyway, hoping my frantic words break through to her.

"Lovie, it's the *attic* that's been poisoning you." I point to the chimney poking through the roof. The walls around it are smeared with hideous yellow-brown stains like nicotine. Only it's not nicotine.

"You see that?" I say urgently, and her eyes dart to the back wall. "Those are carbon-monoxide stains. The house has been poisoning you ever since you moved in."

She eyes me with confusion, like she's debating if I'm lying to her. But I'm not. I should have figured it all out earlier.

"Don't you see, lovie?" I plead. "Your headaches, the nausea, the light-headedness." I reel them off on my fingers. "They're all symptoms of carbon-monoxide poisoning."

"The notes . . ." she says, eyes glinting with madness. "I found those notes. Someone's been threatening me."

"No," I tell her gently. "No one's been threatening you, lovie." My eyes are wet with sympathy, and I wish I could pull her into a hug. I take a deep breath. "*You* wrote those notes."

She steps forward threateningly. "Liar!"

"You said it yourself. You never told anyone about your medication or the errands you had to run. *You* wrote the notes."

She goes very still, eyes fixated on me.

"Your system's been poisoned for weeks now," I tell her gently. "Carbon-monoxide poisoning causes extreme confusion." I step forward. "You wrote the notes. You just don't remember doing it."

"Amanda . . ."

I shrug helplessly. "Maybe Amanda succumbed too. You said she was finding notes. She was being poisoned, just like you."

"Then where is she?"

"I don't know," I admit. "Her mind would've been cloudy." I frown at the chimney, thinking. "She could be anywhere."

I don't want to stand in this poisonous room talking. I want to get the hell out of here. Now. Sarah's been in here for hours with the attic shut, breathing the toxic air, and look what it's done to her.

"The house," I tell her. "This house has been shut up for forty years. There are no windows, no ventilation. There's nowhere for the carbon monoxide to go. It's built up for years and years." I shudder. "No wonder your cat got sick."

Her head snaps back in my direction. I have her attention now.

"I think the chimney's the source of the leak." I swallow hard, pointing. "Maybe it's blocked or something. That would explain why there are stains in here but nowhere downstairs." I tug at her sleeve. "Lovie, the house has been leaking carbon monoxide for God knows how long. We have to get out of here."

"I'm not going anywhere."

"Sarah—"

She steps forward threateningly. "Don't call me that!"

My heart plummets. How the hell am I going to handle this? I can't call Gabe; he's seven hours away. And my phone . . . dammit. Think, think.

Tim. Sarah knows Tim. She trusts him, I think. I bite my lip. "Do you have your phone on you, lovie?" Her eyes flick back and forth like she thinks I'm trying to trick her.

"We can call Tim, okay?" I say softly. "If someone's coming for you . . ." I feel terrible about playing into her delusions. But if Tim can help me get Sarah out of here, it will be worth it. "Tim can help us.

"Lovie . . ." I glance over my shoulder, pretending to listen. Pretending to be frightened. "Let's call Tim, okay?" I whisper urgently. "We'll need him on our side when they come for us."

She mumbles under her breath, but her eyes are eager. She looks behind her to the cradle, mumbles something louder that I can't quite catch. Then she snatches up her phone and gives me a distrusting look.

"*I'll* call him," she announces, and I nearly gasp in relief.

I chew my lip anxiously as she types the passcode in twice. I'm thinking only of my kids and Gabe. God, after this mess is over, I'm going to call them. I really need to hear their voices. Hell, I might even drive up to their grandad's and surprise them there! Yes, I think gratefully. I'm going to see my family when I get the hell out of here.

She's calling Tim. The sound of ringing echoes through the attic. Please, Tim. Pick up. Please.

"Hi! This is Tim's voicemail!" My heart plummets.

Wordlessly, Sarah hangs up and rings him again. Her eyes never leave mine. Goosebumps shoot up my arms. Just how dangerous is she? The silence is growing more hostile. With each ring, she becomes more agitated.

Pick up, Tim. Please, God, pick up.

"Hi! This is Tim's—"

No. No. No. Tears spring into my eyes. I want to collapse on the floor and break down sobbing. Sarah's gaze is terrifying. I don't see Sarah, Lizzy—whoever she was. My friend. I see someone whose system has been poisoned for months. Someone whose mind and reasoning have unraveled. Someone dangerous.

My pulse throbs so hard I wonder if she can hear it. Sarah presses the redial button. We wait. *Ring. Ring.*

"Know what I think?" Sarah mutters, brushing away a sweaty strand of hair angrily.

Ring. Ring.

I start praying, frantically reciting the childhood prayers my grandma taught me.

"I don't think anyone's coming for me, Emily," she says. "I think the person who's been threatening me is already here."

Ring. Ring.

Tim. Please. *Please.*

"You did it, didn't you?" she says quietly. "The notes. The threats. All of it."

My knees tremble. "Lovie," I say shakily, holding out my hands, "I had nothing to do with the notes. It was *you*."

"Gaslighting," she hisses, eyes glinting madly. "You're gaslighting me."

I hold my hands up like I'm at gunpoint. I step back, heart slamming. The attic stairs, I tell myself. Run for the stairs!

She sneers. "It was you! You were the one who knew about my past. You were the one who knew I was on meds. It was always you! Why are you tormenting me?"

"Hi! This is Tim's voicemail! Sorry I'm—"

She inches forward, and for the first time I realize she's holding something in her right hand. I'm about to run when I see it. Oh God. My heart drops; my feet freeze.

She's holding a fucking hammer.

"Please leave a message after the . . ."

With an animal cry, she lunges forward, raising the hammer.

"Don't kill me!" I cry out in horror. "Don't kill me! Don't kill me!"

I jump out of the way as she brings the hammer down. She swings again, the hammer glinting in the dark. I scramble back, panting with terror, adrenaline surging through me. The stairs, the stairs! I've got to get to the stairs. I can't see Sarah, but I hear her animal cries in the darkness. I press my back against the wall, trying not to breathe, squinting at the exit, desperate to get out. But the hammer shines softly, swinging back and forth. She's blocking the stairs!

Gabe, I think desperately. My babies. I'm going to see them again. I am! I grit my teeth and creep forward, keeping my eyes on the hammer. It's frozen in place. She's listening. She's waiting for me.

"Emily?" she breathes in a singsong voice. I charge forward and throw myself at her, grabbing for her arms, trying to pin them as we fall back into darkness and crash heavily to the ground. I groan as my elbow hits a floorboard, but I scramble forward on my knees, panting in terror. Sarah swears, grabs my plait, and yanks hard. I scream when my cheek hits the floor with a sickening crack.

She grabs my waist, tries to throw me off her. Dazed, I realize her hands are empty. She's dropped the hammer. I shove her down with my left hand as pain roars through my head. Sarah kicks at my legs, and my sandal flies off. She swears in rage, gobs of spit landing on my chin. The hammer. The hammer. Where's the hammer? Gabe. The kids. God. I choke on tears. My babies, my babies.

Sarah goes still. I glance down. Her eyes are so dilated they're black. Her face is dripping sweat, and she's staring at . . . We see it at the same time. The hammer. Just inches above her head. For a brief moment, we stop struggling.

We both lunge for the hammer.

Chapter 39

Twelve days later

Dear Diary,
   I'm going to burn you! I can't have someone finding this.

The waiter sets my tea down. Lavender. It detoxes the body and boosts the immune system. "Lovely cat," the waiter says, smiling. "Enjoying the sun, is he?"

I shield my eyes from the afternoon sun. Reaper is lying in his cat carrier, purring contentedly, watching the small stream of customers come and go from the Power Plant Café. It's got a vegetarian-friendly, sort of hipster vibe. They sell crispy salt-and-pepper tofu pieces, king oyster mushroom skewers, and silky steamed spinach. I discovered it yesterday. I'd placed Reaper on the passenger seat of my rented Toyota Tarago (family van, seats seven!), and we cruised the town streets while I pointed out the sights.

"Yes, he is." I smile gently, pushing my plait over my shoulder. I spent eight hours dying it yesterday. It's honey blond and tied with a blueberry bow.

"Haven't seen you here before?" He raises an eyebrow, grinning.

I study him curiously, taking my time to answer. I shape my words carefully now, softly, languidly. I want them to melt from me. "I just moved here yesterday," I breathe. "I'm originally from Darwin."

"This your first time in Tasmania?" His eyes are hungry. Good. He'll do. I wonder if he wants children, because I do. Three.

"Yes." I smile warmly. "First time."

It took nine hours on the ferry to get here from Melbourne. I won't be going back. I can't.

"Shout out if you need anything else." He winks meaningfully, wipes his hands on his black apron, and reluctantly steps back inside the half-filled café. The Power Plant Café is within walking distance of the hotel I'm staying at. It's nothing much, but they let me pay in cash. I couldn't take any furniture from Black Wood House, obviously. Not with Emily lying dead upstairs and the police snooping around for days on end. I'd grabbed Reaper, and we'd hidden out for a week in the forest, sleeping on the bloody ground in a sleeping bag and cooking two-minute noodles on a little gas burner. That was a strange week in the forest, to say the least. By then, I figured the newspaper had revealed all my secrets. It's a shame I wasn't there to watch it unravel. That would have been interesting.

One night, I lay awake under the ghost gums, thinking. I've spent all my life running. Suddenly it was just me, Reaper, and all the terrible things I've done. Somehow I always end up lost and completely alone. What did Emily say? *You repeat what you don't repair.*

It was time. I needed to turn myself in and confess it all. I needed to get help.

But if there's one thing I know about me, the real me, it's that I *don't want* to change. I like slipping into people's skins.

I'm good at it.

I mean, I *do* feel like shit about Emily. I didn't mean to kill her. Carbon-monoxide poisoning makes people do very strange things . . . like accidentally murder people. The whole thing is a nightmarish blur. All I remember is trying to protect my sister. I was certain Sarah was in that attic with me. Hallucinations are common after long-term exposure to carbon monoxide. I wish I'd known that earlier, but it makes so much sense now. Poor me. Poor Amanda. Her bones were found on the roof. The roof! I don't know how the hell she got up there. Police are still trying to figure that one out. All that nonsense about the bug she found in the wall. All my suspicions that Jeff Johnson was poisoning me, when it was actually the house. He *did* pay his cousin to break into my office and get some dirt on me to drive me out. But other than that . . .

I stare off into the distance. It's very green in Tasmania; everything smells clean and brand new. I find myself gulping in the air, trying to flush Black Wood's toxins. I don't miss Melbourne. But I do miss Emily. It's too bad. All of it. I *loved* Emily. She was so, so nice. And now . . . I sigh heavily, leaning back in the stiff wooden chair and smiling at the passersby. Poor Emily. Poor Sarah. That's two people I've had a hand in killing. And Emily had so many unfulfilled dreams. But no matter! I've got a plan.

I place the ceramic mug on the nut-brown table, and Reaper stares at a sparrow picking at a crust on the sidewalk. His tail flicks back and forth; his eyes are clear and focused. It's a miracle he survived, my boy. But he's a fighter, like me.

Carefully, I glance over my shoulder, making sure I'm alone. When I'm certain no one's watching, I look down at my brand-new smartphone on my knee. I click on the ABC News website, Melbourne's number one news source, and reread an article from yesterday.

FIRST BODY FINALLY IDENTIFIED IN BLACK WOOD MURDERS

July 6

ABC News, Melbourne

The mystery of the first body found at Black Wood House has finally been solved. Police have identified missing Beacon woman, Emily Thompson, as the first victim. The mother of three was found in the Black Wood attic with blunt-force injury to the head. Police revealed that the family of the 36-year-old were visiting relatives in Canberra and did not report her missing for days.

In a tragic twist of events, it seems Thompson told her husband that she wouldn't be answering her phone for a while. She'd also taken annual leave at Mercy Community, where she worked as a grief and loss therapist, so her colleagues did not report her missing.

"Unfortunately, neither the family nor her colleagues realized she was missing," police reveal. "Until today, we couldn't find a next of kin to identify her body."

"It's so sad to think she was lying there dead for days and no one knew," neighbor Jeff Johnson said. "Black Wood has such a tragic history. For too long now, Black Wood House has been the blight of Beacon. God forbid, something's happened to Sarah. We'd love to see it bulldozed."

Police still hold grave fears about missing homeowner, Sarah Slade. It's understood they're currently interviewing a person of interest in her disappearance.

I flick to this morning's headline and read it over and over again. A wild giggle bursts out of my mouth, and I quickly cover it with the back of my hand. I devour the headline, beaming.

JOE COSGROVE, HUSBAND OF MISSING WOMAN SARAH SLADE, ARRESTED FOR BLACK WOOD MURDER

There he is. My darling, shiny-haired, cheating husband, front and center of the website. He's wide-eyed and terrified, with a vaguely guilty expression on his face. Wonder what his new girlfriend thinks of this.

I snort my laughter, feeling like I've won a war. I hum a little tune and sip the lavender tea. I truly didn't expect the police to pin Emily's murder on Joe. But it's a nice little bonus for all he put me through.

They'll never find the murder weapon. All I really remember after the incident with Emily is waking up in the forest with my fist around the hammer. I buried it at the foot of a ghost gum.

If he's got a good enough alibi, he might still get off. But for now, good riddance, Joe! They'll find out you're Liam Martin soon enough. And . . . I smile so hard my cheeks hurt. That letter I sent Andy. I'm sure he thought I was a nutter when he read my rambling message. But once he finds out that his best mate is really Liam Martin, maybe old Andy will take that letter to the police. Maybe they'll start an investigation into my sister's "suicide." And maybe one day soon there will be another headline: JOE COSGROVE ARRESTED FOR MURDER OF SISTER-IN-LAW.

I stop humming. If they figure out who Liam Martin is, then they'll soon discover who I really am too. The Sarah Slade skin is over. It's bittersweet, like moving away from home. Tears sting my eyelids, but I'm ready. Goodbye, sister, I tell Sarah. Goodbye for good. Goodbye, Black Wood House.

I bring the mug to my lips, feeling the steam warm my cheeks. I shake my head, wry smile on my face. Black Wood House had me so crazy that I actually thought it was *alive*. I thought it was speaking to me. I even thought we understood each other. Me and Black Wood House, rotten to the core.

I take a sip of lavender tea, thinking. When I was hiding out in the forest, freezing in a sleeping bag with Reaper curled at my feet, I wondered why I was still alive. Susan Campbell. Bill Campbell. Amanda Vale. Emily Thompson. Four Black Wood victims. Why was I spared?

Maybe, I finally decided, it's because we *are* the same. I am Black Wood House. I am horrid and awful and poisonous. All along I was peddling that self-help shit to hide my rottenness. I was an Instagram queen with perfect hair and teeth and a heart of darkness. But now— now I am free.

The house didn't want to be fixed, pulled apart, made new and clean again. And neither do I. I ceased the renovations. I listened when it told me to stop. Maybe that's why the house spared me.

Or maybe . . . I shake my head. Maybe I'm just crazy.

I open Google and type in "vet nursing courses near me." The waiter appears at my side again. He looks down at my phone, blatantly snooping. "Vet nursing? That's cool!"

I smile broadly. "Thanks! Time for a change of career, I think." I look away dreamily. "I've always loved animals. Been a vegetarian for twenty years."

"I'm a dog person myself." He smiles and refills my lavender tea while somehow maintaining eye contact. "Free refill on the house."

"Thanks, lovie." I tilt my head, letting my blond braid swish over my shoulder. "What's your name?"

"Anthony." He grins eagerly, and I suppress a frown. I wonder if he'll let me call him Gabriel.

He slides a biscuit next to my cup. It's buttery yellow, the size of my palm. He smiles so hard I feel like his face will crack. "What's your name?"

Ah! I've been waiting for this. I take my time, adjusting my paisley skirt around my ankles. I reach up to shield my eyes from the afternoon sun, and the wooden beads of my bracelet click together like ice cubes.

"Emily." I smile at him. "My name is Emily."

Epilogue

He drives slowly up the snaking driveway, past the lone tree in the front yard. Its trunk and branches are so bare it looks like a charred hand in the dark. The night is cold and still and silent, lit only by a sliver of moon and one headlight. He got lost trying to find the house. He's been driving for six hours now, and his calves and wrists ache.

He stops the car, stares up at the house, and thinks, Oh God, what the hell have I done?

He swipes at the layer of sweat on his upper lip. Helplessly, he turns to his silent, pale wife. She stares straight ahead, clutching her handbag to her chest.

From the back seat, his young daughter leans slowly forward, her breath hot against the back of his neck. "Daddy?" Beth says in a strained voice. "This isn't it . . . is it?"

What have I done? What have I done?

He reaches for his wife's hand, feels it trembling. Or is it *his* hand shaking? He swipes at his upper lip again as waves of panic crash over him.

I did what I could, he tells himself resolutely, eyes on the horrid house. A man's gotta provide for his family, and they'd long worn out their welcome at his father-in-law's place. He and his wife worked four jobs between them, scraping every damn dollar together to save a deposit. But God, the bloody housing market is ridiculous. They're asking for a 30 percent deposit these days! Who can afford that? Not him.

Black Wood House was a *quarter* of median house prices. A quarter! He'll demolish it himself if he has to. Brick by bloody brick. He'll build a new home on these massive grounds for his growing family. But for now, thank God his daughter isn't old enough to google the house's terrible history.

"This is the one!" he says brightly, steeling his voice so it doesn't crack. "This is your new house!"

Silence.

"There's four bedrooms. Two bathrooms!" He rattles them off, voice tinged with hysteria. Silently, his wife slides her hand out of his. He knows he's scaring them, but he can't seem to stop talking. "Plenty of room to run!"

In the back seat, his daughter begins to cry. He can't bear it. He exits the rental van crammed full of their meager possessions and lurches to the front door. Wordlessly they follow as he pushes the front door open. The smell hits him first. Stale air, stuffy. Terrible.

Creeeeeak, went the porch. *Creeeeeak,* went the door. He takes a step forward, and the door slams shut in his face.

He jumps back, shocked. He reaches for the doorknob and rattles it. "What the hell," he mutters, rattling it again and again. The door is locked.

The wind, he thinks. But despite the cold night, the world is still. There *is* no wind.

Shit, he thinks, shoulders slumping. How the hell am I going to get a locksmith to the house at this hour? The panic roars again, sliding over him like a skin. Not that a locksmith would even *come* here. Not to Black Wood. The realtor admitted as much.

"If you run into any problems," said the balding realtor, clapping a hand on his shoulder, "you might have to fix them yourself. You won't find a builder within fifty k's who'll touch the place."

The town tried to bulldoze it years ago. But the realtor didn't tell him that.

"I read about Black Wood House," the other man said slowly. "Four dead bodies in fifty years. Horrible."

The realtor hesitated. "Yeah" he said. "Four."

Five, actually. There was that nasty business with one of the demolishers. Poor bloke was found in the Black Wood kitchen, head smashed in. No charges were ever laid. The realtor didn't tell him that either.

"Good luck, yeah?" the realtor said to the new owner. "You look after yourself."

"Of course," the man said shortly, giving the realtor a strange look.

The realtor waved him off, thinking about the dead women. Emily Thompson and Amanda Vale. Both showed signs of carbon-monoxide poisoning. Likely even Susan and Bill Campbell were poisoned by the house. But they couldn't very well exhume their bodies after they'd been rotting in the ground for so long.

The strange thing was, the house had been inspected thoroughly, and they couldn't find a source for the leak. The chimney was unblocked, the attic walls clean. No telltale signs of a leak anywhere. No soot, no smoke, nothing. You'd swear the house was doing it on purpose. You'd swear the house wanted to be left alone. Undisturbed.

You'd swear it was killing off anyone it could.

After that mess with the demolishers, the town finally gave up and left Black Wood to rot. Nobody stepped foot there anyway. Except the occasional podcaster, snapping pictures on their iPhone and posing soberly at the boarded-up front door.

He kicks at the door, swearing.

And the house roars, *Get out. Get out, get out, get out!*

But he does not hear. He does not listen.

He's frenzied now, panting and sweating and kicking the front door until it bursts open.

Silence.

He stands breathless at the front door, sucking in the dirty, stale air. He steps inside, and his wife and daughter reluctantly follow.

The house speaks a final time. *You're going to pay for that.*

He freezes in the dark.

"Daddy," Beth cries, latching on to his arm. "I'm scared!"

"It's okay," he whispers hoarsely, pulling her to him, eyes darting around the dark house in alarm. He stands protectively in front of his terrified wife, shielding her trembling body with his. "It's okay . . ."

But it's not. Because a horrible sound rings out in the darkness. An echo of laughter so deep, he swears it's coming from the foundation of the house itself.

And then, without anyone touching it, the door slams shut behind them.

Author's Note

Hello reader! There is a part in this book where Emily is gently trying to steer Sarah in the right direction. She warns her: *You repeat what you don't repair.*

On May 1, 2021, I was 11,000 words into this book when I had a breakdown. I have always struggled with mental health issues, but this was the darkest period of my entire life. I found myself living in a caravan park with my mum and my dog, with no money, no job, no self-worth, and no hope left for the future. I was suicidal and rang Lifeline daily.

For my family, I kept going. But, God, it was hard. Anyone who has ever battled mental illness will understand.

During my breakdown, I faced the realization that I was repeating the same mistakes over and over. I projected all my issues and fears onto Sarah rather than face them head on. Because just like Sarah, I did not want to change. Confronting fears and past trauma is, frankly, terrifying, and who the hell wants to do that? (Hint: not me).

In story writing, there's this thing we call the *Dark Night of the Soul*: This is when the protagonist has tried and failed, they are alone, and they are beat. They think the story is over and there is no chance to win.

For months, I was lost in that darkness, thinking my story was over.

Maybe you've been there too. Maybe you're there right now, stuck in an impossible situation with no way out.

But the thing is, *that's not how the story ends*. I knew that if I wanted to finally break free of the cycle and save my life, I had to seek help for my destructive habits and behaviors that had always held me back.

Here's when the fourth and final arc comes in. It's called the *Resolution*.

This is where the protagonist learns how to overcome. Where they finally learn the central lesson that has been holding them back. This is where they grow stronger, stick it to the enemy, and break free. This is where they finally win.

Little by little, I inched my way out of the Dark Night of the Soul. I got on a mental health plan, got re-trained for a job, and continued writing this book even when I didn't see a point.

Exactly one year and two days later, on May 3, 2022, I woke up at 5 A.M. to this email from my agent, Naomi Davis: Lisa!!! I have great news.

An editor wanted to buy this book. And then another one did. And another, and another, until this book went to a four-house auction, and now you're holding it! Thank you!

My point is: You repeat what you don't repair. If you're lost in the Dark Night of the Soul, please keep inching forward. One day soon you'll stick it to the enemy, reach your amazing resolution, and finish your story. I encourage anyone struggling with trauma, addiction, or mental health issues to reach out for help. Yes, it's scary, but 1000 percent worth it in the end.

If you or a loved one needs extra support, please call:

In Australia:
Lifeline: 13 11 14
Beyond Blue: 1300 22 4636
OCD and Anxiety Helpline: 1300 269 438 or 9830 0533
Suicide Call Back 1300 659 467

In the United States:

988 Suicide and Crisis Lifeline

Substance Abuse and Mental Health Services Administration: 1-800-662-HELP (4357)

National Mental Health Hotline: 1-866-903-3787

National Depression Hotline: 1-866-629-4564

Last but not least, in America alone, 430 people die each year due to carbon monoxide poisoning. Please check that your detectors are working.

For more information, please visit wikihow.com/Test-a-Carbon -Monoxide-Detector.

Acknowledgments

And now for the good bit!

To my agent, Naomi Davis. I don't even have words for what you've done for me. From day one, you have believed in me, encouraged me, advocated for me, and I AM NOT CRYING, YOU ARE. You have changed not only *my* life for the better, but my family's lives, too. I am forever grateful.

Also, to the whole team at Bookends Literary, particularly James McGowan and Jessica Faust. Thank you so much for your early help and guidance on this book.

To the wonderful team at Penguin Random House! I am so, so lucky to work with you all. I squeal each time I get an email from any of you. Seriously, I am one step away from tattooing all of your names on my face.

To my editor, Jenny Chen. My life got so much better as soon as you entered it. Thank you for your rabid enthusiasm, your openness, your excellent notes, and for loving this twisted story as much as I do.

Mae Martinez, thank you for being a pleasure to work with and for all your help in getting this book over the finish line!

Thank you to my production editor, Jocelyn Kiker, and my copy editor, Kayla Fenstermaker! You are both absolute word magicians, and I'm so thankful to you for catching all my errors and for not shooting me for my overreliance on "ly" adverbs. *I'll be more careful of that in future, I thought grimly.*

To my favorite people in the whole world who just happen to be my family.

Mumsy, for making me look out the window of a parked car, and asking me the question that changed my life: "What can you see?"

My brother, Dan, thank you for making me do all your Year 12 English homework; it sure paid off. And thank you for always, always, always encouraging me. If this book sells enough copies, I'll buy you that bloody superyacht.

My sister, Joels, Hello, it's me! Thank you for all the wonderful memories we've made over the last few years. Especially that time you got wasted during the wine tour and did the chicken dance in a crowded restaurant. That was gold.

My darling pork chop. I know sometimes it's easier for you to communicate through song lyrics, so here are mine:

> *No one's gonna give you love like I give you love*
> *No one else is gonna fight*
> *Not like I'd fight*

Hurricane and Matty! Thank you for all your encouragement and for the years and years of friendship.

H, I couldn't love you more. I honestly don't know what I would have done without you. Love, your bestie from another testi.

Matty, I officially hire you as my security. You start Monday.

To Noah, the Fortnite king! I love you so much. I'm so thrilled that you love to read, but maybe don't read this one until you're way, way, *wayyyyy* older.

To Jay, I couldn't have asked for a better brother-in-law. We love you so much, Possum Lips.

Vick, for screaming when I got my book deal, and for my awesome Black Wood spoon!

Thank you to Sera, Zoe, Sandra, Tristen, and Damon, and all of Kyle's fam for your encouragement over the years.

To every member of the #llamasquad. Thank you for four years of screaming, consoling, rabid encouragement, and for always laughing when I post the sexy toast GIF. Extra special thanks to Katy, Suse, and Miep.

To my Melbourne writing mates, especially Bridie, Kat, Steph, and Riona! Thank you, Bridie, for reading those early chapters of this book and saying, "This is the one! I *feel* it!"

To my beta readers, Kim (#floridamanforever) and Katy, for wanting to read more pages of the early draft. And for not saying "Yep" when I kept asking if it was shit.

To everyone at Open Colleges. Especially my wonderful marketing team!

Thank you, Lynn, for being the coolest, kindest human being on the planet. You've always got our backs, and you go above and beyond for all of us. If we ever get another boss, we're all gonna be such shitheads to them.

Rach, for not only being an awesome leader but also a great friend to me. Thank you for all the memes, your generosity, and for just getting me.

Arpita, for being our lifesaver and the easiest person to work with ever. You are an absolute treasure!

Keith, my dear Machan, who has better stories than I do. Thank you for making us laugh all day long.

Jono, for always being so gracious and especially for being so kind to me during the interview process. I will never forget that.

Aaaaaaaand, to YOU! The wonderful reader! *Thank you* for buying this book. You are freaking awesome. Please stop reading and say, "I'm awesome. Lisa says so."

Go on, say it, I'll wait.

My dogs have always been my little lifesavers, my friends when I had none. To my lovely girls, Layla and Esmerelda. And to the beautiful souls I've lost, Shadow, Jack, and Axe. Mummy will always love you.

(Also, reader, please send me your dog pics. PLEASE I BEG OF YOU.)

And lastly,

To my heavenly Father,

For the promise that saved my life.

About the Author

Lisa M. Matlin was a guitarist in a rock band before switching from songwriting to story writing. She lives in Melbourne, Australia, with her husband, pug, and golden retriever. She's probably re-watching *The Walking Dead* right now and trying not to laugh at her own jokes. Lisa is a passionate mental health advocate and your dog's number one fan. *The Stranger Upstairs* is her debut novel.

About the Type

This book was set in Baskerville, a typeface designed by John Baskerville (1706–75), an amateur printer and typefounder, and cut for him by John Handy in 1750. The type became popular again when the Lanston Monotype Corporation of London revived the classic roman face in 1923. The Mergenthaler Linotype Company in England and the United States cut a version of Baskerville in 1931, making it one of the most widely used typefaces today.